# MINDTALK

# MINDTALK

A. ALEX COME'

**ARPress**
45 Dan Road Suite 5
Canton MA 02021

Hotline:        1(888) 821-0229
Fax:            1(508) 545-7580

Ordering Information:

Quantity sales. Special discounts are available on quantity purchases by corporations, associations, and others. For details, contact the publisher at the address above.

Printed in the United States of America.

ISBN-13:        Softcover        979-8-89330-880-8
                eBook            979-8-89330-881-5

Library of Congress Control Number: 2024902397

# CONTENTS

# CHAPTER ONE

The warehouse interior lay draped in the final, fast fading darkness of predawn. Morning wasn't far away, minutes at best. Alone in this abysmal darkness, hunkered down behind the rear end of a long-abandoned forklift, I listened.

They were here. I could hear them; their footsteps faint tapping sounds against the dirty cement floor...mere seconds of muted sound, then silence again.

I knew what they were doing; moving a few steps then stopping to listen. I also knew why they were here. They intended to kill me.

I could tell one was in the darkness straight ahead, thirty, maybe forty feet. Another moved to my not so far left, just this side of the neatly stockpiled 55-gallon drums. There may have been a third man further out, but I couldn't be sure. I was sure of one thing, though; they were closing in fast.

One would stop and another would start, then they'd move together, almost as if they had rehearsed their timing under the direction of a trained choreographer.

To know their exact number would have been nice, but like they say, "you may as well wish in one hand and..."

Well, you know the rest. Besides, for me this was just one more opportunity to provide clear, indisputable evidence that 'Murphy's Law' does exist, which happens to be the story of my life. And in case you're not familiar with Murphy's Law, it's a simple little philosophy that says, 'whatever can go wrong, will'. Up to this point my search had been fruitless anyway, no evidence of anything.

And certainly now, with men hunting me, the probing was over. At best, the most I could hope for would be just to get out alive.

Frompy, though a pimp by trade, had always been a reliable source of information. He had said—guaranteed—we'd find cocaine. Lots of it, he had told us, stacked crates filled with plastic bags packed in coffee grounds. Quantities valued in excess of two million: just the evidence our client, the district attorney, needed. But now, the way it looked, the only thing the D.A. was going to get was a corpse...mine.

I'll admit my palms were sweaty. I was a little nervous. The situation wasn't exactly an entertaining episode of Magnum P.I. I mean, these guys were real killers with real guns, probably fitted with silencers.

In my moist little hand, I held a nine-millimeter Beretta with a fifteen-shot clip. Hell, even with the spare in my pocket, that gave me thirty rounds total. If there were, in fact, three of them, and each carried a similar handgun, also with spare clip, then they would have at least ninety rounds. Nice odds, right? Now you can see what I mean about me and Murphy's Law!

The warehouse sat almost isolated on the north side of the city, Indianapolis that is, certainly not the largest metropolis in the country but certainly one of the biggest in Indiana.

And to fill you in, my name is Alex Stone, Private Investigator. No Tom Magnum, no Mike Hammer and no Hollywood stud type. Just a low profile five-foot, six-inch guy whom obviously needs to get into another line of work...if he lives that long.

And like most private eye firms there's a partner. One whom at this very moment is standing vigilant watch outside ensuring no one sneaks in on me. His name is Joe Hardon. And while he is not, by standard of the law, a criminal, he does have an alias. Alias, of course, by Webster's definition, meaning pseudonym, pen name, stage name or assumed name.

As for me, right now I could personally think of a dozen justifiable names to call him.

But when we were in the Marine Corps together several years back, Joe was best known as 'Big Joe Hardon' and not because he is some big overgrown giant behemoth; you know the kind I mean, that mountain of a man who's first glance says 'don't screw with me pal', but when he opens his mouth he reveals a soft teddy bear persona. Believe me, that is not Joe. Actually, the man I call partner is only two inches taller than myself. But to help you get the picture, stick a space between the d and the o in his last name. Why such an alias, you wonder? You'll understand that later!

Still, I must give credit where credit is due. Although the guy is only five-eight, he's bad. And in lack of understanding on my part, has an impelling influence over the ladies. To them I guess he's the Mel Gibson type; born with that rugged boyish look women go for in today's man of the millennium. Things just seem to always go his way. When it comes to our individual lot in life, we're total opposites. Joe's Guardian Angel has always been Lady Luck. As for me, it's freaking Murphy.

But with what I believe to be a clear conscience, I can say there is no green-eyed monster rearing its ugly head. In fact, I love the man like a brother.

Still, opposite as we are, we do see eye to eye on several things. First, we're not in the least prejudiced; we believe everyone in this world is an equal unless they choose not to be. And as far as our line of work is concerned, we irrefutably agree on this. When it comes to three particular dregs of society, mercy doesn't exist. I'm referring to the lowest forms of human life, cold-blooded killers, rapists and the sickest ones of all...child molesters.

We consider their kind human insects, overgrown pests worthy of extermination. Actually, they were the very reason we had gotten into this business in the first place. Ridding the world of them was to be our contribution toward the betterment of society.

But as it turns out, far too many have an umbilical connection with lawyers 'of the dark side' and end up with more rights than people like you and I.

One more thing about Joe, and it does my heart good to share this since it really bothers him. Although he's straight as an arrow and happily married with three beautiful daughters, he has an uncanny appeal in attracting gentlemen of the gay community. And aside from the fact a few of our closest friends are gay, if you ever get to meet Joe, be sure and ask him about 'Don'.

The only exit I knew about for sure was straight ahead about twenty aisles down and to the left. And if these guys were the pro's I figured them to be, there would be a guard on it.

But if I could get to the door and take him out, I might have a chance at making it outside and across the open yard to the car. The rusted chunk of iron hiding me now would offer security only so long; sooner or later they'd spot me.

Oh, there is one more tidbit about Big Joe I nearly forgot, and I consider it his greatest flaw. He carries a.45 auto and actually believes it is the ultimate handgun. I personally think he's read too many Mickey Spillane novels.

Reaching down I slipped off my shoes, a hundred-dollar pair of Doc Martins. I tied the laces together then flipped them over my shoulder. Wiggling my toes, I concluded that if I could hear them, they could hear me.

Besides, I've got this thing with shoes. For some it's toy trains, old coins or antiques. For me...I'm into footwear and not in a kinky way. When I was a young kid growing up in the streets, an old black cabby once told me that clean nails, a neat haircut and a pair of shined shoes make the gentleman.

He had also informed me, with a smile, that a woman judges a man's prowess by his shoe size. And just for the record, I have bigger feet than Joe.

Crouching low, I darted from behind the forklift, crossed the open walkway, then stopped just inside the first aisle. Down on one knee I paused, listening with teeth gritted, anticipating the sting of a silent bullet, but it didn't happen and I thanked Murphy. Satisfied, I moved again, two aisles down this time.

The inside of the warehouse was stifling. A river of sweat was streaking its way down the middle of my back and pooling at the belt-line; it felt cold.

If I got out of this alive, my mind was made up. I was getting into another line of work. Actually, I had quit a dozen times before, but Joe always talked me into staying-this time he wouldn't.

I had no idea what I'd do, only that it would be something different and a hell of a lot safer.

I was a cop once, trying to do the same job within the legal margins of the law, but it never worked. There were too many Darth Vader in black robes tapping gavels. I'd been a Marine, a Sailor, a Firefighter/Paramedic, and even sold pots and pans once. None satisfied me and each had its drawback-one was too frustrating, one too restrictive, another too boring and one gave me VD twice. And besides, the Gumshoe business was becoming the Amway of law enforcement… everybody owned a piece of the action.

Rising again, I scurried down three more aisles moving to the opposite side this time, careful not to establish a pattern.

Wiping sweat from my forehead, I strained my ears for the sound of footsteps. They were on both sides of me now, close, one just ahead to the right, another almost opposite to the left.

Far down the long walkway, a broken window laden with soot revealed a filmy ray of morning light over the city's skyline.

Daylight would explode into life any second. If I wanted to live, I had to get to the door. What I needed was a diversion, to draw their attention away long enough to make a run for it.

On the shelf in front of me I began groping carefully for something to throw. Sweat continued to trickle down my face and into my eyes. They stung and I tried easing the pain with a few frantic blinks, then made a swipe with my sleeve.

Time was running out and I wanted to hurry. My nerves were crawling like ants on a dead bird, but my brain told me to move slow, that a noise now could only hasten the arrival of Murphy's great uncle, the Grim Reaper.

The heat was unbearable and there was no air movement whatsoever. Just my luck, I was going to die right here in the world's largest sauna… with my clothes on and alone.

I thought about Joe and wished he were in here with me; he had a way with situations like this.

My hand felt something hard and it wasn't me, it was a piece of iron. Round stock, maybe? Exactly what it was I couldn't tell. It was thick and nearly a foot long, round and heavy. "Maybe it is you," I told myself.

Whatever it was I kissed it gently then gave it a hard fling into the darkness behind me. It remained airborne for what seemed an incredibly long time.

When it finally hit, there was a thundering crash followed by the breaking of glass, then a loud clanging noise as it struck the floor and rolled to a stop.

For the first time I heard the voices of the men searching for me. The one to my left spoke first, followed by the guy to the right.

"What the hell was that?"

"I don't know. I'll go check it out."

"Bullshit. Stay where you are. It's a trick. The son-of-bitch threw something, you idiot. He's trying to draw us away. He's got to be right here, close."

I cursed my luck...and that freaking Murphy. Hell, throwing something always worked in the movies!

The morning sun burst over the skyline and daylight poured through the big window at the end of the walkway. Then he was there, the man to my left. He stepped right into my aisle and we both yelled 'shit' together, bringing our guns around to fire. I was quicker. My bullet tore into his chest, knocking him backward into the stacked pile of 55-gallon drums. They were empty and came clamoring down around him, making one hell of a racket. For me the hiding was over.

I turned in a split second and caught only a glimpse of the guy to my right bringing up the barrel of his Uzi. I hate automatic weapons, especially in the hands of people who don't like me.

The wild spray of bullets tore up the shelving just above my head, and as I ducked and rolled, I glimpsed yellow flame shooting from the muzzle. Just as I suspected, it was dressed with a silencer.

He was two aisles over and it had saved my life. Had he been any closer, I would have gone to the city morgue looking like a human sieve.

I heard the soft clang of the empty clip strike the floor and a new one slide into place. I didn't say it loud, but I said it. SHIT!

Scrambling to my feet, I took off on a dead run. My shoes fell from my shoulder, and I yelled shit again.

As fast as I could, I covered the distance toward the exit door. Two aisles over the man with the Uzi matched my speed and fired wild bursts each time we crossed an open aisle-way.

The deadly spray of lead slugs tore up everything in their path. Papers flew, glass broke, wood splintered, metal ripped and the cement floor sparked like fireworks behind my heels.

Things didn't look good for me.

As I ran, I fired two wild shots of my own, hoping for a hit but knowing better. The nine-millimeter barked like an echoing explosion through the quiet warehouse. I prayed that if Joe hadn't heard the first shot, he heard these and was now on the run to my rescue. I prayed too that he'd take out the guy at the door. If he didn't, they'd soon be zipping me up in a black body bag.

The Uzi fell silent again and I knew another clip was going in. The far wall with the exit door was growing close very quickly. Sweat poured over my face and my breathing was coming out in painful rasps. I was never a record-breaking sprinter, but I was sure this was probably my best time ever.

The Uzi was back. A spray of lead trailed my heels and then it happened...I took a hit-kind of! One of the bullets, I'm not proud to say, sliced across my right cheek...posterior cheek, that is. Not very glorious, I'll admit, but it sure as hell stung and I yelled above the clatter of the zinging bullets.

Outside, over a now waking city, the morning sun continued to climb. A wide transparent beam of blinding light filled with floating particles shot through the glass of the big window, forming an almost perfect square on the dirty floor. Strangely, I thought of that beam as my guiding light.

As I covered those last few yards another odd thought flashed through my mind. It was morning. I didn't want to die; I wanted to go get breakfast.

Crossing to another aisle, I spotted the door and the guy guarding it. He was waiting for me, gun raised.

Behind me the Uzi continued to demolish the shelving and tear chunks of cement out of the floor.

I wondered when the guy at the door would shoot? The gun in his hand waved as he parried for a clear shot. There was no place for me to go. If I stopped, the wild Uzi would rip my body apart, and if I continued on, the guard at the door would put a bullet through my frantic, pounding heart.

I screamed the words at the top of my lungs for lack of nothing else I could do: "Shit, oh smelly shit!" It didn't help!

Again I fired two more shots, this time at the guy guarding the door. They were misses, of course, but what did I have to lose? I had never thought about it before now, but shooting at a target while on the run is like trying to hit the urinal in an aircraft toilet during turbulence.

It looked pretty certain Murphy was going to get the last laugh when the door behind the waiting guard opened suddenly.

A bright patch of blinding light poured in and engulfed him. When he turned, Joe caught him across the face with the barrel of the .45 and he went down, dead weight.

Then, moving swiftly, Joe darted to the aisle up which the man with the Uzi ran.

Poised with feet spread and looking like the main star of a B rated cops and robbers movie, I heard him yell down the aisle.

"Drop it now or you're dead." A couple of seconds elapsed.

Somebody didn't listen to Big Joe! I heard the .45 auto boom twice-then caught a split-second glimpse of a body sliding across the floor past the aisle to my right.

Heart pounding in my temples, I came to a tired and very welcomed stop. Placing my hands on my knees, I leaned over to help catch my breath. My chest ached. Sighing, I closed my eyes. Sweat poured from my face, forming a small puddle on the filthy floor between my feet. It was over and I thanked God repeatedly.

Joe came walking up while sticking the.45 back in its holster. Smiling, he asked.

"You all right Alfie?"

ALFIE! That's what he calls me. Not my favorite name, but I had made the mistake once of telling him I didn't care for it...some friend, right?

Straightening, I looked him in the eye and let sarcasm flavor my tone.

"Of course I'm all right. I'm just fine! For the past several minutes, which felt like hours, I've been hunted like an animal, shot at with automatic weapons and had a good pair of pants ruined. I've lost five years off my life from fright, dropped my shoes somewhere, which are probably scuffed beyond repair, or worse yet, full of bullet holes, and on top of all that I got hit in the process."

His face grew serious. "Hit! Where?"

After I'd said it, I cringed, wishing I'd kept my mouth shut, but it was too late. Pointing over my shoulder with my thumb, I mumbled the words as I shook my head.

"In the back there."

Moving around behind, he saw the little red blood stain over the right buttock then laughed out loud; a laugh louder than the bark of my Beretta. It filled the warehouse. I hated that laugh and continued to shake my head.

"And you used to be a Paramedic," he said, bordering hysteria. "I hate to tell you this, Alfie, but that wound isn't in your back."

My jaws tightened and I sucked in a deep breath. "I know it, you rock brain." There was solid irritation in my voice that I couldn't help, and he loved it.

"I didn't say 'back', anyway. I said back *there*!"

Putting a hand on my shoulder, Ile gathered his composure then told me, wearing a stupid grin.

"It's no wonder you were so out of breath when I busted in. I mean, if someone had shot me in the ass I'd have run like an Olympic champion, too." Biting my lip, I slammed the Beretta back into its holster.

In the distance we could hear the wail of approaching sirens, and to me they were a beautiful sound.

Outside, morning had fully arrived and the sky over the city was bright with warm, beautiful sunshine.

Gingerly I grabbed hold of my right cheek, took a deep breath, then ambled on toward the door. Joe put his arm around my shoulder and walked along side, smiling to himself.

My walk resembled a man with a corncob stuck where the light doesn't shine, but I didn't care-I was alive.

The wound burned and I could feel it seeping a little blood. Joe glanced over at me, started to speak, but burst into laughter instead.

I called him a name not fit for the ears of children and he laughed even harder…some friend!

It was three hours before we cleared the red tape at the police department. We filled out forms, wrote reports and underwent an interrogation a North Vietcong General could have learned from.

From there it was a trip across town to the Emergency Room-Joe's idea.

The female physician working E.R. liked his smile, so she let him watch while she bared my bottom and sewed three sutures into my posterior.

When I limped out, my friend and partner tried to soothe the hurt by singing a tune for me, 'Shake, Shake, Shake, Shake your Bootie.'

This morning's activity had created an insatiable appetite for both of us so we stopped at Mac's Diner and ordered burgers and fries. I made Joe go through the drive up and we ate in the car on the way back to our office in Lafayette.

Just out of curiosity, have you ever tried a burger in a speeding vehicle during rush hour, balanced on one cheek? It's a trip!

## CHAPTER TWO

arly Monday morning I walked into the office and closed the door on a hard hammering rain. It had me soaked by the time I got in since my key always sticks...Joe's works great.

The rain was cold and turned my hair into a dripping, soggy mess that sent hair gel running into my mouth. I didn't care for the flavor. The old commercials were right; a little dab will do ya.

Joe wasn't in yet, so the place was dark. After switching on the ceiling light, I hung up my coat then went into the bathroom to towel dry my hair. The mirror was too honest; I looked like a Private *Dick*, all right.

When finished, I went around behind my desk and eased gingerly into my chair; my butt still hurt. The chair squeaked and I made a mental note to oil it later. The clock on the wall read 6:34 a.m. It was too early for anyone to be up and about, especially Alex Stone.

But this morning was different. On and off all night I had wrestled with insomnia. Deep inside a strange feeling, an odd sense of uneasiness, had poked relentlessly away at my brain. It was as if some sixth sense had been trying to get a message through; a warning if you will, but one I just couldn't quite figure out.

Sighing, I slipped open the top drawer of my desk and pulled out the two darts I kept there. They helped me relieve stress and served as the barometer for my day ahead. Aiming with a squinted eye, I threw the first one across the room at the huge poster to the right of the door. It sailed true, striking with a soft thud between the big-lettered words-'Murphy's Law.' Then I launched the second one, which struck lower, stabbing into one of the 55 listed Murphy truths.

This one read; 'never play leapfrog with a Unicorn.' I thought about the possible consequence and made a face.

Outside, the rain was loud. It pounded my ears as I watched it slain into the countless puddles scattered over the dirt parking lot. By noon the place would be a nasty arena of mud. The kind of muck to ruin a good pair of shoes.

For a fleeting moment Joe came to mind. He was always lecturing me on the merits of being optimistic. Hell, maybe he was right. Maybe I leaned a little too much toward believing the glass was half empty instead of half-full.

Gently propping my feet on the desk, I closed my eyes and laced my fingers behind my head and let a smile come to my face.

I envisioned the rain stopping suddenly and the sun popping out. I imagined a dozen bikini clad women knocking on the door, asking permission to use the lot as a mud wrestling pit-then begging me to referee. Of course, I agreed.

Picturing it, my smile widened. There were three blondes, three brunettes, three redheads and three beauties with hair as dark and shiny as black marble. Then the vision vanished! My eyes opened. I lowered my feet to the floor and listened to the chair squeak again. No way, I thought! Never happen! Knowing my luck, the moment I stepped outside the sun would temporarily nova and I'd go blind; then along would come Joe to take over. He'd explain everything in explicit detail as if it came from the pages of some erotic best seller, and I'd try to kill him.

After filling the coffee maker, I pulled off my shoes and rubbed on a little polish. During the last buff, a rusty Escort station wagon splashed its way close to the front of the building and tossed out the morning paper. It struck hard against the front door then bounced back down the steps, coming to rest in the pestilent downpour.

"Thanks, Murph." I mumbled under my breath.

Throwing my shoes back on and a coat over my head, I ran out and grabbed it, then darted back inside.

The plastic bag they had it wrapped in had come undone and it was partially soaked. Figures! I shook my head.

The coffee was ready, so I threw the paper on the desk then poured a cup. After a quick sip I went back to my chair and sat; it squeaked again. Opening the paper, I turned the soggy pages to the employment section.

There were two pages of jobs, but only a few of interest. One was Head of Security for an electronics corporation located in Honolulu, Hawaii. They boasted a list of benefits that staggered the mind. There was also an opening for a paramedic at one of the local hospitals working twelve-hour shifts, a nearby county was taking applications for a deputy sheriff and one of the smaller, adjacent communities was in need of a full-time Town Marshal. Of them all, the Hawaiian security job generated the most interest. Pausing a second, I pictured myself going to work dressed like Thomas Magnum.

After agreeing I'd look great, I went back to the paper. That's when Joe pulled up.

His red '66 Corvette eased through the puddles and pulled to a stop at his parking spot next to the door. The rain had stopped. How fortunate for him, I thought. The last thing in the world I wanted was for his hair to get wet.

When he came through the door, he hung his coat on the brass rack as always, then silently smiled, as always.

Settling back in my chair, I took a sip of coffee and waited for his customary greeting, as always.

"Morning, Alfie." Cheerfully sickening could be his middle name.

"Morning, Joey." I reciprocated.

Although he's never told me, I think he hates Joey as much as I dislike Alfie.

I watched him pour a cup of coffee then move around behind his desk. When he was seated, he glanced at the paper and up at me. He bit hesitatingly at his lip while gathering the words he wanted to say. But I beat him to it.

"Save it Pal. Don't waste your breath. There are jobs in here that sound good, one in particular, and I'm calling later today."

"Come on, Alfie." he began, letting his face grow somber with phony worry lines. "You can't be serious; you know you care too much. And besides, the community needs you."

I put my hand up. "Cut the crap! This time I mean it, I'm OUT! History!"

He sensed the assertive tone and took evasive and semi-tactless action.

"By the way," he said, concealing his grin, "how's the little bottom today?"

"Sore!"

"You know," he continued after taking a sip of coffee, "you were shot doing a great service for the folks of Indiana. I mean, you risked life and limb to make their community a safer place to live. I've been thinking about writing a piece for the paper. You know, let them in your act of heroism. It could make you famous."

After rolling my eyes I stuck a finger down my throat and gagged for him. That's when the phone rang. On the second ring he picked it up and began what was almost a one sided conversation.

"A.J. Investigations."

For several minutes his head moved like a bobber at the end of a fishing line. The person at the other end talked non-stop. And although I couldn't make out the words, I could hear the voice. Whoever they were, there was excitement in their tone. Periodically Joe would say something brief or ask a question.

Then he grabbed a pencil and started writing. Glancing out the window, I noticed it had begun raining again.

"No problem." Joe said finally. "Within the hour." He then hung up and I turned back to look at him.

For a few seconds he sat staring at me in silence. I waited patiently then, against my better judgment, asked.

"Well?"

Following a sip of coffee, he leaned back in his chair and tossed the pencil on the desk.

"That was a man named Bordenwell; that is, James W. Bordenwell. He wants to talk to us about a job."

I raised a hand again.

"NO, not talk to us. Talk to *you*. I'm history, remember? As far as I'm concerned, I've never even worked here."

At that, Joe rose and went to the coffee maker where he topped off his cup. Holding out the pot he gestured, but I shook my head no.

"The man's problem is serious, Alfie." He said the words while turning to place the pot back on the burner. "At least let's go talk to him."

When he turned to face me again, he had a look in his eye, a look that said he had all but agreed to take the case. It was an expression I didn't care for, and one that brought to mind my restless night's sleep and its strange forewarning.

And although my mind was made up about quitting, I had to admit I was curious. What could be so dramatic as to win him over in a two-minute phone conversation? Sure, money was part of it, but there was more.

He returned to his chair, and I followed him with my eyes.

Seated, he told me finally.

"Alfie, the man's wife and two little children have been abducted."

I whistled under my breath. "That's big-time stuff, Joey. Why would he call little peanuts like us?"

"Don't know. Guess we'll have to ask him when we get there. He's waiting for us right now."

I frowned. Talk about Murphy's perfect timing. Turning my eyes to the poster hanging by the door I read the truth that says, 'In case of doubt, make it sound convincing.'

Shaking my head I rose slowly from my chair and stuck my hands in my pockets. Then I walked to the window and stood gazing into the rain.

I could feel Joe's eyes on me and in the glass I could see my reflection. Staring at myself, I relived the ordeal in the warehouse. I recalled how close I'd come to taking that walk through the valley with the big shadow. The memory was strong.

Turning, I told Joe.

"NO pal, not this time, I'm out, strike three, no more, conclusion, culmination, finale, finished, THE END! I feel sorry for this Mr. Bordenwell, but I'm through playing detective. You're in this case alone. And I'll warn you up front, I've had this bad feeling all morning."

With piety on his face, Joe moaned, "You're not going to desert me now, are you? This is serious, Alfie. You're the only person in the world I trust to cover my ass. Where is your heart?" He looked like a little puppy whose bone was just taken away. Joe Hardon should have been an actor.

I shook my head and moved to my desk where I grabbed my cup to gulp down what little coffee was left. It was cold and tasted terrible. He started in again.

"Show some compassion, Alfie. I mean, just think what some scum life, child molesting, kidnapping doper might be doing to those little kids right now."

I turned and glared at him. He knows his psychology. Pointing a finger, I told him, "That was low, Joey."

"I know," he said, rocketing from his chair and grabbing his coat. "You ready to go?"

Rolling my eyes, I sighted out loud. "YES, you gumshoe bamboozler." He smiled and didn't try to hide it.

On the way out the door I told him firmly, "This is the last time, pal. The very last case-no matter what!"

Giving me a quick glance, he clambered down the steps to the car, still smiling. The rain was still cold.

"You got it, Alfie," he said with a cheery voice, sliding in behind the wheel of the Corvette. "I swear on Murphy's head this one is it…no more, no matter what."

As we pulled out of the muddy lot onto the highway, I stared blankly through the windshield. Rain hammered madly against it, streaking down in heavy streams. The wipers labored vigorously, squealing and sloshing against the heavy weight of the water.

Glancing over at Joe I shook my head. Softly, just under my breath, I repeated his words.

"No more, no matter what!" So why in hell didn't I believe him?

Bordenwell lived in the city on upper Ferry Street, in one of the older, restored mansions. It was a posh place, three stories with giant pillars, a circular drive, and huge, meticulously manicured lawn. The place sat high on a hill and masterfully overlooked the city below. It must have been some view at night when the town was lit up. A yellow Porsche sat out front parked beside a gray Cadillac Seville. This man had money. Probably more in his checking account then both Joe and I would earn in a lifetime. The wealth around me brought to mind another Murphy truth, 'anything good in life is either illegal, immoral or fattening.' I wondered what Bordenwell did for a living?

At the front door we were greeted by a tall, white-gloved butler in a long-tailed tux who obviously had been expecting us.

He was polite in every respect but hustled us quickly inside and closed the door hastily. When he did, the sound echoed eerily through the house as if we had stepped into a giant vacuum. The interior was extraordinary.

We stood in a massive open room, a huge ballroom of sorts. It seemed to stretch out forever and opened high above to the very top of the house. A polished mahogany stairway climbed to all three stories with balconies and railing surrounding each. The place looked more like the spacious lobby of a grand hotel than someone's home. It was easy to let the imagination run and envision the gaiety of a party given here a century ago.

The walls were covered with expensive paintings and murals, and I would have enjoyed time to look at them all. But the butler led us down a long hall into a large study eloquently done in a 1930's decor. I expected to find Sherlock Holmes sitting in a tall-backed chair waiting for us.

The room was filled with irreplaceable antiques from that era and reminded me of one of those roped off rooms in a museum. The kind that captures the imagination and compels you to climb over the rope and just touch every little thing.

The butler led us to twin oak chairs positioned near a polished roll top desk then left us alone. When he was gone Joe got up to snoop.

"Some house, hey Alfie? Talk about nostalgia. This place is incredible, don't you think?" He glanced over his shoulder at me and smiled. "Someday we'll own a house like this."

I stared at him and returned the smile. He was serious.

"You really believe that don't you?" I said admiringly.

"Absolutely."

"Well Joey," I said, folding my arms. "It's like Murphy says, 'whoever has the gold, makes the rules.'"

He returned to his chair and sat down. Looking at me, he winked. "Exactly Alfie. And someday we'll have the gold." Smiling, I shook my head. I had to admit his dynamic optimism was almost infectious.

When Bordenwell came in, we rose to greet him.

Like the Butler, he was tall. Obviously muscular and around our age, Bordenwell was casually stylish. Long blond hair touched his shoulders. He wore a light blue T-shirt with blue sport coat, Levi jeans and Nike running sneakers.

I could tell he was tired and had been without sleep for some time.

After we shook hands and introduced ourselves, he gestured to the chairs. We were no more than seated when the butler came in with coffee. When cups were filled, he asked if that would be all? When Bordenwell nodded his dismissal, he left with a bow. We talked.

"Gentlemen," Bordenwell began anxiously, "I am at my wit's end. As I mentioned over the phone, someone has kidnapped my wife and two children, Elizabeth and little Bradley."

"Ages ten and seven, right?" Joe cut in.

"Yes, that's correct. Elizabeth ten and Bradley seven."

Joe continued. "You said it happened yesterday. Where exactly?"

Bordenwell' s eyes filled with wetness and his bottom lip quivered just enough to notice. He hesitated a second before answering. This was difficult for him but necessary.

"Yesterday in Indianapolis, at Grand Station."

"What happened?" I asked. He looked over at me.

"Well, we were returning to the car; that is, the children, my wife Emily and myself, when suddenly three people wearing nylon stockings over their faces appeared out of nowhere and attacked us. I was struck over the head and the last thing I remember was being shoved into the back of the car...the Seville out front." Following a deep breath, he continued." When I awoke, I was still in the backseat, but the car had been moved to an alley and it was dark. I was alone."

"Did you go to the police?" Joe asked.

"No!"

"Why not?"

"Because of this."

Bordenwell handed him a folded piece of paper. Opening it slowly, Joe held it so both of us could see. It was a note written in hand, in a penmanship that looked unquestionably feminine.

We have your wife and children. If you go to the Police, or anyone else, we will kill them. Go home and wait. Keep your mouth shut. We will contact you in one week. Make a mistake and we will send them back to you in pieces.

Joe re-folded the note but held it in his hand for a while, then looked back to Bordenwell.

"The note warned not to call anyone, yet you called us. Why? Surely if you intended to call anyone at all you would have contacted someone better skilled in this area?"

Bordenwell sighed again. "I called you because I didn't know what else to do, because you're small and low profile. I was afraid an agency from Indianapolis might secretly go to the police there. My God, man, I couldn't just sit around on my ass; these people have my family!"

He looked away for a few seconds, then back. "Will you help me? Please!" His lip was quivering again.

Joe looked my way and I shrugged. He knew it was up to him. We stared a few seconds then he turned back to Bordenwell.

"Normally, this is an FBI thing. But given the fact the note warned of any interference, we understand your predicament. However, you must realize that even with us operating in the shadows, there is still no guarantee of your family's safety. We'll do what we can, that's a promise. The advantage of hiring us lies in the fact we have access to the underworld's local grapevine. Something the Feds won't have. We need to drive to Indianapolis immediately. Hopefully we can pick up a lead and act on it before the kidnappers get wind. Don't get your hopes up too high and keep your fingers crossed. This does not appear to be an ordinary case."

Bordenwell raised his eyebrows. "What do you mean?"

I sat quiet while the wheels turned inside Joe's head. He was right. Something was smelly about the whole thing. He just wasn't sure how much to tell Bordenwell at this point.

After throwing me a fast glance, he turned to face him again.

"As a rule, when kidnappers snatch someone, they make contact within a day or two. This lessens the chance of getting caught by giving law enforcement agencies less time to follow up clues. Your note stated a week's wait. The question is, why so long a time?"

A thoughtful look appeared on Bordenwell' s face as he considered what Joe had said. But it lasted only a few seconds.

"Look, I don't care why they are waiting so long." His words were sharp and angry. "Damn it, all I want you to do is find these sons-of-bitches and get my family back. That is the kind of work people like you do, right?"

He leaned back in his chair and folded his arms. "Now, what about money?"

Looking at Joe, I made a face. He was thinking the same thing I was, that Mr. James W. Bordenwell could be a sharp, irritating pain deep within the brown-eyed sphincter muscle.

We came to terms on four hundred a day for expenses, a Visa and an oil and gas credit card. Plus twenty-five thousand cash if we got them back.

Our stay at Bordenwell' s house lasted another two hours. It was good for us but harried for him.

We sat him in a chair, took out a notebook and gave him a first-class interrogation. The information he gave went together like a puzzle and shined with a glimmer of promise.

The incident had taken place around 6 p.m. in a small, isolated parking lot north of Union Station.

As was mentioned, there were three assailants. One might possibly have been a woman, but he couldn't be sure. If so, I thought, it would explain the handwriting on the note. Two of the attackers were Caucasian, one of which being the possible woman. The third he described as a giant black man.

Bordenwell had actually been struck over the head twice. The first blow had only knocked him to his knees while the second brought down the curtain. There had been a short time lapse of semi-consciousness before the actual blackout came. He had been struck with something long and black in color, something resembling a Policeman's nightstick. We made a note of that. That could have been exactly what it was.

He remembered his wife screaming, but only briefly. She was probably knocked unconscious, too. He stated that two of the attackers had been dressed in jeans, one with a short sleeved blue shirt and the other a tee shirt, light brown in color, military issue type, he thought.

The third person wore dark pants, like dress slacks, blue or black, he wasn't sure. This one he described as shorter and skinny, maybe because 'he was the possible 'she'. Bordenwell couldn't recall what type of shirt that one wore. The two in blue jeans both had combat boots on their feet while the one in slacks wore some type of slip-on loafer.

Bordenwell also recalled catching a fleeting glimpse of the arm that swung the club; it had been the white guy, and he remembered a large dark tattoo of some sort on what he described as a very huge arm.

The only other thing he remembered was that the black man held some sort of large knife in his hand. I asked him about the blade, whether it had been shiny or subdued. When he told us subdued, Joe and I both looked at each other...possibly military issue. It might mean something; then again, it might not. Those types of weapons could be had, anywhere.

The questioning ended with all of the standard inquiries, like any enemies, bad debts, recent threats, beneficiaries of insurance policies, personal family problems with the wife or relatives, etc. Nothing he told us appeared out of the ordinary.

Satisfied we had covered everything; we took a tour of the children's rooms located on the second floor. It appeared they were typical kids, but on the same token, lucky ones, too.

The little girl's bedroom was filled with countless dolls and stuffed animals. A canopy bed with pink silk curtains and pink comforter and pillows stood near a set of large French doors leading to an outside balcony. The walls were covered with pink paper patterned with kittens and puppies. And there was a vanity and matching dresser of pink, too. It wasn't difficult guessing Elizabeth's favorite color.

A walk-in closet held enough clothes to outfit two city blocks of not-so-fortunate children. And on one wall there was a large bookcase filled to the ends with books I would have expected in the possession of someone much older. There were subjects on algebraic math, English, space exploration, how to fly small aircraft, health and many others. Either this little lady qualified as borderline genius, or her parents were trying very hard to impress the company.

As for little Bradley, his room was boy all the way. On one wall hung a different colored pennant for every major baseball team in the league. A bat and glove stood in one corner and at the foot of a bed shaped like a racecar, an overstuffed box of toys sat silent. All other walls were covered with giant theater posters; an array that, because of his age, surprised me. There were two different Indiana Jones posters, one of John Wayne holding his round-levered Winchester, Mask of Zorro with Antonio Banderas and Catherine Zeta-Jones, The Lion King, The Mummy with Brendan Fraser and sexy Rachel Weisz. Also, Steven Spielberg's Fievel Goes West, the Power Rangers posing in a martial arts stance, big bad Rambo in First Blood and my personal favorite, a life size blow up of Michael Douglas in Romancing the Stone. The thing that made this my number one choice was Kathleen Turner standing at his side showing a lot of leg and smiling like only Kathleen can.

I grinned back at her sharing a little telepathic gumshoe reasoning. "You know Kathleen," I told her, "little Bradley has quite a collection of posters, most beyond his years. So that makes me think two things; one, Dad has had a hand in helping the youngster select what will hang, and two, like his sister, he must be one very intelligent little person."

My mind's eye watched Kathleen's smile widen and in that sexy, raspy voice of hers she told me, "Forget the shop talk, stud. Remember my hot torrid love scene at the foot of the stairs in Body Heat? Well, it should have been you there with me, we'd have really steamed up the screen."

Turning my grin into a big smile, I pictured myself throwing a lawn chair through the locked French doors and clearing the broken glass away with my bare hands, then with a John Wayne walk mosey across the open floor to where she stood waiting with bated breath. Hands on my hips I stood tall and silent as she ripped open her blouse. Her breath was wild, her chest rising and falling madly. She had it bad for me. But hell, I couldn't blame her, I was a Private Eye with a big gun. Her eyes closed then, and she muttered the words every man longs to hear from the lips of a sex Goddess. "Please, I need..."

Joe yelling from the hallway startled me. Blushing, I turned and looked at him. His eyebrows were raised. Waiting a few seconds, I sighed then joined him and Mr. Bordenwell there.

At their side I explained to them both the importance of gathering a psychological profile on the person you hoped to find; and to accomplish that, the best way was to study that person's personal possessions.

Bordenwell nodded, then walked on ahead. Joe leaned over and whispered in my ear.

"Nice try you dirty middle-aged man...and that was just a poster, too!"

Grabbing Joe's shoulder with one hand, I rabbit punched him over the right kidney with the other. He yelled out and Bordenwell turned. When he did, we smiled for him.

# CHAPTER THREE

Before leaving Lafayette, we made a stop at Bordenwell' s bank to cash our first four-hundred-dollar advance. While at the counter Joe charmed a blond teller he knew into spilling the goods on our client's net worth; over seven million in cash alone and much more yet in assets all over the world. He was a business genius with fingers in every pot except the one you go to the bathroom in, and we weren't sure about that.

On the drive to Indy, we sorted through what we had-a probable kidnapping with a note that didn't fit. The week's wait was wrong so it could be they were inexperienced? But if not, then why would they take such a risk? Were they just a group of spaced-out psychopaths vying for attention as well as money?

Bordenwell was rich, to say the least, with big bucks readily available. So, if I had kidnapped his family, I'd want my money right away. And I'd want the freedom to spend that new gained wealth as well; something you can't do behind bars if you're caught because of stupidity.

Insurance perhaps? Maybe! Although we doubted it-at least as far as Bordenwell as a suspect was concerned. He was already immensely rich and certainly not in need of blood money, especially that of his wife and children.

However, his wife Emily was another matter. Although she was one of three kidnapped and Bordenwell had assured us things were wine and roses between them, she was still his primary beneficiary, and that made her our primary suspect.

It could be she had masterminded the whole thing, from authentic kidnapping to the note warning of interference. Yet Bordenwell had assured us the handwriting on the note was not hers.

As his wife, she would know better than anyone the way her husband would react, figuring he'd be too afraid to go to the police or FBI. Instead, he'd call someone small and virtually unknown, a low-profile organization like us; people who he believed could move fast, do the job, and safely restore the old home front.

She, on the other hand, would think the opposite. That this same agency, being small and inexperienced, would bungle things-maybe even by way of a little unsuspecting help. And in the process, her beloved would somehow get himself murdered while she and the children got rescued...and rich.

There had been no one else to even remotely point a finger at. According to our interview with James W., friends, relatives and even enemies all appeared clean.

A State Trooper sped around us and shook his finger at Joe, whose eyes diverted immediately to the speedometer. I felt the car ease up as he lifted his heavy foot. When he looked over at me, I smiled wide.

In my pocket was a group photo of the Bordenwell family. Reaching in, I pulled it out. It was one of those studio poses in front of a fake backdrop. In this case, a big stone fireplace. Four happy faces stared out at me, everyone smiling and seemingly content.

Bordenwell sat to the right wearing a blue pin striped suit. Emily, blond like her husband, sat close to him on the left. This woman was what I'd consider an above average attractive lady, maybe not a *Kathleen Turner*, but definitely a Head Turner; no pun intended.

She was in a bright red dress with white, wide brimmed southern bonnet, wearing two dimples that put little Orphan Annie to shame. The children sat side by side on the floor at their parent's feet.

Elizabeth had her mom's smile and dimples, big blue eyes too. Her hair was done up in twin ponytails and there was sweetness in her smile. Little Bradley was the reflection of his room. With mischief in his eyes, he radiated what I'd bet was one strong, all boy constitution.

It appeared Bordenwell had it all, lovely children, a beautiful wife, wealth, good health, everything. Surely he wasn't connected in anyway, and probably his wife wasn't either. But until the fat lady does her number, all things had to be considered.

We came into the city around noon and our first stop was an eatery called The Spaghetti Place. Our reason for stopping was not lunch, but rather to wait on an old acquaintance. It was Frompy's number one dining spot.

Religiously he ate lunch there every day between eleven and noon, regardless of the season or trouble in the world. And although he was every bit a six-foot four inch, black, hardnosed, dyed in the wool soul brother, Italian food was always first choice with him.

We drove around the block five times before finding a choice place to park. It was across the street almost directly in line with the front door. My watch read eleven-ten, so we settled back to wait.

The rain had stopped some time ago and now a sweltering sun blared down like the blast furnace of a Chicago steel mill; and with it came a murderous humidity. No air moved and our clothes clung like soaked cotton. Even with the windows down there was no relief.

Snooping through Joe's glove box, I rummaged for something to fan myself with and came up with an Indiana State map. He watched me cool myself for a short time then began lecturing on the merits of sharing.

I let him finish then ripped the map in half and stuffed his share in his hand. His face twisted into the dumbest look I'd ever seen but he never said a word.

In front of the restaurant a long crowd waited patiently to get in. Personally, there are three things that totally turn me off: watching someone puke, someone spitting a big green hocker on the sidewalk in front of me, and long lines at restaurants; and as the cliché goes, not necessarily in that order.

Almost one hour to the minute from the time we parked, Frompy stepped out into the sunshine. He was dressed in a bright yellow double-breasted suit with black tie. On his head he wore an Indiana Jones fedora with a big yellow feather stuck in the headband. Had he been with us, Indy would have kicked the shit out of him and ripped that stupid feather from the hat.

As expected, Frompy was with his bodyguard, Cue Ball. Cue, unlike Frompy, was well educated holding a degree in Law and Society from Purdue University. He was a monster of a man and one who Joe and I both considered handsome. Mr. Ball, as he was so referred by friends and enemies alike, was well known for two things and his education was not one of them; even as far north as Chicago he was reputed with being, bald and bad. And oh ya, a killer if so ordered. Although a friend, he was someone to be reckoned with. Joe and I both had learned long ago there was only one way to deal with either one: serve up their own medicine-and the restaurant was not the place for that.

Frompy's Caddy was parked a half block down and we watched as Cue opened the door for his boss and let him in. Then he slipped in behind the wheel and drove away. Joe started the Corvette and we followed.

They took Meridian to Washington, cut over to Northwestern, then twisted and turned through a number of alleys and narrow streets until finally they pulled in behind an old two-story brick building. We knew the place. It was an all-black bar and grill called, 'The Pussy Cat Lounge,' home of Frompy's office and, much to Joe's dissatisfaction, a hangout for local gays. It was all black, I should say, except for the white hookers who came and went to turn in their night's earnings.

We watched Mr. Ball get out of the car, open the door for Frompy, then the two of them disappeared inside. Joe eased the Corvette up beside the Caddy and shut off the engine, glancing my way.

"You ready Alfie?"

"Ready pal."

Frompy was a typical pimp. He loved all the nice things in life: good food, fine clothes, classy cars, beautiful women, wild parties, plenty of attention and everything, else that could bring the human body pleasure. But of it all there were two things he cherished most: power, and pardon my slang, his Dick, although I could never understand why. I had stood beside him once at the urinals in the courthouse and happened to see him shake it when finished. As far as I could see, he looked just like me...except of course for color.

When Joe and I walked into the lounge the jukebox was moaning a sad blues tune. Seven men, all at the bar, turned our way and stared in silence as we crossed the floor to where they sat. Leaning over, I whispered in Joe's ear, telling him to keep his hands to himself. He failed to see the humor.

Mika, a fat Ethiopian we knew, was tending and offered the only warm reception we could expect. Wiping a glass dry with a bar towel he moseyed over and asked our pleasure. I ordered a Michelobe lite, and Joe asked for a Diet Pepsi. Shaking his head, Mika grinned.

"Man, I see you still drinkin like a white honky pussy."

"Don't waste your breath Mika," I interrupted, smiling while staring at Joe; "he knows what he is." The song on the jukebox ended and Nat King Cole came on.

Our man Frompy was nowhere to be seen so we figured he and Mr. Ball were in the back office. When we stretched the truth and told Mika he was expecting us, he just nodded his head toward the dim lit hallway and we knew it was okay to go back. Letting the drinks set, we left the stools.

I can honestly say we were the last two people Frompy expected to see. When we walked through the office door he was sitting behind his desk and looked up. His eyes widened and lips stretched into a long thin line. After the warehouse incident he probably figured me to be a ghost.

Mr. Ball was seated in a chair to the right looking nonchalant. His expression never changed. He was chewing on a toothpick and never missed a chew as we approached the desk.

I spoke first, forcing a smile.

"Frompy, old buddy. How are you?"

Recovered from the initial shock. he leaned back in his chair and folded his arms. Grinning now, he tried hiding his nervousness.

"Hey, I'm doin' fine. bro. Heard you almost met the bad, MO-foe reaper the other day?"

"No thanks to you." I said, still smiling. "I'd put a bullet right smack dab in the middle of that high glossed forehead of yours, but if I did, shit the color of your suit would ooze out and get all over my painstakingly shined shoes." His grin disappeared and he sat upright in his chair.

"Hey cracker. who you think you talkin' to?"

"I'll put it plain" I told him. "I'm talking to a low life, black assed traitor who damn near got me sent to the morgue. I went into that warehouse trusting in your word. And I'm thinking maybe you set me up."

Frompy's nostrils flared. Things were beginning to get warm, but now was no time to ease up.

"Moment of truth, my friend." I said pushing, "and no bullshit. Was it or was it not a set up?"

There was a long run of silence with our eyes locked. Although I knew Joe had him covered, I made it a point to watch Cue Ball with peripheral vision. Both of his hands were in his lap and I kept them in view as best I could.

"Okay man," Frompy said finally, "the night before you went in I got this call, warnin' me. They say they're gonna waste ya. That if you was to get the word, I was dead too. These dudes were heavies. What the hell you expect me to do?"

Joe cut in sharply. "I'll tell you what I expect you to do." Frompy frowned and turned his eyes to him. Joe continued with notable irritation. "Be a man of your word. Since when did you start running scared? You damn near cost my best friend his life and I don't like it. And on top of that, all that shit poison is now on the streets."

Frompy laughed at Joe. "So who the fuck are you man, great cracker crusader?"

Joe lost it. His hand darted across the desk and grabbed Frompy by his black tie, pulling him down so his chin lay nearly touching the desktop. Mr. Ball started to get up but my Beretta came out and the barrel landed between his eyes. "Not a smart move, Mr. Ball." I told him. My expression showed sincerity and the barrel of the nine-millimeter probably resembled a cannon at that close range. Even a man the size of Cue Ball couldn't stop a bullet with his skull.

Joe pulled his.45 and we all heard the hammer click. In the same instant he drug Frompy part way across the desk till he was lying on top belly down. A pile of papers flew to the floor and a round plastic holder filled with pens and pencils tipped over.

Still holding the tie with his left hand, Joe moved around to the side of the desk and buried the barrel of the.45 between Frompy's legs, hard into his crotch. The big man jerked and cried out in a tone highlighted with pain and fright- "What the hell you doin'?"

Joe got right to the point.

"I'm getting ready to blow your cowardly balls off. Tell you what, if you want to live long enough to have to use Viagra, you better answer a few questions. If you do, and we like what you have to say, we'll call things even. But, if we get no answers, or the wrong answers, your pimping days are over and you'll be well on your way to a free sex change, understand?"

Beads of perspiration were forming on Frompy's brow. Considering the warehouse, I had to admit he looked good in sweat. Joe pressed a little harder on the.45 and he yelped like a kicked dog.

"Shit, easy with that thing, man."

"Question number one." Joe began. "Ever hear of a man named Bordenwell?"

"No."

"Bad start. Let's try again. What's the word on the street concerning a recent kidnapping?"

Frompy hesitated briefly and that gave him away.

"I ain't heard nothin'."

Joe lifted up on the butt of the 45 and pushed down harder. Frompy's body jerked and a scream that made me almost feel sorry for him left his throat. Tears filled his eyes.

"All bad answers." Joe told him. "I'll ask you one more time. But before I do, let me tell you this. A woman and two little children have been taken. It happened right here in your city. I want them back and if anything, anything at *all*, happens to those kids, I'm coming after you. And all the help you can muster for protection won't do any good. No one will stop me. I'll hunt you until I find you. And when I do, I'll cut your pecker off and paint it yellow to match your suit. You got that?"

Frompy nodded in silence.

"Now," Joe continued. "What do you know about a recent kidnapping?"

"Okay, man. Word is some people come down from the east lookin' for white market meat."

"White market meat?"

"Flesh, man. You know, white slaves, to sell across the pond."

Joe looked at me and he didn't have to say it. I knew the bad word he was thinking. Then his eyes went back to Frompy.

"What's the word on these people?"

"Last, I heard they was stayin' at some old farmhouse south of the city."

"How many?"

"I don't know for sure, three, maybe four. Hell, I don't know man. That's not my thing. I stay clear of that shit. I make enough jingle right here with my ladies, mindin' my own business."

Joe thought a minute before he spoke again. The room fell silent. Music from the jukebox drifted faintly down the hall, it was Nat king Cole again. A fly buzzed past me and landed on Mr. Ball's arm, but he didn't move to brush it away. It landed, walked to his hand, then flew again. A trace of sweat trickled down between my shoulder blades and tickled; I wanted to scratch but didn't.

Above the desk, a large window air-conditioner hummed away but wasn't working worth beans. With the money the girls brought in, you'd think Frompy would have it fixed or replaced.

"OK, one more thing," Joe said finally, "and we're out of your hair." He glanced over at Cue then and smiled." No pun intended, Mr. Ball." Cue grinned back.

"If you give us an address, we're history. You have my word."

Frompy swore. "Shit man, I don't know. You askin' too much."

"Bull!" Joe explained. "You owe us after the warehouse deal, and you know it. Now either you tell us, or I blow off your little black toy."

Not taking my eyes off Cue, I chimed in. "Hell Joey, how did you know it was small?" Mr. Ball burst into laughter and Frompy told him to shut the fuck up.

Then there was silence again. Joe shook his head with impatience.

"Screw it." he told Frompy. "I'm through playing around. I'm counting to three; if you haven't answered by then it's goodbye pee-pee and hello vagina."

That was the ticket. As they say in those old detective movies the man spilled his guts, ratted, and sung like a canary.

"Shit, man." Frompy told him. "You fuckin' up big time, but okay. I got to make a call."

Joe let loose of the tie and Frompy chambered back into his chair, rubbing his crotched like a cherished gem.

After giving my partner a nasty look, he jerked up the phone. A short conversation followed as he wrote down an address on a piece of paper. When he hung up he gave it to Joe and grinned.

"These motherfuckers are bad. We talkin' top of the line world-class killers. Mess with them and they will blow your shit…a-way!"

"Well if they do," Joe told him calmly, "then you'll never have to worry about us again. But if by chance this address leads us astray, word of honor, I'm coming back."

Joe winked at him then and Frompy's face went sober.

We left the office and the bar walking backwards, with gun still in hand.

Outside the sun was bright and I squinted. We climbed into the Corvette and pulled away. Two thoughts were running through my mind: "It's hot, and oh shit."

# CHAPTER FOUR

Just as Frompy said, the address led to an old farmhouse. It sat nestled in the middle or a cornfield at the end of a long gravel drive. We cruised past the turn off taking in what we could, then pulled over and parked.

Fields of high green stalks surrounded the place on all three sides, and we could smell freshly cut grass from the yard. Bushy Walnut trees towered high over the house, draping it soundly in shade. In the back a huge red barn with twin silos stood silent and run down. The place appeared void of any type of machinery or livestock, not even an old, gray-haired dog to bite Joe. We felt good about the corn; it would provide the cover we needed to get in for a closer look.

Together, we entered into the rows of corn running parallel to the right side of the drive and advanced at a fast crouch. We had no idea what we'd find.

It was possible Frompy had lied about everything, wanting only to get us off his back. Then again, maybe he hadn't; if so, we had to consider the possibility he tipped them off since we hadn't left his office throwing hugs and kisses.

As we moved along, I gave thought to the statement he had made about these people being world class killers. If they were, I wondered what our chances would be of succeeding; or just staying alive for that matter.

The dirt in the stalk rows had turned partially muddy from the past rain and it stuck to the soles of our shoes. I looked down and couldn't wipe the scowl from my face.

As we moved, I thought about Joe. He was my best friend, the best I'd ever had, a brother by heart. And although he was one hell of an investigator, he was not invincible. The bad feeling I had earlier was coming back and I found myself wishing Bordenwell' s call had never come.

If Joe were to get wasted things would never be the same; he'd been in my hair too long. It's funny; all our lives friends come and go but when that certain one comes along, they're more like a good wife than friend-someone you can truly trust and fits like an old shoe-despite their being a pain in the ass.

Birds were chirping in the trees around the house and above our heads the sky was a vivid ribbon of blue and white. Just as towering mountains capped with fresh fallen snow are one of God's exquisite creations, so is a beautiful summer sky.

After wiping sweat from my brow, I thought about how great a big glass of ice-cold well water would taste. The sun was hot and sweat beneath my sport coat created cold, irritating wet spots on my shirt.

In line with the house finally, we kneeled and looked the place over. In addition to the big barn and silos were two long open-faced pull barns, a chicken coop that had seen better days, and an old outhouse that leaned way too far to the right.

Poised there studying the surroundings, we began forming a plan we hoped would get us inside alive. The safety of Emily and the children had to be considered too; if in fact they were in there?

Waiting for dark was something we talked about but nixed. Too many things could happen by then. Besides, if it turned out they weren't here then it would have a great bearing on what we did next, and all of the time we spent waiting would have been wasted.

Once these people left the state, or worse, got out of the country, the odds of finding them would become hopelessly grim. So, all things considered, it was now or never.

We decided Joe would circle around back and use the buildings for cover while working his way to the back of the house. I was to return to the road and walk right up the drive like any red blooded, stranded American motorist would do.

When I asked Joe why it was him who got to go tip the back, he said it was because he was the sneakiest. That alone lost any argument I might have had. With a quick nod we separated.

Back at the car I pulled off my sport coat and laid it on the seat, then removed my shoulder rig and threw it on the floor out of sight. I stuck the Beretta in the inside pocket of the coat, then hopped in behind the wheel. I made a U turn in the middle of the highway and swung onto the long drive leading up to the house. Alternating the gas and brake, I made the car buck and jump halfway up the drive, then killed the engine.

Grabbing my coat off the seat I got out, slammed the door, kicked the tire and cursed like a drunken sailor denied an extension on his shore leave. Turning, I started for the front door of the house. By now Joe would be making his way up the back...I hoped.

As I moved toward the porch my nose picked up an even stronger scent of the fresh cut grass. The yard hadn't totally dried from the morning's rain and dozens of little grass slivers were clinging to my feet like metal filings to a magnet. First the mud in the corn row and now this! If shoes had eyes, I could imagine the looks I'd be getting.

There was a narrow sidewalk in the middle of the yard, so I walked over and stepped onto it. Stomping my feet, I knocked off a good portion of the little wet devils, then continued.

The porch was screened. Inside, the front door sat in the center with black shuttered windows on each side. I couldn't see who, but someone pulled back a small corner of a curtain and peered out, then it dropped back and they were gone. I really didn't like this plan, especially my part, but it was the best we could come up with.

Above my head-miles up-a jet skirted across the blue sky. I couldn't hear it, but it was leaving a long white stream in the wake of its trail.

At the front door lay a black oval welcome mat that read, 'Howdy Neighbor' in big red embedded letters. Stepping onto it, I wiped my feet then rapped lightly. The door rattled noisily.

The jacket was draped over my arm with my free hand ready to grab the Beretta. Trying not to look obvious, I strained to see through a small window in the center of the door, but a lace curtain distorted the view.

The sun was growing hotter by the minute and it felt good to be in the shade of the porch; the walnut trees made a difference of twenty degrees or go. As I waited, I bit at my lip. I didn't care for standing in front of the door like this, but the idea was to sell myself as a troubled pedestrian, not a private eye anticipating a house full of killers. In reality, like it or not, if we had any chance at all, this was it.

Then the door opened. A dumb look appeared on my face and the little old gray hair lady saw it. Looking up at me, she let a faint smile curl at the ends of her mouth.

"Yes, can I help you?"

Trying not to stutter over my words, I told her with a thumb pointing over my shoulder, "My, ah, car broke down. It's acting strange; a fuel problem or something. I was hoping I might use your phone to call a mechanic?"

She hesitated momentarily as her eyes swept over me. Then she opened the door wide and invited me in.

I stepped into a small foyer with a big rubber tree plant and moved out of the way so she could close the door behind us.

The house was much cooler than the shade outside and at once I knew she had central air. From the front door I followed her into a perfectly square living room and over to a small round table holding a figured lamp and black dial telephone. It sat on top of the phone book, which I pulled free and opened to the yellow pages. Throwing the old lady a smile, I pretended to finger through it while scanning the room with apprehensive eyes.

The place had the personality of a senior citizen. Old, light creme colored furniture from the sixties brought back memories and blended well with the two toned, brown shag on the floor.

There were a lot of green plants and hand knitted doilies about, with three paintings on the walls, all country scenes.

The couch was a sixties reminisce as well, with green, close-knit carpet like covering. An antique piano buried beneath a clutter of standing pictures sat centered on the west wall with a chair on each side. There was a wooden rocker and a green recliner whose color came nowhere close to matching the couch.

I saw no used ashtrays, no candy wrappers, no dirty dishes and no clothes lying around. Nothing to indicate the presence of other people in the house.

Pretending I found what I was looking for I dialed a bogus number, then hesitated a few seconds and continued looking around. After three rings, the phone clicked at the other end. A women's voice came over and I tried to hide the surprise as she talked.

"Speaking is the great Madam Constitine-Psychic and Counselor. Do you have a problem, trouble in your life, searching for someone special? Your higher self has directed your hand. Trust it. I am your answer, your solution, and your servant. Would you like to make an appointment? I do sense a great deal of trouble in your life, so for you, your first enlightening consultation is free."

Madam Constitine went silent, waiting for my answer. The little old lady lowered herself into the wooden rocker and sat staring at me. Looking at her, I widened my smile and spoke into the receiver.

"Yes on the first part, no on the second. The problem, you see, is my car. It's been acting strange, bucking and jerking and making strange noises. Nothing like this has ever happened before. I was hoping you might tell me what's possessing it?"

Madam Constitine promptly hung up but not before telling me her lack of appreciation using the kind of language a different sort of madam might use.

Continuing to hold the receiver at my ear, I went right on talking into the tone. "Yes, I see. Okay. I'll try it. Thanks."

I cradled the receiver and looked at the old lady.

"He thinks it's just a small problem, something I can repair myself." I paused a second then asked. "Ma'am, do you suppose I could have a glass of water? I'll bet you've got the coldest well water in the state."

She eased herself out of the chair and smiled sweetly.

"Why, sure you can have a drink. Water is good for you, ya know. It's God's miracle elixir. That's why he put it here. Doctors say we folks don't drink enough of it anyway."

I followed her stooped little figure out of the living room and down a long hallway with entrances to three separate rooms, each with closed doors. My hand gripped the Beretta tightly and my ears strained for any kind of noise, but the old house remained silent.

The kitchen was at the back of the house where a single window to the right of a back door looked out over the yard. The sink faced the opposite wall, so while the old lady turned to draw my glass of water, I made sure the door was unlocked and quickly searched for Joe. I didn't look long.

He popped his head up and peered in through the window. Raising a hand, I gave him the OK sign and watched him nod his head in acknowledgement. Then he put his fingers in his mouth, pulled his cheeks apart and stuck his tongue out at me. Ass!

After thanking the old lady for the phone and water, I returned to the car and lifted the hood, pretending to fumble with the plug wires. Satisfied, I slammed it, got in and started the engine.

The old woman was standing on the porch watching intently, so after waving good-by, I backed out onto the highway and drove away, pulling down to where we had been parked earlier.

Joe showed up about three minutes later. When he got into the car, I told him once again the house looked clean.

"Maybe so," he said beaming, "But the barn wasn't."

"What are you talking about?"

"In the red barn I found an old van. Someone had tried covering it up with hay. Guess what I found inside?"

"What?"

"An old military duffel bag."

"And?"

"And guess what was in it?"

I felt my heartbeat quicken. "What?"

"Two pair of combat boots, a policeman's night stick, and three pair of nylon stockings."

I couldn't help grinning. I opened my palm, flipped it over and Joe gave me five.

"But that's not all." He continued. I stared at him, waiting anxiously.

"There was also some rope, a half dozen green army cravats, a doll, a toy truck, two pictures...one of a puppy and another of a kitten, and two fake police identification holders with badges, no ID pictures." Reaching up, I ran my fingers through my hair. "Damn," I said out loud, "every tool of the trade."

"You got it, buddy." Joe came back. "Everything you need to lure a trusting kid into your car." Joe motioned back toward the house with his thumb. "Are you sure the place was clean?"

"Well, I didn't exactly do a room to room you know. I mean, it is fairly possible they were hiding inside somewhere. At the time things seemed kosher, but without a thorough look, who knows? Think we need to go back in?"

"Yep," he said, "We need to question the old lady."

"You got it, pal." I said. "Let's do it."

We repeated the same scenario. I pretended more car trouble, while Joe went around behind.

The old lady was just as friendly as before and let me in with no hesitation. Once again, the house seemed quiet and empty. But this time I didn't go to the phone. Instead, I went straight through to the kitchen on my own cognizance.

The old woman followed silently behind, surprised that I'd be so audacious. She stood speechless as I opened the door and let Joe in. When he stepped into the kitchen, she spoke out finally, her voice demanding.

"What is going on here?" I sensed no fear in her tone. So either she was one brave lady or had good reason not to be frightened.

Joe already had the.45 in his hand, so I pulled the Beretta free of the coat pocket. The old lady turned pale and clutched her chest with a sigh.

We regretted scaring her, but if these people were in the house, it would be a small price to pay.

With caution we began our search. The old woman reconciled there was little she could do, so she returned to the living room and sat in her rocker.

We left no stone unturned, checking every room, every cubbyhole, the attic, the basement and everywhere else a person might conceivably hide. We found no one. The place was clean.

Returning to the living room we sat side by side on the couch to face the old woman. For several minutes we just sat staring, no one saying a word.

Exactly how to handle it I wasn't sure but having worked as a paramedic I understood fairly well how elderly people thought and felt.

After several minutes of silence, I finally said to her. "Look Ma'am, my friend and I are Private Investigators. We mean you no harm. We're searching for some missing people, a young woman and her two little children." She continued to stare in silence with an expression that said, "save your breath sonny, I'm one stubborn senior citizen who doesn't have to say anything and you wouldn't dare hit me."

I went on anyway.

"Out in the barn, there's a van hidden under some hay. We believe it was used in a kidnapping. Do you know who the van belongs to?"

She still refused to talk.

"Please," I continued, "It's very important. The life of the people we're looking for may depend on it. "

She remained tightlipped. I looked at and he curled up the ends of his mouth. I knew the key here would be patience.

Rising from the couch, I put the Beretta away and knelt on the floor beside her chair. Taking her hand, I looked into her eyes. She didn't resist and stared back.

"Please, help us." I began again. "You've lost a loved one in the past, I'm sure. It hurts, and it's the kind of wound that leaves a permanent scar the rest of your life. These people were taken from a happy family. We think the children are going to be taken to bad people who will hurt them. They don't deserve that, they're just innocent little kids who put their trust in people like you and me."

Recalling the statement she had made earlier concerning the water, I added, "Ma'am, even the Bible tells us how precious little children are, how very special they are to God. If you know something, anything at all, and don't tell us, he will not be happy with you. God wants us to help these people. He's working through us. So please, find it in your heart to tell us if you know anything at all."

Surprised, I watched as her eyes began to water and a single tear suddenly trace its way down her cheek. Then she began to cry, and she cried hard. I looked at Joe and he shrugged in dismay.

Helpless and feeling strangely responsible, I held her hand while the tears fell. On the piano was a box of Kleenex, so rising from the couch Joe grabbed a couple and placed them in her other hand; she was trembling. Then he knelt beside her too, putting away the .45.

Her crying lasted for some time, and once I thought I saw a tear in Joe's eye too.

Finally, after a long while, she eased her sobbing. She looked at us and motioned with her hand.

"Go ahead," she said sniffling, "sit down, please."

Together, Joe and I returned to the couch.

"Lennie was here," she began, "and he had two friends with him, a young woman and a black man."

"Lennie?" I asked.

"My son, and not the kind of boy to make a mother proud."

"I'm sorry." I told her.

After a sniffle she continued. "Someone in an old beat up car dropped them off and they got the van; the one in the barn. Then later they came back again. There was another woman and two beautiful little children with them this time, just like you said. The children were so frightened. Every time I went near them, they shied away. It was so sad. It just broke my heart."

"Where did they go?" Joe asked her.

She looked at him and shook her head. "I don't know. The only thing I remember is something about New York. That's all."

"New York City?" I asked.

She blotted her eyes and thought a second. "No, but I remember it was a place with a famous name, European I think."

Joe and I glanced at one another a second then turned our eyes back to her.

"Ma'am," Joe said, "the van is still in the barn. How did they leave? Did they all go in the old beat-up car?"

She blew her nose, then wiped out each nostril with the tissue.

"No. Some fancy white limousine drove right up to the door and picked them up. Lennie didn't even kiss me good-by when he left."

Scooting to the edge of the couch, Joe rested his elbows on his knees.

"Did you get a look at anyone from the limousine?"

"Why, yes. The driver!"

"What did he look like? Do you remember?" She nodded.

"He was all dressed up in black; had long pretty blond hair. A good-looking young man he was. Course, I hate black and he looked like he belonged at a funeral instead of driving a fancy car."

"About how old would you say this man was?"

She blew her nose again.

"Not sure, really. Probably in his thirties. It's hard for me to tell anymore, you know. You younger folk all look alike."

Joe cleared his throat, hesitated a second, then asked. "I know this may sound silly. But did you happen to get a look at the license plate?"

She nodded her head proudly. "Yes, I did! Got a look at it when they drove away. I don't remember the numbers, but I know what state it was from-New York. Across the bottom it read, The Empire State! I remember that from a trip my late husband and I took to Niagara Falls." She blushed and smiled sheepishly. "It was our second honeymoon, you know."

She remembered little else. They had left early, around seven or so, right after breakfast and all in the limo.

The van belonged to her son Lennie, his since high school. He kept it parked in the barn all the time, except when he'd return home, once or twice a year.

Several times in the past he had used it and returned with strange people, mostly children, and always frightened ones. Until now, she had believed they were abused kids, that he was taking them to a happy home somewhere.

All the while she was telling us a thought ran through my mind. In this country alone, over two thousand kids come up missing every year, fifty percent of which are between the ages of 10 and 12, and many never come back.

With all information expended, we each thanked the old lady with a warm smile and kiss on the cheek. You'd have thought we gave her a million dollars.

Lennie's mother was really a sweety and our hearts went out to her.

Should our paths ever cross-we made it a point to have a man to man with her little boy and explain the importance of parental love and respect.

Outside, we returned to the barn and sifted through the van one more time. We found nothing else, but did take notice that there was no plate or registration to be found.

After taking possession of the duffel bag, we returned to the car and headed for Lafayette. An old friend of ours, Jake Jenkins, Indiana State Trooper extraordinaire would be more than happy to dust the items, run a check and put together a makeshift file. And all without asking questions-we hoped.

# CHAPTER FIVE

W e were back in Lafayette within the hour. Our first stop of course was Jake's house and naturally he wasn't home. So leaving the bag in his garage, we attached a short note explaining what we needed.

From there we returned to Bordenwell' s house. Back in the den, sitting in the same chairs, we filled him in. Joe began voice edged with the glimmer of hope Bordenwell was in need of hearing.

"We've got some encouraging news. As of right now we have a promising lead and they're not that far ahead of us. At this point your family is alive and doing okay."

Bordenwell cut in excitedly.

"Thank God. Did you see them?"

"No, but we have a good idea of what is going on now and where they are, or at least where they're headed." Bordenwell nodded as Joe continued.

"As we had anticipated this was no ordinary kidnapping. It's our belief they were not taken for ransom."

Bordenwell swallowed noticeably, "What do you mean?"

Pausing, Joe looked quickly at me then back to our client.

"Your family has fallen into the hands of white slavers." Bordenwell' s face went pale.

"What! You must be mistaking! That's barbaric; this is the twenty-first century for God sake."

Joe shook his head. "I'm only telling you what we know so far."

Then Joe said something else, something that made good sense.

"Mr. Bordenwell, I'm sure I speak for both myself and my partner when I say you really should call in the FBI on this. If these people make it out of the country...well the world is a big place."

Eyes glazed over with fear and speechless, Bordenwell stared a long time at Joe then turned his gaze to me, desperate for reassurance, as if he were waiting to hear one of us say it was all a joke. But what he wanted to hear could not be said.

Like an iron claw, horror gripped his heart. Slowly he rose from his chair and walked away. Joe and I remained quiet, respecting his moment of decision. It was tough for him.

There was loneliness in the way he had looked at us, desperation, a silent pleading and I was glad I wasn't in his shoes.

The butler came in and started to speak.

"Pardon me, sir, but there is..."

Bordenwell snapped at him. "Not now Howard, take care of it."

The Butler gave a curt bow and left immediately.

Bordenwell returned to his chair at the desk.

Looking at the both of us he said, "Gentlemen, had I contacted the FBI in the beginning, instead of you, would they have gotten this far?"

"Probably not," Joe told him without hesitation, "but things are different now, we have leads to give them and it could make the difference."

Bordenwell was up front.

"Frankly, I do not trust them. I think they would bungle it, take too long, they're just too damn bureaucratic about everything. You two, on the other hand, have proven reliable and trustworthy. Please," he pleaded, "I've got a gut feeling about this and generally my hunches are successful-they've made me a lot of money in the past. I'm asking you to take the case and leave the FBI the hell out of it!"

I looked soberly at Joe, and he shrugged.

Bordenwell added. "Look, I know you can find them. I'll double your fee to eight hundred a day, more if you need it. This very afternoon

I'll have an affidavit drawn up by my lawyers stating that when you do find them and bring them home, I'll give you $50,000 each, no, $100,000 cash money if you so prefer. Is that suitable?"

We shrugged and he went on. "I really don't care what it costs, or how long it takes, just find these bastards and get my family back!"

Joe glanced over at me again and I knew just what he was thinking. Neither of us had ever had that kind of money before. The offer was excellent, but the job nearly impossible. A one in a million shot. There was no misgiving about this being an FBI case. We would at least have liked them working with us. All facts on the table, we were small time; never had we handled a case of such magnitude. It could require a lot of travel, predictably both in and out of the U.S., and would become extremely costly and time consuming, not to mention potentially hazardous to our health.

Leaning back in the chair I folded my arms and said to Joe. "Well, what do you think?" He stared at me thoughtfully for a long while then turned to Bordenwell.

"Understand, we may never find them. And even if we do, you may not like what we bring home. Usually women are forced on drugs until they become dependent, then are sold into prostitution on foreign soil somewhere. For children, it's often worse. More times than not, they end up in the hands of child pornographers or molesters. Right now, we believe they're being transported to New York State. Where exactly, we're not sure. I'll tell you up front, if we don't catch them there, the Lord only knows where we might end up, could be anywhere in the world...South America, Middle East, the Orient, your guess would be as good as ours. However, you can take this to the bank. If we do get lucky and find them, it will have cost us greatly. The world they're being taken to is dark and deadly, a slice of hell itself filled with drugs and murder and powerful people; the worse kind of people. The kind of people who worship money and kill for fun. I won't t sugar coat it, Mr. Bordenwell; it's the devil's playground, a human sewer of psychopaths and perverts. And constantly, once they learn we're on their trail, death will be a persistent threat to us, for your family and maybe for you too. So here's the bottom line. Dead or alive, if we bring them back or supply you with proof they're deceased, the money stands, because either way we will have earned it. You do have our word, however, that once we start, hell itself won't stop us...not until all three have been accounted for or we're dead."

Bordenwell' s face was strained, but there was relief too. He was pleased we were staying.

Joe appeared confident, optimistic as always, reasonably sure we could succeed. I truly admired that. But as for me personally, another one of Murphy's truths went rumbling through my mind... "The light at the end of the tunnel is the head lamp of an oncoming train."

While Joe said good-by to the wife and kids I returned to Jake's house. He still wasn't home so I bought a New York State map at a filling station, then pulled into a restaurant and ordered a sandwich and coffee.

While waiting for the order I opened the map and read down the column listing cities and towns. The famous name of a city in Europe the old lady had said. With a pointed finger I slid down the list, picking out potentials...Amsterdam, Delhi, Dunkirk, Geneva, Jerico, Naples, Norwich, Poland, Rome, Syracuse, hell they all qualified and there were others besides.

Looking at things logically, it would make sense that they would head for New York City. There they could meet any one of a hundred ships with which to smuggle out their cargo overseas. Maybe the old lady was wrong.

Sighing, I tapped my fingers on the tabletop. If I had kidnapped someone, was planning to sell them into slavery overseas and was headed for New York State, the Big Apple would sure as hell be the place I'd head. Yet the old lady had been emphatic-a city with a European name. I scratched my head, letting a scowl show on my face. Assuming the old lady was right then why go elsewhere? Why go inland? Pondering led to possibilities. Maybe they were headed to an area used as some sort of holding place, for the purpose of drugging their victims until rendered helpless and dependent, thus lessening the chance of escape or resistance? With that accomplished then would come the trip to the city.

My food still hadn't arrived so I went to the pay phone, dropped in my change and dialed Jake. This time he was home and picked up on the second ring.

"Yo, Jake here."

I was glad to finally hear his voice.

"Jake, Al here. Get our package?"

"Yeah sweetheart. What's the deal?"

"Promise me, mum's the word?" He hesitated but I trusted him.

"You got it. So what gives?"

"Joe and I are on a case. Kidnapping, white slavers we're pretty sure."

Jake whistled.

"So who's throwing in with ya, us or the Feds?"

"Neither; we're flying solo."

He laughed out loud. "Did you two guys get into the Ex-lax and shit your brains out? You're talking real heavy weights here. The Feds lose men to these people all the time."

"Jake, please. Save the lecture. We need a favor. We need you to do like the note says, plus one more thing.

"What might that be?" He asked.

"Kiss the department's computer and make it hot. We need a list of all registered white limos in New York State, with a name and address for each. Can you do that?"

He laughed again; this time quick, abrupt.

"Shit man, you don't want much. It's my ass if I get caught."

Now I laughed. It was time for politics.

"Jake, Jake, Jake." I said musingly. "You want to talk about somebody's ass? Might I remind you it was less than two years ago when you yourself had your eye on a tight little tush belonging to someone we both know very well? Let me refresh your memory-down at Nicks, standing at the bar? What was your opening line that night...? "Say, aren't you Harrison Ford?" To help you better recall, reach up and touch your throat, you know, the spot where Joe grabbed it."

"Okay," Jake said hoarsely, "I get the picture. But just why is it, every time you two want something you bring up my sexual preference? It isn't fair, you know."

"Sorry Jake. I agree, but Joe told me to."

He made a funny noise over the receiver then laughed lightly. "It figures," he said softly, "but you tell that handsome stud he's still got a cute walk."

"You got it," I said, smiling to myself. "I'll be sure and tell him for you. But Jake, we need this stuff right away, we've got the life of a young woman and two little kids at stake. Our client wants no interference from anyone so please keep it quiet."

He paused a long time at the other end.

"All right." he said finally. "I'm on my way in right now. I'll have it all for you by five this evening. Meet me at the donut shop on the west-side at six-fifteen."

We hung up and I returned to the table. Just as I sat down the food arrived. It was a French dip combo and the hot broth steamed from the little bowl. My taste buds experienced instant erections and I could feel myself salivate. My arteries didn't need the cholesterol, but I needed the energy. This whole thing was beginning to drain my brain.

Dipping a corner of the sandwich, I took a bite and gave thought to the case.

A white limo from New York! There were a lot of underworld figures in New York, and that fit. The Big Apple was a major point of worldwide shipping-regardless of cargo type, and that fit too. How much was a white, attractive female worth in today's flesh market, twenty-five grand, fifty, maybe? Emily Bordenwell was not only beautiful she was also educated. Such a woman might bring an even higher price. Still, something didn't settle.

Even if her worth were a hundred thousand, that wasn't much to the people we were dealing with. Their main stay was the drug business. Hell, one drug deal alone often brought down millions. A hundred thou to them would be petty cash. And if money were what it was all about, just a plain old ransom would have brought them more than all three together.

My guess was they didn't want her for the cash profit; she was trading material. Probably to someone who had all the money he wanted with lots of drugs to trade. I guess it's like they say, when you have everything, what else is there short of kinky desires? So, the important question was...who is it that wanted her?

The children would be worth something too, especially at their age- old enough to scare into submission, yet young enough to brainwash and teach new habits, or should I say nasty habits. The whole thing made me sick, and I wanted to get to New York, A.S.A.P.

My coffee cup went empty, so the waitress came over and replenished it. I watched it swirl in the cup as she poured. It gurgled and threw up a warm mist. When it was filled, she smiled and was gone.

Alone again, I gave thought to the ad in the paper, the one about the security job. Hawaii! What an opportunity! Clean, 9 to 5, tropical weather, paid vacations, free medical and more. Plus, people wouldn't be shooting at me, either.

I took another bite of sandwich and followed with a sip of coffee. Then wiped the corners of my mouth with the napkin. Maybe the job would still be there when we closed the case. Maybe.

Jake was waiting for us in a corner booth. His patrol car was out front and he was in uniform. We sat down opposite him he gave us a worrisome frown while he shook his head. "Do you guys have any idea what you're getting into?"

Joe grinned at him.

"Of course, Jake."

He shook his head again. "And I suppose you think you can handle the whole thing as simply as a routine surveillance?"

His mouth widening into a smile, Joe told him.

"Nooooooo problem."

Under his breath Jake said, "Shit." Then he threw a large yellow envelope across the table. "Everything you asked for is in there. Take my advice and throw in with somebody. You guys are good, but this thing is bigger than you think. Even we plan cautiously and move slow in this kind of game."

"Precisely, Jake." I said looking at him. "And if we move slowly now, we may lose them forever. We have no choice; our only chance is to strike fast and hard. To the FBI, fast is bypassing Congress and taking a week of their own to make a decision. We just don't have that long... the woman and her children don't have that long."

Jake frowned and wrinkles formed around his eyes.

"You fucking guys think you can save the world. You can't you know, not alone anyway. There are a lot of bad guys out there, in case you've forgotten. And in our line of work, citizens don't recognize heroes. Every time one of us goes down-it's tough shit Jack; you were just doing your job anyway. Damn it, ask yourself...is going out on the ledge alone worth it? It's a long way down if you fall, with one hell of a sudden stop. And just in case you've forgotten, the golden rule of police work is safety in numbers."

Jake got up from the table then and grabbed his cup, draining the last swallow of coffee. He looked down and grinned. "You two saps need any more help, call me." Then he winked at Joe and left.

We watched him leave the restaurant, climb into the car and drive away. Jake was a good man and a good cop. Like he promised, everything was in the envelope. There were two computer-imposed photos of the men belonging to the gear we had turned over, along with their respective rap sheets. Enough can't be said about fingerprints. There was no information on the third person, the possible woman. Whoever she was, she was clean.

Together we studied the photos and appropriate information for each.

Steven Leonard Barkin was Caucasian, 34, and 240 pounds of six-foot, four inch ugly. He had either done time for, or was now wanted for, armed robbery, rape, child molestation and assault with the intent to kill. The photo showed a mean face, sober, with eyes that gave away the insanity that motivated him. His hair was long, reaching down between his shoulders and, in this case, tied up in a ponytail. He claimed two aliases, Steve Barns and Stew Bains. Interesting to us was the fact that both his real name and aliases maintained the initials S.B. He was ex-Army, Captain, 101st Airborne with 9 years accumulated service. He had been dishonorably discharged on March 8, for assault on an MP, who he nearly beat to death with the man's own nightstick.

Two tattoos, 101st airborne eagle on the underside of the right forearm, and a small black widow spider on the very end of his penis. Joe and I both cringed when we read that. He was no dummy; educated at Harvard, he had graduated with honors from the school of Engineering.

The second photo belonged to one Carlo Mandagon. Afro American, 246 pounds, six foot six inches. I frowned. Why did these guys have to be so big? Born February 12, 1964, he was 37 years old with a fifth-degree black belt in Aikido. He was wanted for armed robbery, extortion and murder. It seemed he killed two men in a barroom fight, needless to say with his bare hands and feet. All the while I read, I kept thinking how much I loved my Beretta. Mandagon was a good-looking man, even in his mug shot; prominent cheekbones with straight, narrow nose and long beaded strands of hair. He too was a college grad, Purdue University, School of Aeronautics. And there was one more notable fact worth mentioning-he was gay. When I read that I looked at Joe and smiled. In response, he held up the first three fingers of his right hand and told me to read between the lines.

As for the other info requested, the computer had turned up 168 white limos registered in New York State. All but three were located in the Big Apple, so our work was made easy. We had three stops, two in Syracuse and one in Rome.

If we were on the right track in our thinking, it had to be one of these three since they were in towns or cities with European names. As requested, Jake had provided us with basic info on each of the owners. Process of elimination would be our approach. We would go into New York via the thruway, stopping at Syracuse first, then on to Rome. If both of these cities turned up clean, then it would be on to the Apple.

Outside the sky was turning into dusk and darkness wasn't far away. New York would be a 12 to 14 hour drive and we would travel through the night. Time was ticking away quickly, growing more and more precious by the second.

I thought about Emily and Elizabeth, and little Bradley, about the fear they must each be feeling. I thought, too, about Mr. Bordenwell, and how he must be pacing the floor, and at night tossing in his bed, dreaming of the horrible things that might already be happening to his family.

How ironic, I thought. Together and happy one day, torn apart the next, perhaps never to see one another again.

In my mind there were also thoughts of the people we would eventually confront. Killers, who loved the thrill of holding the power of life or death over another human being; sadistic men and women whose only interest was in themselves. They were a concealed race of underworld people deriving their pleasures and fortunes from the suffering and death of others.

Sighing, I made a face. Jake was right. We couldn't save the world. Truth be known, some people didn't want to be saved, but that was their business. Somewhere in the State of New York were three people that did. And come hell, high water or a bullet, those three would taste their freedom again.

# CHAPTER SIX

t was raining again, hammering the Ohio Turnpike in a mad frenzy. Water washed over the windshield like the jet stream of an automatic car wash and visibility was practically zero.

Joe had the bird dog scanning and we were streaking along at an insane 80 miles an hour.

In addition to the dangerous hydroplaning we were no doubt doing, the monotone click of our bouncing tires created the perfect rhythm for putting you to sleep.

Joe was driving and despite the fact he had once driven big rigs down this very highway, I stayed awake to make sure he stayed awake. The wipers squeaked methodically while the dark veil of rain hid the taillights of the cars in front. It was enough to turn a big fearless man into a bundle of shredded nerves.

I'd have told Joe to slow down but the risk was something we needed to take. If the Bordenwell family got shipped out before we reached them, then the plot would thicken and I hated to think of how the end of that book might read.

No doubt flying would have been faster, but that would have meant surrendering our guns at the airport, which would mean notification to New York State law enforcement agencies upon landing, and we did not desire that. Theirs were among the strictest gun laws in the country, even when the men carrying them were licensed investigators like ourselves, and even though having a firearm in our possession might mean saving the lives of innocent people.

Somewhere along the way New York police developed the philosophy that anyone carrying a gun other than themselves infringed upon their almighty authoritarian image.

Around 3 a.m., we pulled into a plaza for a sandwich and fuel since the gas tank was as empty as our stomachs. It was a nice break from the monotonous ride too, not to mention I was ready for the little boy's room.

With the necessities out of the way, I grabbed a coffee and barbecued sandwich, Joe a burger, fries and Diet Pepsi. Despite the late hour there were a lot of people around. While Joe waited for his turn at the cash register, I stood back and watched the busy array of people. I wondered where they all came from? Where each lived and worked? It was hard to imagine our humble little planet was capable of feeding so many.

I was curious about them in a friendly sort of way. And I was sure many were curious about me too. So why, I wondered, was it that the most inquisitive and intelligent of all species on earth, made it a point to go out of their way to avoid having to talk with someone they wondered about?

Back on the road we ate in silence. The rain was still there but had lightened noticeably. Twice in a ten mile span the radar detector sounded and we slowed to 65.

Just the other side of Cleveland we hit single-lane construction and lost time for at least a twenty-mile stretch. Then somewhere shortly after, I fell asleep.

Head rolling softly to the motion of the car, I dreamt. I found myself as Humphrey Bogart in a dark gray double-breasted suit with a beautiful dame at my side...the one and only, Kathleen Turner. We were lost inside a big warehouse being hunted by a dozen thirsty killers with.50 caliber Thompsons. The shoes on my feet were blue suede and the hat on my head was a porkpie pulled low over my brow. There was a.45 in my hand-which I didn't understand-and an unlit cigarette dangled from my lips. Kathy clung to me like the wet shirt she'd look spectacular in, and there was admiration in those beautiful eyes. Somehow I knew when it was all over and she was safe, she'd insist on giving me a reward—and I like rewards.

In the dream there was a lot of gunplay and near misses, fifty caliper slugs were slamming all round us and the ratta-tat-tat of the Thompsons was loud. As for me and the.45, each shot was a hit. We ran from aisle to aisle with me pulling Kathleen along behind and firing at the same time. It was semi-dark in that warehouse, but Kathy glowed like an angel. And as for the remuneration afterwards, well, to be honest, I couldn't remember. But it must have been good because when I opened my eyes Joe asked what I was smiling about.

My blurry eyes caught a sign that said New York State line, forty miles. The wipers were off and although still dark, everything seemed incredibly crisp and clear as though the all night rain had washed the world.

On the horizon to the east, the very tip of a huge orange ball was cresting quickly. The light of day would soon be waking the sleeping planet. Yawning, I looked over at Joe. He smiled.

"Morning Alfie. We're almost to the New York line."

"I know." I said, following with a stretch. "I just saw the sign. Why didn't you wake me?"

"Why?" He asked, making it sound like I'd asked a silly question, "Alfie, when I drove truck, it was many a night I cruised these highways from sundown to sunup with no one to talk to. I enjoy driving at night; it's an experience all its own, especially in the dawn of morning when the sun comes up. Look."

Glancing again to the eastern sky we watched the now fully exposed sun complete its float above the earth and spill golden warmth over everything in sight.

"Beautiful, isn't it? Joe said.

"Yes sir." I said, not taking my eyes from it. "The good Lord certainly knew what he was doing when he hung that in the heavens."

"Yep." Joe replied. "That's for sure. Ready for breakfast? We've got a plaza with a Mac's diner ten miles ahead. We'll pull in, get something to go, and continue on. We should be in Syracuse around eleven or so."

"Sounds good, pal." I said. "I could use a hot cup of coffee right about now, and besides, I have to use the bathroom pretty bad."

Joe grinned and shook his head. "Alfie, I swear, you have to go more than my three daughters put together."

"Bad kidneys." I told him, trying not to fidget.

He laughed, then quickly changed lanes to hit a big pothole. The nerve endings surrounding my bladder screamed at my brain and I gave Joey a look that said you're one step away from being shot with a nine-millimeter.

Syracuse was a big place, but we only had two stops to make. The first address was in a wealthy suburb called Brightland Heights. Houses here easily started around the hundred thou mark, no questions asked.

220 Court Drive was the address we sought and after an information stop at a filling station, we drove right to it; the place was owned by a banker named Fremont Bullshort. I tried not to smile at the name, imagining what they called him in college.

Pulling up to the house, I glanced at my watch and read 12:05. There was no limo out front but the garage door was closed and it may have been parked in there, so we figured why not give it a shot.

At the front door a Spanish woman answered and in broken English explained that Mr. Bullshort was at work and the Mrs. was out. Joe fabricated a story about Mr. Bullshort meeting us at 12:15 and asked if we could wait in his den; luckily, he had one. She was more than happy to show us in, then excused herself to go about her household chores.

Alone, we went through his desk and small file cabinet on the floor beside it...nothing. With little else to go on we gave him a clean bill of health, at least for now, and left. Just as we pulled away, a red Chrysler Le Baron pulled into the driveway...probably Mrs. Bullshort. I looked at Joe and grinned. "Nice timing."

At the second address we found no one home, so we checked the info sheet and decided to go to the owner's place of employment. William Creston, like Bordenwell, was a self-made millionaire with his fortune coming by way of real estate. He had an office in one of the high-rise buildings downtown.

Finding a place to park was like pulling hen's teeth. We finally located a pay lot for all day parking only, and shelled out a five-dollar bill for what was probably going to be less than a half-hour stay. Even with Bordenwell' s money, that price rubbed me the wrong way, but I didn't say anything since New enjoy the art of arguing and I was too tired Yorkers thoroughly to partake.

Inside the building we located Creston's name on the locator plaque then climbed into the elevator. It was on the eighth floor, which turned out to be entirely his. The receptionist was a gorgeous redhead with a sweater that showed just enough cleavage to stimulate your neurons. Romeo Joey did the sweet-talking for us.

Standing in front of her desk, he cleared his throat, and she looked up, then smiled. He returned it with one of his own. His eyes moved to the sweater then back to hers, and she blushed slightly.

"May I help you?" Like a sensing device to a hot target, her eyes locked onto Joe's.

Joe widened his smile and let his breath out slow.

"That would be very nice. I'm always needing help."

"Oh?" She said coyly. "And just what kind of help is it you need?" Joe started to speak, but she cut him short.

"If it's secretarial, I happen to be very good at shorthand, typing, correspondence, and, from time to time...*dictation*. I've also had some training as a nurse, so I'm very, very good at backrubs and taking temperatures."

"And making them climb, too." Joe said smoothly.

I couldn't believe what I was hearing. It was all I could do to keep from getting sick. If that had been me standing in his shoes, security would already be doing to me what they did to Axel Foley in Beverly Hills Cop... throwing me through a glass window.

"Actually," Joe went on, speaking in a deliberate slow voice, "We really need to talk to Mr. Creston. It's very, very important."

"I see." she said slowly, batting her large eyelashes. "Do you have an appointment with him?"

"No, we don't." Joe replied in a sad, apologetic manner.

"Oh, that's too bad." She puckered her lips as if to say, "You poor little baby." I couldn't take it anymore. Turning to Joe, I told him to cut the shit. Instantly the secretary looked my way with an expression suggesting I go play in the Syracuse traffic.

Then, turning back to my pal Joey, she smiled again.

"Perhaps I can call Mr. Creston and see if he has time to talk with you."

"That would be wonderful." He cooed. "You know, you really are a great secretary. Your boss is very lucky to have you."

Blushing again, she asked, "And what may I say is the nature of your business?" Joe hesitated a second, looked up toward the ceiling as if thinking, then put his eyes back on hers. "Tell him, White Slavery."

For the first time she broke her stare. Her big lashes fluttered again, and she frowned, smiled for a second, then went to a sober expression. Not sure how to receive what Joe had said, she searched his face for reassurance. But now he was giving her his serious look. Reaching for her intercom button she dumped over a container of pencils. There was a click and she spoke into the speaker.

"Um, Mr. Creston, you have two gentlemen out here who say it's urgent they have a word with you."

"Concerning?" Creston's voice reminded me of the late Walter Brennen.

The secretary hesitated. "Uh, White Slavery, sir."

"What?"

"You heard me right sir, White Slavery. That's what the gentleman said."

There was a long pause before he answered.

"Okay, show them in."

Without rising from her chair, she pointed to a thick mahogany door just behind her.

"Through there."

When we filed past her desk, she asked. "Hey, are you guys the FBI?"

I didn't give Joe time to answer. "No." I said over my shoulder. "We're salesmen"

William Creston was a slender, grey headed man probably in his early sixties. No resemblance to the late Mr. Brennen, though. He was alone in the office and asked us to sit as soon as we reached the front of his desk.

"Now gentlemen," he began, "what is this bunk about White Slavery?"

Joe settled back in his chair and crossed his legs, making himself comfortable. He was direct and what I felt might have been just a little bit too informative, but I didn't question his approach since usually his hunches were right.

"My name is Joe Hardon, and this is my partner Alex Stone. We're private investigators from Indiana representing a client whose family was abducted four days ago in Indianapolis."

If Creston knew it had only been two days ago and not four, he gave no indication through facial expression.

A series of questions and answers followed. We talked nearly fifteen minutes and never once did this man say anything to raise our suspicions. In fact, Mr. Creston never once swore or said anything off color.

He remained a gentleman always and several times made reference to biblical scripture.

During the talk I noticed a plaque on the wall sporting a Christian Icthus. There was writing below it on a small brass plate, but it was too far away to read.

Often, a lot can be learned about a person by way of personality and choice of environment. This man was genuinely nice, a gentleman in the true sense of the word. He had a natural way of making you feel comfortable and at home around him. When we finally left he shook our hands and with a warm smile said he would pray for us.

It's said that God hears the prayers of a righteous man. I was glad Creston was one such person. For I couldn't shake the feeling that not very far into the future we would need all the prayer we could get.

In the elevator on our return to the lobby, the Beretta felt full in the holster beneath my coat, and it was a comforting sensation. Christians believe there is power in Prayer-I believe that too. But I also believe in the old adage: 'Praise the Lord but pass the ammunition.'

# CHAPTER SEVEN

Rome, New York was a mid-sized city with a population of Rome, according to our atlas census, 39,100 people. Maybe 39,103 I thought, plus a couple of visiting bad guys. While it had no giant cloverleaves or city blocks of high-rises and skyscrapers, it was once a thriving military community with a large and active Air Force Base. But like so many others, the Clinton administration had closed it sometime ago and that, along with many of its factories moving out, had turned the once bustling city into a quiet but well-kept community. And much to my interest it possessed a colorful historical past.

During the Civil War it played a spirited role in the Underground Railroad, and I was willing to bet the countryside was filled with hidden caverns and tunnels used just for that purpose. According to the map, the area was well saturated with streams, brooks and creeks-the primary navigational route for that era. If things hadn't been so grim I'd have taken time to do some backpacking.

The limousine we were searching for belonged to one N. Billy Robbinson, president of First Federal Merchants Bank on Black River Boulevard. The N. stood for Natalie. I wondered if Billy stood for Tomboy?

Precisely at 3:00pm we pulled into the parking lot of the bank. Both in need of a shave and change of clothes, we agreed we weren't exactly dressed to meet a lady, but the way we saw it, if Robbinson was in any way connected to all of this, she was no lady anyhow.

Inside, the tellers looked us over with suspicious faces. I suppose we did fit their perception of what a bank robber should look like and when we told them to fetch the president their faces all developed worry lines. But we didn't pull a gun or yell stickup, so after a short consultation among themselves they gave her a buzz. In seconds she was there.

The Billy in her name most definitely did not stand for tomboy, at least in the looks department. The lady president was unremittingly a looker, movie star material. No Kathleen Turner, but really attractive.

Standing five-six or seven, she was dressed in a solid black three-piece suit. Dark, round rimmed glasses highlighted her shoulder length blond hair and a pair of made-for-the-bedroom blue eyes stared out from behind them.

Her walk radiated grace and self-assurance. It was the kind of stride that turns heads and says, "this is nothing, you should see me in my Victoria's Secret teddy."

After brief introductions we followed her into a plush office and sat in high-back mahogany chairs. Settling in, I glanced around.

Soft yellow carpeting covered the floor. Her desk was mahogany too and matched the chairs; it was all very neat and well organized.

An attractive flower arrangement sat at one corner and on the wall behind her, oak-framed pictures of her posing with famous movie stars hung in a rectangular pattern. I was not entirely impressed-there was not one of her with Kathleen!

"Now gentlemen," she said in a soft business tone, "what is it I can help you with?" I watched her eyes dart back and forth behind the dark glasses.

While Joe cleared his throat she fixed her eyes on him while methodically interlacing her fingers and laying her hands to rest on the desktop.

"Well, Miss Robbinson." He began politely. "I'm really not sure just where to start."

She smiled briefly, a curt smile void of courtesy.

"Well, why don't you just start at the beginning, Mr. Hardon?"

I sensed the belittling undertone and if anything can ruffle Joe's feathers, being belittled will do it. Glancing down at the carpeting I quietly shook my head.

Joe's lips pressed hard together. When he replied his tone was controllably abrasive.

"All right, Miss Robbinson, we'll start at the beginning. Two days ago in Indianapolis, Indiana, a kidnapping took place. It involved a woman and her two little children."

Robbinson's expression never changed; she shook her head.

"That is unfortunate. But what does it have to do with me?"

Joe folded his arms and crossed one leg over the other. "My partner and I represent the husband/father of the kidnapped family. We're here because a limo registered in your name was seen in this location on the day of the kidnapping."

Her lips perched slightly but quickly changed to a pretentious smile. Leaning back in her chair she too folded her arms.

"So?"

So. I thought to myself, did I just hear an outright admittance to being there?

"So," Joe went on, uncrossing his legs and sliding to the end of his chair to lean forward, "we think people who kidnap are low life assholes."

Robbinson pulled the corner of her lip between her teeth and held it there while staring directly into his eyes. Her mind was racing but if Joe's remark upset her it could not be read on her face.

Perched there on the edge of his chair Joe stared back coldly. It was obvious he did not like this woman and whether his provoking was intentional or personal I wasn't sure.

Finally, shaking her head with a grin that really said, "You son-of-a-bitch," Billy rose to her feet. "I believe it's time for you to leave, this meeting is over."

"I think we had better end it too," Joe snapped, almost before she had finished her statement, "because if I stay, I might forget you're a woman."

Billy became obviously miffed.

"Don't try bullying me, Mr. Hardon! Who the hell do you think you are coming into my office making accusations and talking to me in this manner? I will not be intimidated. I could have you arrested for threatening me."

Joe rose from his chair too and I followed. Leaning on her desk, he grinned. "You might consider having me arrested, but you won't."

Billy leaned forward, now face to face with Joe. "And just why in the hell wouldn't I?"

Dropping the grin, he told her. "Because of two things. One, you're involved and don't want the press. And two, despite your pompous, tough girl, bullshit attitude, you're a good judge of character. And you know damn good and well that if you did have me jailed, as soon as I got out, I'd come back and bitch slap your arrogant executive ass."

A grin came across my face. I was surprised at Joe; he never talked to women like this, not even the ones he disliked. Pointing a finger toward the door, Lady Billy told us in no uncertain terms.

"Get the hell out of my office! Out of my bank!"

As we turned to leave Joe paused and looked back at her, saying; "And I suppose it's your city too, your state, your country, and your universe? That's the trouble with slave traffickers, they think they own everything." Pausing a brief moment longer he added, "And by the way, could you recommend a good hotel?"

We heard it one more time; "Get the hell out!"

Leaving the bank, we did not go directly to the car. Instead, we walked around the corner out of sight and stood beneath the shade of a huge Maple tree and talked.

If this woman was the smart person we thought she might be, she would be watching to see which car we got into, and for the time being we didn't want her knowing-since our next move was to tail her.

Within minutes, a white limo pulled around back and picked her up. A blond-haired, soap opera-looking chauffeur dressed in black got out and opened her door. He listened while Robbinson said something, closed her in, then looked around suspiciously. Finally, he got in himself, and they drove off.

During the tail we took a half-hour ride through some of the prettiest countryside I'd seen in a long time. We were in the heart of dairy country and much of the scenery was worthy of a Hallmark card.

Beautiful farms and grazing cattle graced green rolling hills with an aura of peace. Trees: Oak, Pine, Spruce, Maple, White Birch and others, lined much of the road side and added color and beauty to the endless scattered patches of woods and fields.

We crossed several crystal-clear streams busy with trout fishermen and returned a lot of friendly waves from passing traffic.

The limo moved along Highway 69, traveling northwest. I got out the map and followed the little black strip with my finger. There were three little towns within what I'd call a reasonable driving distance from the city: The town of Lee, a place called Taberg, and another west of there ten miles or so, called Camden.

Maybe we were all wet, but it was our guess that if they went beyond Camden, then their destination was not home, but rather to the residence of someone worthy of knowing we were in town.

It was late afternoon now and the sun was beginning to fizzle out. New York temperatures ran cooler than Indiana, and likewise, dark would come earlier as well. As we traveled along, Joe and I talked.

Interesting was the fact that the beautiful bank president never once denied her involvement, or that her limo had been in Indiana the day of the kidnapping. Her idle threats hadn't gone very far and we were sure now that she would be interested in knowing just who we were, whom we had talked to so far, and, just for the sport of it, what we were made of. As far as we were concerned, she was involved.

I couldn't believe our luck stumbling onto the right limo so quickly- Murphy must have been doing Lady Luck while good fortune slipped past.

It was almost 4:30 when they pulled off the main highway onto a private drive lined on both sides with giant Maple Trees.

We drove past the turn off then made a U-turn and came back, slow. The limo was out of sight, probably now parked at some million-dollar estate.

We were nearly seven miles past Camden in the heart of what I classified back woods, so things were iffy as to whether this was Robbinson's place or someone else's.

Just down from where the limo had turned off we found another drive on the opposite side, so we backed in, shut off the engine and waited. If anyone left from the same road they couldn't do so without us knowing.

We were both bone tired. It had been nearly forty hours since either of us had slept, except for my short nap on the turnpike, so I told Joe to catch a little shuteye while I kept a lookout. Without argument he laid his head back and soon dozed off.

Bored as hell, I watched as minutes turned into hours.

I fought sleep, yawning constantly. The sun sank away, and dark shadows slowly inched in around us.

By eight-thirty it was dark enough I could barely see, and a vigorous breeze had begun rustling through the trees. I thought maybe a storm was in the air, but not being from New York I didn't know for sure. The leaves rustled with a loud chatter and those eerie sounds that only the black of night can create, came out to test my imagination.

By nine o'clock darkness had completely swallowed the earth and I noticed there were no stars twinkling in the heavens above. Over the trees beyond the car a full moon made a terrible face at the cold night air growing strong enough to make me shiver.

Pulling up the collar of my jacket I stuck my hands in my armpits and looked over at Joe. He was sleeping peacefully, making a noise that sounded a lot like snoring, although he swears that's not what it is-according to him it's heavy breathing.

I had once asked his wife, Sue, which it was. "After sixteen years of marriage," she said with a warm smile, "I know the difference. He breathes heavy, yes...but not during sleep. The man snores!"

Around midnight he awoke and sat up in the seat, rubbing his eyes.

"Any movement?"

"Not a thing." I told him.

He yawned. "So what do you think, Alfie? Her house or not?"

"Your guess is as good as mine, pal. But given she has been there this long it's probably hers."

He was staring at me, and I could barely see his face, yet I easily read his mind and told him what I knew he wanted to hear.

"Why don't we sneak in and take a look. The Bordenwells may be in there right now just waiting for a couple of heroes like us to come to the rescue."

He grinned and I caught a flash of teeth.

"That's the attitude that makes me proud to know you, Alfie", he said opening the car door and scurrying out. "And to think you're considering getting out of this business. The very thought makes me want to cry."

"Cut the shit." I whispered as we quietly closed our doors.

Quickly we slipped across the road to the private drive. The trees towered high, blocking out nearly all of the moon's light. It was darker than the inside of the Titanic and hard to stay on the road. Several times we strayed off into the trees and had to feel our way back. Crickets chirped to their own accord and somewhere in the woods to our left, a whippoorwill's call sliced through the black obscurity.

Time passed slowly. There was no way of knowing how far the house would be; perhaps a mile or maybe around the next bend?

Steadily we edged along, listening to every sound. The night breeze was turning into a hearty wind despite the shielding of the trees.

Through a gap in the treetops I caught a glimpse of a gray-black cloud encroaching the moon. It was ugly and promised one hell of a storm-then there came conformation. A silent streak of lightning flashed, and thunder exploded the same instant Joe touched my shoulder. I jumped.

"You asshole," I told him.

"Look," he said, pointing straight ahead.

Straining to see through the thick darkness I saw what he was pointing at. Distant lights from a faraway house glowed dimly. A bad feeling swept through me, like the sensation of a thousand ants having been dumped down my shirt and scrambling to find their way out.

Glancing back into the darkness behind me I tried to guess how far we had come-a half-mile maybe? Back there was Joe's corvette. It represented our only haven of safety for a thousand miles. On my mind too were the photos and rap sheets on Barkin and Mandegon.

The closer we drew, the more the place took shape and the larger it became. By the time we were kneeling just inside the massive front yard we heard thunder roll across the sky again.

Pulling our guns, we slid a round into the chamber. We were here now, and it was time to be ready.

The place was big and ritzy, a million-dollar estate, no questions asked. Sixty or seventy feet of grass yard lay between the house and us. The place was built of stone and looked much like a small European castle.

We counted four stories, and all the way around the roof the walls were parapeted. Lightning flashed again and I almost expected to see ancient warriors dressed in heavy armor standing guard with spears and crossbows.

On the south end, a huge, rounded tower climbed high into the dark sky, eerily silhouetted against the moon and cold drifting clouds.

In the center of the main house, beautifully colored stained-glass windows glowed with a kind of reverent glare, giving the image of a giant cathedral. There was a huge three-car garage at the north end with a huge weather vane centered on the roof: it spun madly in the wind now blowing fiercely, and even at our distance, we could hear it squeal.

Motionless, we strained our ears, moving our eyes over the area, looking and listening for guards and dogs. We saw neither and I didn't like it.

The white Limo was parked on an oval drive that swung close by the front door. Beside it was a dark colored convertible Jaguar with the top up-obviously someone was anticipating rain.

A light shined over the front door and several more in rooms downstairs. On the second story we watched someone pass briefly in front of a window-they crossed but didn't return.

All stories above the second level were dark, so was the tower. We knew that at least two people were inside the house somewhere-Robbinson and her chauffeur. But there were others too, we were willing to bet.

The wealthy citizens of New York State certainly were trusting souls. A spread like this and no guards, dogs or security fence. It just wasn't right. Joe looked my way and whispered.

"I don't like it Alfie! What do you think?"

I never answered. Like a violent explosion, bright lights came to life everywhere, totally lighting the area around the house, including where we kneeled.

They nearly blinded us, and we dove for the ground. It was a waste of time-we may as well have been in the middle of a lighted football stadium.

A second later, N. Billy Robbinson opened the front door and leaned against the jam with folded arms and wearing a haughty smile. Her eyes where dead on us.

I frowned feeling stupid and embarrassed like a thirteen-year-old caught by his mother with his hand wrapped around his woody.

The gorgeous blond had changed out of the black suit and into jeans and navy-blue shirt. Western boots had replaced the high heels. It appeared Billy did stand for tomboy after all.

"Gentleman," she began pretentiously, almost yelling above a wind now aggressive enough to whip our coat tails, "we've been expecting you. And just in case you're unsure of who I mean by we...well, take a look on the roof."

We did. There were now six men with automatic weapons and shotguns, all aimed on us. "And" she continued, "at each corner of the house as well." There were two each there.

She unfolded her arms and stuck her hands in her pockets. "Please gentlemen, do put your guns on the ground in front of you, get up, and come inside where it's warm." Turning then, she disappeared into the house.

A loud boom of thunder rumbled above our heads, followed by an insane streak of lightning.

Joe looked at me and shrugged.

"Why not Alfie? It's going to rain anyway."

# CHAPTER EIGHT

Crossing the yard to the house I pondered another Murphy truth… 'If everything seems to be going well, you obviously don't know what the hell is going on.'

How true it seemed. Things at this point looked noticeably unfavorable. But, looking at the bright side, as Joe would do, I concluded that we were at least stirring the feces and getting results. I guess it's like they say when things become stalemated, 'You may as well do something even if it's wrong.'

Inside we found an impressive collection of VIPs all sitting around a huge dining table in high back captain chairs, sipping coffee. There were six all together, and every head turned to look at us with curious faces.

Billy walked deliberately slow to the head of the table, and I followed her with my eyes. Them was conscious effort in the premeditated swing of her shapely hips…as tight as her jeans fit it was no wonder she was so irritable.

As soon as she was seated, she smiled briefly, then motioned for us to sit with a sweep of her hand.

At the opposite end of the table two chairs had been pulled out and stood waiting, so Joe and I slid into them.

As at the bank, Billy rested her hands on the tabletop and interlaced her fingers. Another brief smile followed, and she looked directly at Joe.

"Now, Mr. Hardon. Please allow me the pleasure of guessing why you are here. You've come to...'Bitch slap' me, correct?"

Leaning back in his chair Joe crossed a leg over the other and returned her pompous gaze.

"Given the opportunity."

A hearty laugh escaped her throat. "And I just may give you that opportunity a little later." Her eyes swept over him slowly. "Yes, perhaps later." Clearing her throat, she added. "But first, allow me to introduce these fine people you see gathered. I shall begin to my right."

Our eyes fell on an Army Officer in dress uniform. He was noticeably pudgy with fat, floppy cheeks and nearly bald. He would have made an excellent Army poster character since he resembled an old bulldog in military uniform.

"This is Brigadier General Thomas L. Phieffer, United States Army, Pentagon. He represents the Department of Defense." Smiling, the tubby general gave us a curt nod. On his uniform were enough ribbons and brass to cover half the tabletop, end to end.

"Next to him," Billy continued, "sits Professor Robert Nugent." Looking at him she smiled admiringly. "The good professor has recently been nominated for the Nobel Prize regarding his work in nutrients and human longevity. In addition, he has been highly acclaimed for his work in ESP and physic phenomenon."

I hid the smile that tried to show on my face. This man was in his late fifties, in dire need of a shave, wearing thick wire rimmed glasses and a hair style resembling the great all time boxing promoter, Don King. He had buckteeth, wore an oversized lab coat in need of ironing and a grin that looked more synthetic than the vitamins he created. No doubt his nobel nomination had to be in the brains department; most handsome and best dressed were definitely out.

"Next to him," Billy went on, "We have Doctor Sidney Priveman, MD, Ph.D. and scientist. He is recognized as one of the world's top authorities in human DNA." Looking down her nose at us she added flippantly. "In case you don't know what DNA stands for, it..."

I cut her off. "It stands for Deoxyribonucleic Acid-the genetic material which encodes the structure of living organisms."

Her eyes fluttered a second with surprise while the good Doctor smiled at me with respect on his face. Billy started to speak again but Priveman, without realizing, cut her off.

"Most impressive, young man. Tell me, where did You learn of DNA? I should like very much to talk with you later. Perhaps…"

Priveman suddenly realized his exuberance had cut off the lady at the head of the table. Turning immediately he apologized, his face appeared flushed. There may have even been fear.

Nodding her acceptance, Billy directed her attention to the next seated person. She was now starting up the opposite side of the table.

"This lady is Dixie Barnebin." The two women glanced at one another with an expression that hinted a relationship beyond mere friendship, then both brought their eyes back to us.

"Dixie works for the government also-Federal Bureau of Investigation to be exact, and very closely to the director. Nothing passes to her boss without first crossing her desk. Ms. Barnebin, in addition to criminal law, has a degree in parapsychology and is herself a renowned psychic."

Like Billy, Dixie was an exceptionally beautiful woman. She was petite, well built with long red hair, the kind of face and body you'd see on the cover of Vogue Magazines. She didn't look at all familiar, but I was willing to bet I could identify her handwriting.

Billy's attention immediately fell to the next in line, a tall man with long hair, dangerously well-built and with cruel eyes. Glancing at Billy, Joe spoke up before she had a chance to start the introduction.

"Please allow me the privilege of finishing the prelude, Madam Chairman." He said it brashly. Hesitating briefly, she stared into his face, then grinned and gestured with a graceful sweep of her hand. "By all means."

Joe turned back to the man now staring at him with an inquisitive expression.

"His name is Steve Barkin. Thief, killer, rapist and asshole to his mother. He was a one-time Army Officer, 101st airborne but was dishonorably discharge in 1980. Two tattoos, one on the right underarm and a second on the end of what is probably a very tiny pecker."

At that Barkin turned red and started to rise angrily from his chair, but Billy stopped him with a raised hand. "NO, not now S.B., you can settle it later."

"Yeah." Joe chimed in. "Later, S.B." Continuing on, my best friend with the overactive mouth moved his eyes to the next and final person at the table.

"And this guy," he began, "goes by the name of Carlo Mandagon. Martial arts expert, killer, thief, extortionist and worst of all...faggot. Normally I have respect for homosexuals, in fact some of my friends are of the preference, but you, Mandagon; you're a disgrace to them and deserve all the cold and cruel names they've been given. You're not a homosexual, you're just a cold, insensitive butt-pirate."

Unlike Barkin, Mandagon did not lose composure. Instead, he smiled softly and spoke in a calm tone, his voice well-seasoned with what sounded like a Jamaican accent.

"Woe, Mon." He told Joe, seemingly amused. "You talk like a bod one. If S.B. doesn't kill ya, I will. You have my word." Joe gave him a smile back and told him mockingly.

"Woe, Mon. I'm looking forward to it."

With his eyes locked on Joe's, Mandegon was still smiling when Billy cut in.

"Enough!" She stared at us a few seconds then said. "It's obvious you two have done your homework, and I'll admit I'm quite impressed. However, it's time to return the introductions, so if I may?"

We both politely nodded.

"Ladies and gentlemen," she began, looking at Joe, "The handsome man with the dark hair, mustache and overbearing sense of confidence, is Joe Hardon." Joe gave them a smile.

"And the other," Billy added, "with the scientific knowledge, is Alex Stone. Both are Private detectives out of Lafayette, Indiana. They are here in search of a missing mother and her two little children."

She put sarcasm in her voice. "Do any of you happen to know where they might find these people?" The coffee sippers remained silent.

"Actually," Billy went on, "I believe we all know where they are. And perhaps these two ambitious heroes would like to see them? How about it, gentlemen? Would you like that?"

"That would be very nice." I said. "Yeah." Joe echoed. "Exceptionally nice."

Billy clapped her hands and a door to our right opened. Heads turned.

Through the open door came a man holding an Uzi, followed by a blond woman with two little children. Behind them was another guard, a shotgun cradled in his arms. They paraded family of three to where we sat, then stopped so we could have a good look.

What we saw was infuriating. They were the Bordenwells all right. Emily was obviously drugged and all but out of it. Her eyes were glazed, face expressionless and there were no dimples now. She was far away in another world, imprisoned against her own will, locked helplessly in a drug-induced abyss. She was barefoot and dressed in blue coveralls with the number 48 stenciled across the front. Her hair had lost its luster and hung to the shoulders in straight, uncombed strands.

There were obvious signs of dehydration and malnutrition as well. I'd seen the condition before. There were tracks on her arms, little dark holes from frequent injections of what was probably nearly pure cocaine. Hell, it had been less than three days and already she was this far-gone. They were pouring the shit into her.

Little Elizabeth was barefoot too and stood holding her mother's hand, although her mother was not squeezing back. The little girl standing in front of us was no longer the sweet little darling in the picture her father had given us. She stared at the floor mostly, looking up only occasionally. Frightened and confused by the terrible cruelty surrounding her, she had no way of knowing we were there to help.

If she too had been drugged I couldn't be sure. I could not see her face long enough to search her eyes. And like her mother, she was also dressed in blue coveralls but with a different number across the front, 49.

Holding her other hand was baby brother Bradley. It was obvious he was tired, but he did look a bit more alert than his sister. Unlike her, his eyes roamed the room, staring at the faces around the table. Across his coveralls was the number 50, and like the other two he was barefoot.

In the pit of my stomach I felt a sickness welling. I was wishing the Beretta were in my hand. And like Bradley, I looked into the faces of those at the table; none showed even an ounce of remorse. In fact, several wore a low-keyed smile, as if they were proud of the sad and pitiful state they had put these innocent people in.

Openly, I was confused. Mrs. Bordenwell seemed over-drugged, robbed of her natural beauty, and not attractive at all now. And, too, she was unable to speak; at least it appeared so. In such a state she would bring very low dollar value and certainly no man would want her if she were totally unresponsive!

The kids both looked tired but not molested. If molestation were the case, they would be acting more fearful, cringing away, unable to stare at anyone, and all with shame on their faces. No, that didn't seem to be the case. Drugged, maybe, but raped or molested, I didn't think so.

My mind whirled in search for clarity as I tried to piece it together. Around the table we had a beautiful female banker, an Army General, an almost Nobel scientist, a genius Doctor, two hard-core criminals, and a beautiful, top female FBI agent who was passing herself as an active psychic. The latter credential must have meant something, or Billy would never have mentioned it. Professor Goofie, she had said, was also involved in this psychic hullabaloo. Plus, on top of all that, the house was crawling with armed guards.

In front of us stood three tired, drugged, spaced out peon, who did not look in the least like they were being readied shipment overseas to some anxiously awaiting client. In fact, they looked more like established prisoners in a county jail-settled in for a long stay. N. Billy Robbison was no doubt in charge of the whole mess. Why, I wondered, would a Banker be governing over a Brigadier General from the Pentagon and a top FBI agent. The others I could see, but not these two.

Outside thunder rumbled frequently and lightning flashed repeatedly across the dark sky. Rain was falling now, and it hammered hard against the house.

On one hand I was thankful to be inside where it was dry and warm. However, considering the company, I would just as soon have been staked Indian style out on the front lawn, naked.

Billy rose from the table and stood poised in front of her chair. Just as our heads turned to look at her, a deafening crack of thunder exploded almost directly over top of the house. Lightning followed and for an instant the lights flickered, but it lasted only a second and things were normal again.

Turning to the men guarding the Bordenwells, Billy said.

"Return them to their cell." Her eyes came back to us, and she smiled. "Now. How would you gentlemen like a tour of my humble little home?" Turning her head in the direction of the doorway, she yelled for more guards, then turned back to us again. "The tour will not take long, afterward you'll be shown to a bedroom where you can rest and," her nose wiggled and she made a funny face, "change into something a bit less... noticeable."

Under her breath she mumbled something about incompetency, and we guessed she was referring to her guards since they hadn't shown as yet. Obviously irritated she turned again toward the door and yelled out something in a dialect unfamiliar. However, had I been forced to guess its origin, my answer would have been, Russian.

Whatever language it was, it got results. Almost instantaneously three armed men came bolting through and approached the table. Turning away she snapped, "Bring them." Obviously, she meant us.

Billy in the lead, we were hustled out of the dining room and into a long hallway. From there we entered into a large study to stand in silence while the Russian speaking bank president approached another tidy desk.

There she picked up a small pocket calculator and pushed several of the keys, then looked up and grinned.

Immediately a small section of ceiling to floor shelving receded inward from its adjacent sections then slid out of sight to the right, exposing an elevator door. Joe looked at me and raised his eyebrows.

Moving to the elevator Billy pushed a single red button and stood with her back to us while the doors opened. After stepping inside she turned to face us and smiled. "Well, what are you waiting for?"

Uzi barrels gave us a push of encouragement, so we joined her.

We descended fifteen or twenty feet then came to a stop. When the doors opened Joe and I glanced at one another with surprise. A bright-lighted network of tunnelways led off to...places we didn't want to know about.

Billy took the lead again while the three guards followed behind us, weapons leveled and ready. If we were to hope for a break, now was not the time. These men were experienced; they kept their distance and remained always alert.

As we walked the corridors, Billy's boot heels clicked against a green tiled floor. She talked over her shoulder as we moved.

"These tunnels, gentlemen, were originally the work of white sympathizers during the Civil War. Many blacks were hidden out here while waiting transport to Canada. The place lay dormant for decades, until I purchased the property and built this house. No one knew of these tunnels except the contractor who designed the exact location for its foundation. So, total secrecy has been maintained." Her shoulders shrugged. "Sadly enough, as soon as the place was built the contractor met with an unfortunate accident."

Joe shook his head and told Billy.

"You're one cold bitch, lady."

She chuckled. "Joe my boy, it's like they say in the big city, you ain't seen nothing yet."

The tunnels had been modernized, of course, since their original use. The walls were covered with mahogany paneling; obviously mahogany was Billy's favorite. A drop ceiling had been installed with a single line of fluorescent lights dotting it for as far as we could see, and every fifty feet were banks of emergency lighting.

Also there were movie cameras mounted on the ceiling, with speakers spaced evenly between them. No doubt upstairs somewhere, someone was monitoring our every move.

"These tunnels, gentlemen," Billy went on, "run on for literal miles. Perhaps clear to Rome, although I've never followed to see. I've only restored what was needed here." "And," she said matter-of-factly, "just in case you're giving birth to the illusion of escape, note the movie cameras. In addition, I'll have you know every tunnel has been planted with explosives. Anyone trying to escape would be buried alive long before they reach the surface. Plus, not knowing the exact combination, anyone trying to open the panel door in the study using the calculator will create an explosion so violent, nothing will be left here but a big hole."

Pausing, she said as an after-thought. "You know, I think the worst death possible would be the horror of being buried alive. Don't you think?"

It was a question we didn't answer. We came to a closed door, and she stopped us. Putting her hand on the knob she lulled momentarily and looked our way.

"In this room, gentlemen, you will see the finest, state of the art scientific equipment in the world. The latest in X-ray apparatus, Magnetic Resonance Imaging equipment, CAT Scans, interpretation computers, surgical furnishings and much more. It is the finest, most sophisticated research lab in this hemisphere, with the most brilliant technicians and scientists ever assembled. You, Mr. Stone, I'm sure will appreciate its worth."

She opened the door, and we went in.

Billy was right, I was struck with awe. It was like stepping into a laboratory out of the future, something out of Star Trek.

Spread across the entire wall to our right, a giant computer monitor filled with sharp colored imagery caught the eye immediately. Across the colossal screen lay the graphic image of a human body dissected into a dozen segments; a projection from a large scanning device, the image rotated slowly across the screen while a column of numbers clicked wildly in the lower left-hand portion.

Everywhere the room was busy with activity. A dozen white smocked clinicians and scientists scurried about performing their functions; some wore masks and gloves, and some didn't. Electronic equipment nearly overwhelmed the place and metal shelves held test tubes of various shapes filled with multicolored liquids, brightly enhanced by the room's soft fluorescent lighting. Conversations were almost whispered and soft; easy listening music filled the air.

Pausing a moment at one of the tables, Billy touched the shoulder of an elderly man with white hair. He had been staring intently into a huge microscope and jumped slightly when she touched him.

"Dr. Bonsfield, I'd like you to meet someone." After glancing up over his shoulder, he straightened and smiled politely.

"This is Joe Hardon and Alex Stone, she said, "they have volunteered to run the gauntlet for us."

When she said that, I looked at Joe and together we silently mimicked the word... GAUNTLET?

Dr. Bonsfield widened his smile. "Excellent." he said with enthusiasm. "I'm sure you'll both find it most exhilarating." I knew at once I didn't care for that word. Returning to the hallway, Billy pulled the door closed behind us.

"I have two more areas to show you. There are others, but they are of little importance. I do, however, feel it is only fair to warn you our next stop will no doubt inflame your humanistic side, although I can expect little else from narrow minded imperialistic thinking. Anyway, I shudder at the way Americans 'potty train' their young. It creates such…weakness and limitation." She paused a few seconds then shrugged. "Anyway, we call this next area the holding cell. And please, as we tour, do refrain from becoming overly melodramatic and calling me names."

The tunnel continued straight another twenty feet then came to a T. We turned left. During the walk we passed countless branches shooting off both left and right. There were literally dozens of channels and each without markings-no numbers or letters or names. I also noted there were no markings of any kind at tunnel entrances either-probably for the purpose of keeping anyone trying to escape from logically finding their way to the exit. In all actuality employees probably knew their way around blindfolded. But people like us would be caught quickly and effortlessly just trying to find a way out.

When we finally came to a stop it was in front of a huge iron door held shut by a heavy bar stretched across the front-much like those found in old time forts. In addition, there was an armed watchman. From inside, there would be no chance at all of breaking through.

When Billy told the guard to open up, he clicked his heels and replied, "Yes Comrade." Her face twisted into anger. "WHAT?" The guard flushed. "Sorry! Yes Ma'am."

Turning, he struggled with the heavy bar, setting it to rest finally on the floor out of the way.

I looked at Joe and he shrugged his shoulders. I was beginning to feel like we were the starring cast of a low budget Hollywood espionage movie. The only things missing were Bogie himself and, of course, Kathleen.

Billy had referred to this place as 'The Cell', but 'cells', plural, would have been more befitting. There were a dozen or more, and locked within them were a large number of men, women and children of all ages. Each wore the same type coveralls as the Bordenwell family, and each with a different number across the front.

Some slept, some stared into oblivion, many wept and still others called out to us, pleading for help. If ever I were to catch a glimpse of what hell must be, this was it. Perhaps a just comparison would have been the Hanoi Hilton in Vietnam.

I wondered how long some of them had been here? Many of the men had long hanging hair and untrimmed beards. Sickly in appearance, they looked ancient, just waiting, perhaps even hoping, for death.

By comparison, many of the women were no better off. Their skin pale, hair void of shine and eyes colorless, they resembled zombies, mindless people of flesh and blood, existing only, waiting for the relief death would bring.

In anger I looked at the three guards with the guns trained on us. To jump them was my foremost thought, but they were out of reach; to attempt it would be suicide.

Anger and disbelief raced through my body like a burning, consuming fire. This wasn't real, it couldn't be. This sort of thing only happened in third world countries or creations from the imagination of horror storywriters.

Somberly I stared. Someone would pay for this, someone would die for it, and first on my list was Billy.

As soon as she felt we had enough, she led us out and the guard began closing the thick heavy door. The cries and moans of those trapped inside drifted out into the tunnel in tones of begging and pleading. But with ears tuned out, she watched the door slain close and they were silenced.

The guard replaced the heavy bar. Joe and I stood appalled, filled with a feeling of compassion and helplessness...and hatred. And God willing, we swore in our thoughts we'd return to help these people, return to set them free and give them back their lives. God as our witness we would!

The final room Billy intended to show us was dark when we entered and only the light from the tunnel gave us a hint of what was inside. The place looked to be a vast open area.

Leaving us in the hands of the guards, Billy disappeared somewhere into the shadowy darkness. We couldn't see her, but we could hear the loud click of her heels echo into the openness as she crossed somewhere to the far side.

Several seconds went by before we heard the loud slam of a power switch. Light came into the room and we got a good look for the first time.

The place resembled a gymnasium with tiered seating on one side. Beside each seat, a three or four foot metal arm extended up from the floor, clutching what appeared to be a modified version of black binoculars.

In the middle of the room sat something like we had never seen. A long, giant shaft-looking affair stretched across the floor at least a hundred feet in length. I guessed it to be fifteen or twenty feet high and the same distance across. It reminded me of a gigantic version of vent ducting.

As if it were some live, giant mechanical creature; piping, air shafts, hoses, hydraulic lines, electrical cables and whatever else ran into it like a series of umbilical cords; as if their sole purpose were to nurture it, to keep it alive. Neither Joe nor I had ever seen the like.

The walls and top were constructed of thick, clear Plexiglas, and it was divided into four compartments, or chambers; each symmetrically different in shape and size.

Ten feet above it, opposite side of the tiered seating area, a narrow metal catwalk ran its entire length, giving a full aerial view of each compartment. I'll confess, the very sight of it gave me the willies.

Billy faced us and smiled flagrantly.

"And this, gentlemen, is the gauntlet. Tomorrow you shall see it much closer as well as have an understanding of its purpose. Word of honor, by this time tomorrow, you will have no doubts as to what our business here is all about."

Turning to the guards she told them, "Escort our guests back upstairs and lock them in the North bedroom...and for goodness sake, watch them closely."

They nodded and led us away. I took one more look at the gauntlet as we exited the door. My parting thought was a Murphy truth, 'Never eat prunes when you are famished.' I don't know why I thought of that, I just did.

The north bedroom was just that. A bedroom on the north side of the house with a camera mounted high in each corner. There were steel bars at the window and a door so thick Captain America couldn't have busted through even if it meant spending the night with Wonder Woman.

The place was bugged too. There were two twin beds, a bathroom and a closet apiece, with a pair of blue coveralls just our size hanging in each. Like all the others there were numbers across the front, Joe 51 and I 52. This obviously meant two things; we were being offered a permanent position with their fine establishment and no one appreciated our hard-earned body odor.

Two new toothbrushes lay in their wrappers on the sink counter and there were towels, washcloths, shaving utensils and everything else an inmate might need to make his stay tolerable. Honored guests we were not!

After a thorough search, we located what we felt were all the bugs and ripped them out, the cameras we covered with towels from the bathroom. Then settling in, we each took a welcomed shower and crawled into bed.

For the time being, at least, we let ourselves relax. We had looked and there was no way out. Tonight there was nothing we could do short of letting sleep come to replenish our strength.

For a while Joe stared into the ceiling, his hands laced behind his head. He was silent, lost in his own thoughts, pre-planning no doubt. He was like that. Whenever something bothered him, something he couldn't do anything about, he went inside himself for answers and reassurance. After twenty minutes of sober staring he looked over and told me calmly.

"Tomorrow Alfie, our chance will come. You can count on it so be ready."

"No doubt about it, pal." I said, rolling over and switching off the light. I wondered how convincing I had sounded.

The room fell dark, and silence swept through the blackness. As the minutes passed I lay awake. Before long Joe was asleep and breathing easy. I thought about our situation.

Guards were coming out of the woodwork, no one knew where we were and certainly no help would come our way. I wanted to believe Joe was right, tomorrow we could get the break we needed. Miracles happen, the Bible was full of them. Before drifting off I'd say a little prayer. And come tomorrow first thing, I'd begin watching for that big opportunity.

Sure we had a chance; sure we could be successful. So what if they outnumbered us, outgunned us, and held all the trump cards…we were good, Joe had said so!

My eyelids flickered and grew heavy; sleep was coming for me. Just prior to drifting away, Murphy crept in and whispered another truth in my ear…

'The race is not always to the swift nor the battle to the strong-but that's the way to bet.'

He laughed and sleep carried me away.

# CHAPTER NINE

Early next morning we shaved and showered. Then under gunpoint slipped into the coveralls hanging in the closet. Like the others we were ordered to remain barefoot, so after waving good-by to my hundred-dollar wingtips I filed in behind Joe and they escorted us out.

Eight p.m. sharp found us back in the dining room having breakfast with the crew we had met the night before.

All were present along with the addition of one new face-and not pretty one. Another chair had been placed near the head of the table and in it sat or squatted I should say, sat a six-hundred-pound GORILLA, hairy body and all.

At first, we thought it to be a man in costume, but it turned out the real McCoy.

When I glanced his way, Joe was wearing the same dumbfounded look I was. We didn't ask; we were sure Billy would get around to an explanation sooner or later.

The lady banker had put on quite a food bag. Stretched before us were eggs, bacon, toast, home fries, biscuits and gravy, jellies, fruits, coffee, juices and everything else that has ever been served for that most important meal of the day.

For the first several minutes everyone ate in silence, seemingly tuned out to the unfamiliar medley of breakfast sounds and fully content with the lack of conversation.

The funny looking Professor was obviously a vegetarian since his plate held only fruit. As for the two women, together they may have taken enough food to meet the nutritional needs of an ailing humming bird.

Mandegon had only pancakes and coffee while Barkin piled his plate with the works, a real farm boy appetite.

For the Doctor it was toast and coffee only; for the General the same with the addition of two strips of bacon. So much food and so little appreciation.

Popping a bite of scrambled eggs into my mouth I looked around the table and studied faces. These people were a gathering of upper crust snooties with the attitude that the world couldn't run without them. Even if I lived within their means, I could never develop such an outlook, and I was sure Joe thought the same thing.

On one hand, the silence was fine with us, but we wanted more information too. It wasn't until halfway through the meal Billy broke the repose.

"I trust you two had a restful sleep?"

"Not bad." I told her. Joe took a sip of coffee.

"It was great; we slept like a baby locked in its crib."

Billy made a face. "Please do try and understand. Had we not locked you up, your attempted escape would have brought about the means to your end. And to be quite honest, we have something much more exciting in store for you."

"It wouldn't be the gauntlet, would it?" Joe said.

"As a matter of fact, yes." Billy replied.

She turned her eyes to the gorilla. "This is Godzilla."

"Godzilla the Gorilla...catchy," Joe said before taking a bite of toast.

Billy flashed him a second long smile. "Yes, it is rather catchy Mr. Hardon. And our hairy friend has something very special in store for you later on."

Swallowing, Joe told her. "I certainly hope he's not going to try and molest me. Carlo might get jealous, and karate chop him." Everyone except Carlo burst into laughter. But quickly realizing what they had done, fell silent.

One by one their eyes turned to the Jamaican. It took no effort to realize how much this man was feared.

But Carlo himself was grinning too. And across the hush of the table he told Joe, his voice so calm it was unnatural.

"No Mon, I won't chop him. But with Miss Billee's permission, I will molest you. Even now I grow hard thinking of it."

Joe's face lost all expression. He stared at Mandegon a long time, took another bite of toast, swallowed, then replied.

"Let me tell you something Mandegon...up front, no bullshit, man to man. I have no idea of your religious preference, whether you believe in heaven or hell. But if you ever come near me entertaining any such idea you'll find out very quickly if either place exists. Because word of honor, I'll kill you and send you to one or the other. Understand?"

There was a long stretch of silence as they stared, their faces chiseled stone with eyes precariously cold. Each was sizing the other and each, I knew, could be a dangerous man. It was one of those queer moments when something way down deep tells you to keep your mouth shut. All of us waited motionless as tension mounted.

Billy was thoroughly enjoying it, her face aglow with a smile as sinister as the wicked witch of the North. Ardently her eyes danced to the vision of the two men battling to their death. But quickly realizing what she was doing and fearing things might get out of control, she gathered her composure and purposely broke the heated silence.

"Please gentlemen, do realize this is not something to be discussed over breakfast. Besides, I believe Dr. Priveman would like to enlighten our guests as to what is going on here at this house." She looked his way. "Doctor."

He nodded and smiled.

"Thank you, Natalie." Shifting in his chair to face us he cleared his throat then paused a few seconds to gather his thoughts.

"Gentlemen. For several years now we have been investigating... researching, the possibility of communication through mental telepathy. And I'm quite proud to say have made phenomenal progress. With the help of my fellow colleagues," he gestured to them with a swing of his hand, "we have been able to develop a serum that allows such conversation between two people for a run of twenty minutes-and sometimes longer. They need not be in the same room and it makes no difference what is between the two, distance or object. And very much to our surprise we've also discovered that to some extent, we can even communicate with certain animal species, like Godzilla here. If you will, please allow me to demonstrate."

Priveman rose from the table and retrieved a small black container from a nearby stand. Returning to his place, he opened it and removed two loaded syringes. Then he walked around the table to the gorilla.

At the animal's side he stood a moment and glanced thoughtfully our way. "In these syringes lie the most profound advancement mankind has ever known. The doors it will open are phenomenal."

The slightest grin began playing at the corners of his mouth and quickly turned into a broad smile. Beaming, he raised the syringes and announced proudly, "This beautiful little liquid will give the deaf back their hearing and enable science to advance at record speed." His eyes turned to General Phieffer. "And in the hands of the world's super-powers, it will put an end to the threat of nuclear annihilation... perhaps even war itself. It is our belief," he said glancing around the table, "that it may well be the God given answer to complete and total world peace."

Priveman turned then and injected the contents of one of the syringes into a vein he located on the gorilla's arm. The animal accepted it without a flinch; obviously he had been injected many times prior and to him it had become second nature.

It was all beginning to make sense now. The personalities around the table began coming into focus like a slow developing Polaroid snapshot.

Professor Nugent, the pharmaceutical chemist, was an expert in modern drug and nutrient interaction, as well as ESP and physic phenomena. Who better to lead such an endeavor? And who would have ever believed drugs and ESP would mix?

There was Dixie Barnebin, the beautiful FBI agent who no doubt ensured none of this reached the desk of the bureau side, while at the same time playing an active part herself as a known psychic.

My eyes turned again to Priveman. MD, Ph.D. and scientist. The perfect choice for medical overseer to all those unfortunate human guinea pigs locked behind the iron door in the tunnels below.

As for Barkin and Mandegon, they were the strong arms, the stealers of human life, kidnappers and professional hit men when necessary.

And of course the General, whose main interest, if asked, would no doubt be the concern and well-being of this great nation of ours. What was it First Officer Spock had told Captain Kirk while locked dying in the nuclear reactor of the USS Enterprise? 'The needs of the many by far outweigh the needs of the few.' Though fictitious, Spock was a true leader. The difference between him and Phieffer was that Spock sacrificed himself for the many while the General sacrificed the many for himself by turning his head each time an innocent victim was dragged down into the dungeons of experimental hell. And that made him no better than any of the others.

Having gone around the table, only Billy was left. And what her place in all of it was I didn't know for sure. At least, in part, it appeared to be straw boss and loyal company man, but company man to whom? To our government or private industry? Or perhaps herself and a fallen Soviet Union secretly clawing its way back to the top?

So much remained unclear. I was certain of one thing though, white slavery was not the tail we thought we were chasing, at least not white slavery as we had first thought.

When he was finished injecting the Gorilla, Priveman turned and slowly walked to where Joe and I sat. There was excitement on his face, and I thought about the mad scientist in the fifties movie, Frankenstein. It was at my side he stopped and I felt the hairs on the back of my neck stand up.

"If you will be so kind as to lend me your arm, Mr. Stone."

I looked up at him, then at all the others around the table, their faces were aglow with anticipation.

Finally, looking back at Dr. Priveman, I smiled and told him calmly. "With all due respect Doc… Joe has better veins."

"Please," he said, ignoring my remark. "I assure you, except for a small headache afterward, it is completely safe. Mr. Hardon will get his opportunity later. Trust me, there is no other way. If I myself or one of my colleagues were to inject it, there would be room for skepticism on your part. And you more than anyone can appreciate the gravity of it all."

Billy spoke up.

"Perhaps we're being unfair, Doctor. Let us offer the gentlemen a choice." Looking at me and smiling wide she said, "Mr. Stone, either you inject the serum or you inject a bullet-in the head-here and now."

For several seconds I stared back at her then looked up at Priveman and frowned. He gave me a look of reassurance but I had a hard time buying it. The hair on the back of my neck was still stiff. Glancing over at Joe I told him "If anything happens pal, you can have all my shoes."

You'd have thought I told him he was holding a ten-million dollar winning lotto ticket. And to be perfectly honest, that was not the reaction I was anticipating.

Turning up a sweaty palm, I surrendered my arm to Priveman and watched him through squinted eyes. It was a good stick with only the slightest pinch. When he was finished, he stuck on a Band-Aid and smiled with a wink. Trying hard not to be fidgety, I waited while everyone stared with euphoric faces.

For the first few seconds there was nothing. Hands resting on my thighs I tapped nervous fingers. Everyone kept staring and that didn't help. I felt like the poor sap on death row strapped to a tabletop waiting for the lethal liquid to run through the tubing and into his body.

Seconds passed but they felt like hours. Then suddenly the serum entered my heart. I could feel its beat quicken wildly and abruptly I sat up. I was truly frightened now.

I began feeling lightheaded followed by a moment of blurred vision and the strange sensation of stepping out of my body then quickly back in.

All fingers and toes tingled just enough to notice, then I shuttered with one quick forceful twitch and things instantly returned to normal. Looking at Priveman, I raised my eyebrows as if to ask, "Is that it?"

"Wonderful," he said, smiling again. "You're ready. Now you and Godzilla may communicate. Much like a trained dog, he understands all basic commands: sit, stand, turn around, etc. So please, with your mind only, speak to him. Give him an order."

For a few seconds I continued to stare at the doctor, my expression telling him he was crazy. Then I looked over at the gorilla and shook my head. The six-hundred-pound beast was busy picking at the hair on his legs.

"What the hell," I said out loud, "why not?" I'd give him a hard one to start and put this silly game to bed right away.

Concentrating in thought only, I called his name and told him to pick up his glass and take a drink of water. Immediately, he stopped his picking and slowly brought his head up to look at me. His dark brown eyes locked onto mine and we stared. Strangely, the word 'water' popped into my head more in the form of a question!

Wrinkling my forehead, I repeated the command. "Water. Drink."

Then, much to my surprise, Godzilla looked down at the table, picked up his glass and drank it dry, never spilling a drop. I said it out loud in shock and disbelief... "SHIT!"

Again, the gorilla brought his eyes up to mine.

In the form of a question, the word 'shit' popped into my thoughts and instinctively I repeated the word in thought process... 'shit'. Godzilla bobbed his head up and down then raised himself up in the chair and squatted; at the same instant I realized what I'd done.

I started to shout 'NO!', but it was too late. My hairy friend dropped a big pile right there in the middle of his chair. That's when everyone left the table mumbling and casting not so friendly looks my way.

Priveman grabbed my shoulder and informed me with embarrassment.

"I forgot to mention. Please be mindful, if it's a command the ape understands. he'll obey."

Looking up at Priveman I made a face. "Sorry."

The room was already beginning to fill with the terrible odor but he grinned and patted my shoulder. "Quite all right. Now try another command. And do be selective...please."

Looking once again at Godzilla I planted the thought to leave his chair and walk in circles behind it. Without hesitation he jumped down and did as he was ordered.

I couldn't believe what was happening. While watching the hairy creature walk in small distinct circles, I picked up a banana from the table, peeled it, and then took a bite. The moment I began chewing, it dawned...I had no desire whatsoever for that banana. Puzzled, I put it down and looked at Godzilla. What the hell was going on here? Why would I take a bite of fruit I didn't want, and worse, do it without even realizing?

Turning to say something to Priveman I caught myself, and instead brought my eyes slowly back to Godzilla. A small smile came to my face and in thought only I said to him, "It was you; you told me to do that, didn't you?"

The ape's head bounced rambunctiously, and the word "yes" exploded in my brain. "You giant, loveable, smelly primate." I thought, widening my smile. "Are you hungry?" Again, his head bobbed wildly and again the word 'yes' exploded like a cannon inside my head.

"This can't be happening." I said under my breath. I couldn't contain my excitement; it was building like a volcano. Not only were we exchanging thoughts, communicating. We were feeling what the other was feeling as well, much the way twins share the other's sensations.

Exhilarated, pumped up with a feeling of power and control, I gave the order to lay down and roll over. That's when he opposed me for the first time.

Coming to an abrupt stop he just stood there motionless, silent, his dark eyes locked onto mine. Thoughtfully I bit at my lip.

What was wrong? Was he angry, confused, perhaps not sure of the command? Priveman had assured me he understood all basic requests. Maybe the serum had run out? Glancing at my watch I shook my head. It had not been anywhere near twenty minutes yet.

Whatever the reason for the strange behavior, the ape's look grabbed me, reaching clear down into my soul. In my heart I felt a sense of remorse. Why?

The others were mesmerized, their eyes darting back and forth from the ape to me. The room was silent, no one moved.

A minute passed, then another. The house was hot. Godzilla never once broke his stare.

I began to grow uneasy. What the hell was going on? Was he contemplating an attack? If so, he would kill me in seconds. Taking a deep breath I let it out slowly and asked him in my mind, "What's wrong with you?"

They must have been magic words. He never replied but he did break the stare finally. Lowering himself to the floor he began rolling over and over as he had been told.

As he rolled, I ran my fingers through my hair in wonderment. That's when three words burst into my mind.

"Godzilla no dog!"

I went pale! I felt shock, disbelief, fear, and joy all at once...THIS GORILLA SPOKE AN ENTIRE SENTENCE!

Dumbfounded, I looked over at Joe, my mouth open wide. He shrugged, not knowing what the look was all about. Slowly I brought my eyes back to Godzilla who was still rolling on the floor.

Slowly my shock wore off, or at least subsided enough to allow me to get a grip. I said the words harshly to myself and meant every word... "You stupid ass, Stone."

Rising from my chair I walked to where Godzilla was rolling and knelt beside him. Reaching out I put a hand on his shoulder and spoke softly to him in my thoughts.

"That's enough fella."

He stopped moving and looked up at me. Those same dark brown eyes that had reached into my soul were filled with wetness. One single tear streaked its way down his cheek and I shook my head calling myself a dumb ass once again.

Feeling like the heel I was, I apologized and asked forgiveness for the humiliation I had caused him.

Reaching up like a little child, he took my hand and sent one more thought to me. This time his words were accented with feelings that felt like my own "Want go home!"

Inside my head flashed the sudden image of a huge cage, its floor covered with straw. He was asking me to take him back to wherever it was they kept him.

For the first time in my life, I realized just how human the apes really are.

Still holding his hand, I smiled warmly.

"Okay Buddy, you got it." Then a sudden thought came into my head and I said to him, "But what do you say we give them one more show before we call it quits. Get the last laugh?"

He cocked his head, puzzled. Obviously, he wasn't capable of understanding what I meant.

Everyone was still watching closely, remaining silent. I had the feeling Priveman and the others had no idea just how truly smart Godzilla was. Had he become so intelligent he knew enough to keep the majority of his progress hidden?

Looking into his eyes I tried one more time to explain myself. "What I'm saying is let's do one more trick before you go. A trick that will really piss them off! Make them angry! Mad!"

His eyes widened and the puzzled look disappeared. His thoughts came into my head clearly. "Piss off. Like!"

I gave him a wink. "You're my kind of Gorilla, pal. Return to your chair, pick it up and smash it against the tabletop...like you really mean it."

For several seconds my new friend looked at me, and it was obvious he was searching for words. "Then come them-Make mad all, hurt you." His vocabulary amazed me, not to mention, his compassion.

I'd never admit this to a psychoanalyst, but when I told my hairy friend I didn't give a shit how mad they got and that I wasn't worried, he actually smiled.

In seconds he was off the floor and back at the table with the chair in his hands. Violently he crashed it against the tabletop. Dishes shattered and wood splinters flew everywhere. He began grunting and making frantic wild noises. It was a bit more than I had suggested but I liked his style.

Throwing down the remainder of the chair he swept the tabletop with his arm and sent dishes and food flying through the air. Everybody scrambled to get out of the way. Then he was on top of the table beating his chest like the King Kong of the big screen. I was proud of my hairy friend and at the same time happy for him too, because somehow I knew it was well over due.

"Go Kong." I said, smiling to myself. That's when something smashed against the back of my head and knocked me to my knees. I saw stars as blackness rushed in and chased away the world around me. The room grew distant and as I toppled over to greet the floor, I thought of only one thing-Alex Stone, you've created a monster.

When I opened my eyes things were blurry, but I realized I was back in our room.

Blinking, I cleared my vision and found Joe leaning over me saying something that I couldn't quite make out. I strained to follow the movement of his lips.

My head hurt, my sockets ached and my ears felt like the inside of a church steeple with the bells ringing.

Sitting up, the room began spinning so I lay back down. Joe stuck a cold washcloth on my forehead, and it helped.

Whatever had hit me, it hit hard. I remembered too that Priveman had said the serum would leave the subject with a headache. Well he was right, and certainly the blow to the back of the head added fuel to the fire.

Trying again, I sat up and steadied myself with my arms braced behind me. Joe gave me support and asked with legitimate concern.

"Are you sure you're all right?"

This time I understood what he said and nodded a 'yes'.

"Let me tell you Alfie," he continued, "that hard noggin of yours took one hell of a blow."

Moving my head slowly I looked at him and reached back to touch the huge bump on my skull.

"What in the hell hit me anyway?" I asked, "A cannon ball at close range?"

"Worse," he replied sympathetically. "Mandagon's trained foot. He had you kicked so fast we didn't even see the blur. I went for him, but two-gun barrels landed under my chin."

Gingerly working my head back and forth I told him, "Well. thanks anyway Pal. It's the thought that counts. At least now you know what you're in for when he comes around to steal a kiss."

Swinging my feet over the side of the bed I paused a few seconds then stood up. Weakness ran down into my legs, but I managed to stand.

My head began to spin again but I fought it. I ambled into the bathroom and re-wet the cloth Joe had been holding over my forehead. Returning to the bed I sat, then held it in place over the lump. I flinched but it felt cool and helped.

"So what happened?" I asked.

"What do you mean what happened? The gorilla went ape shit."

"Bull!" I said the word excitedly and looked over at him." Then quickly glanced up at the cameras. They were still covered so I went on. "Joe, I talked with him. I had a running conversation with that gorilla. In our minds, we communicated. He knew what the hell I was saying, and he talked back to me, as if he were human."

Joe puckered his lips and looked up at the ceiling.

"Alfie, let me ask you a question. Isn't that part of the brain that allows a person to think, and reason located in the frontal lobe just behind the forehead? I mean, it's not in the back is it? Because I'm concerned that Mandagon might have kicked you just a little too hard."

Irritated, I pointed a finger at him. My head spun again but I didn't care.

"You know something, Joey? Sometimes I think you're just an overgrown Dick with a dark mustache."

His face went sober. "You're serious, aren't you?"

"You bet I am. Go look in the mirror."

"No!" He said with a smile. "I mean the ape. He really did talk to you, didn't he?"

"Yes! Y-E-S." I spelled it for him. "Man, I can't believe it, Joey. Godzilla the Gorilla is more human than Billy the blond wench. He knows happiness, he knows humor, he hurts, he feels sad, and he even felt embarrassment in what I was making him do. The hairy rascal actually talked to me. We had a running conversation I tell you. It was at the adolescent level, granted. But he did talk, forming actual sentences!"

Still looking a little skeptical Joe walked to the bathroom for a glass of water. When he returned, we sat back on the bed and he took a sip.

"So you're telling me all this hocus-pocus, psychic ESP stuff has merit?"

"Absolutely! Joe, I tell you Priveman is right. This serum is undoubtedly the greatest discovery, ever. The impact it will have on the world-the entire human race-is beyond comprehension."

He took another drink.

"Yeah," he said, "impact all right. Impact like Hiroshima."

I started to reply but clammed up.

Together our eyes turned to the door. Someone was there on the other side. And whoever it was, they were clumsily fumbling with the lock.

# CHAPTER TEN

A finger to his lips to signal silence, Joe motioned for me to answer the door while he slipped in behind it.

Maybe this was to be the chance he had said would come. Whoever worked the lock was doing so in haste. There was eagerness inside of me as I waited. Nothing in the world was as desirable as the want of a gun in my hand, and I hoped this would bring that opportunity.

Aside from the soft metallic clicking of trying the lock, we heard no other noises, no voices, no footsteps, and no movement of any kind.

Whoever was out there, they didn't know what they were doing. They were jumping from key to key trying for the correct fit.

I still had a headache and the knot on the back of my skull throbbed like a thumb hit with a hammer. I owed Mandagon and I was one who believed in repaying my debts. If it turned out to be him, it would suit me fine.

The clicking stopped and my eyes followed the slow turn of the knob. Arms folded, I stood silent, waiting.

This was one of those last minute, play it by ear plights that life so often throws at you. A time when the heart pounds, the adrenaline pumps, and in your mind you prepare for fight or flight. Only here, there would be no options; for us it would be fight only.

When the door swung open my eyebrows raised...it was Nugent, the nutty professor.

He stood alone, holding a huge ring of keys in his hand.

For a minute he stood staring, trying to decide whether or not to enter. Realizing the importance of luring him in, I shrugged, then glanced toward the bathroom door and yelled out.

"Joe, hurry up in there, we have company."

Nugent was taking it all in with cautious eyes. Looking at him I forced a smile.

"Well, it's more your place than mine. I'm just a guest, remember. Come on in."

Turning, I walked to the bed and sat.

He paused another few seconds then walked in. Joe exploded into action by shoving him toward me and turning to close the door at the same instant.

In a heartbeat, I was off the bed spinning our guest around. One arm went around his neck and the other bent one of his behind his back.

Holding him like that, I waited for Joe to slip a chair under the door handle. As soon as that was finished, he came over and gave Nugent a thorough frisking. There was no gun, so I turned him loose. Gasping he grabbed at his throat and told me hoarsely.

"My God man, that was a bit barbaric wasn't it?"

"Not half as barbaric as what you're doing to those people in the basement." I told him coldly.

He stared a second thinking it over, then raised a hand and nodded. "Yes, yes, it is. I'm sorry." Glancing at Joe, he said.

"Look, I... I don't know where to begin. In fact, I shouldn't even be here, but I want to help you."

He looked quickly to me. "Help both of you, of course." Then eyes back to Joe, he continued. "Believe me, I don't like what is happening here anymore than you do." He paused, looked my way again then went on. "Natalie is...well, pitiless. Her job here is to keep this project alive at any cost. She is, as you know, a very steadfast individual."

Joe put his hands on his hips and nodded his agreement.

"You won't get an argument from us, professor," he said, "but while you're on our least favorite subject, tell us, just who in the hell does she work for?"

Nugent lulled a second before answering.

"Our government. They fund this entire project. Secretly of course but fund it nevertheless."

Joe smirked for him. "Don't blow smoke up our butts, Nugent. Earlier we heard her speaking a lingo that sounded one hell of a lot like Russian, and if you've forgotten, our government hasn't gone totally communist yet."

The professor raised his hands and gestured.

"All right, all right! The whole story. What you heard was Russian. The whole thing is rather complicated, but I'll try and condense it."

Joe and I looked at one another then back to Nugent.

"You see, while Natalie is in fact working for our government, she is actually a soviet agent. What has happened is that she has...sort of been assigned to us...to our government that is. This project, code named MINDTALK, is a top secret American/Russian collaboration. Under this one roof the two superpowers, and yes they are still a super power, have gathered the very best in the way of American and Soviet Scientists. All of us have been here nearly eight years now, but only recently have we reached the success level of which we're all so proud."

Nugent walked to the bed and sat. Side by side Joe and I stood in front of him with arms folded, waiting. Looking up he glanced at both of us. "Natalie is going to kill the two of you."

Looking at Joe I frowned. "You're right, pal. She is one cold bitch."

"Look," Nugent began again. "In the beginning I was filled with excitement, exuberance. I saw this as a way of helping my fellow man. But now, the whole thing has become hideous, out of control. I think we all started out on the right foot but..." He looked down at the floor and I got the feeling he was actually hanging his head.

"What do you mean, out of control?" Joe asked.

He looked up and there was fear in his eyes.

"Natalie represents the Soviets, and General Phieffer the United States. Half here are American, half Russian. The idea was that both sides would get the formula when it was developed. That way they would be equals and forever keep it out of the hands of all other countries, on both sides."

"But now that it's developed both sides want it for themselves, right?" I said.

Sighing, he nodded his head. "Precisely."

I patted Joe on the back and smiled for him.

"Well friend, old buddy, I hope you're happy now. I could have been in Hawaii. Head of security for some low-keyed corporation drinking pineapple juice through a straw...in an air-conditioned office. But NO! 'Where is your heart?', you said. 'Show some compassion,' you said. You know what we are, Joey? We're the Laurel and Hardy of the new millennium and this is just one more fine mess you've gotten us into, you ass."

He winked. "Relax Alfie, I'll get us out too. Besides, where would we be without excitement?"

"I'll tell you where we'd be. Looking forward to retirement."

Nugent rose slowly from the bed. "I'd better be getting back to the lab before they miss me. I just wanted you to know what they were planning. I've had my share of hurting others and I guess this was the only way of trying to make things right. It's not much, but it's all I have." He started for the door but I stepped in front of him and held my hands up.

"Professor, before you leave, one more thing. Very briefly, how does the formula work."

Ignoring me he said. "I'm afraid I really must be getting back."

"Professor please, our lives may depend on it. The entire world may depend on it should we ever get out of here alive."

Staring into my eyes he said. "I doubt very seriously you would understand anyway."

"Try me!"

Following a shrug of the shoulders, he returned to the bed and sat again.

"OK. First let me say the formula consists of a high concentration of selected minerals, vitamins, and amino acids. All of which have specific effects on selected body organs. There are other ingredients, which are known only to us... if you know what I mean. For the exact formula you would have to get into the safe here, and that would be quite impossible I'm afraid."

"That's fine," I said, "just explain what goes on inside the body and how the messages get from one person to the other."

He made a face. "Well, physiologically speaking, the central nervous system is affected primarily. Basically, the serum stimulates the cholinergic system by use of acetylcholine, which of course is made naturally in the body from chlorine, which we trigger through mega doses of B-5 and B-12. To stimulate EEG activity in the brain we use a special mixture of morphine, phenylalanine, lecithin and the like. By use of specially modified EEG and parapsychology telemetry we know that brain waves are literally shot out into the atmosphere, much like rays of light. Science has known now for some time that everything in the universe vibrates. This we believe is the key to thought transfer. Somehow the sound waves are broken down, or perhaps better phrased... disassembled. Then somehow, they are reconstructed according to vibration pattern. When a mental thought leaves the brain of an inoculated participant, a designated receiver picks it up, and hence you have your commutative connection. The catch, of course, is that the receptor is that person who has been 'cloned,' by the same serum."

"What about the brain? Does the serum effect it, genetically restructure it somehow?" I asked.

"Yes, although we do not thoroughly understand how it happens. Actually, the entire central nervous system undergoes a mild metamorphosis."

"Doctor Priveman said the telepathic communication lasted only twenty minutes or so. Out of curiosity, is that due in part to synapse depletion?"

Nugent nodded with a trace of surprise on his face.

"Why yes, it does. How do you know about that?"

"Basic anatomy and physiology in Paramedic school." I told him quickly, wanting to get on to another question, but Joe cut in.

"Wait a minute," he said waving a hand. "I'm picking up some of this, but you lost me on the synapse thing. What is that?"

Nugent moved his eyes to Joe.

"Putting it simply, Mr. Hardon, synapses are like bridges, they connect the hundreds of nerve fibers inside our bodies, much like a bridge connects a road over a river. Certain chemicals are released from synoptic vesicles that construct the bridge, thus permitting an impulse, or message, to pass to or from the brain. After twenty or so minutes these vesicles deplete themselves of chemicals and need time to reproduce. Hence, end of transmission."

I took the questioning back. "Are other Psychic areas affected by the serum?"

He shook his head yes. "Most definitely. As a matter of fact nearly all of them, at least to some degree...physical readings, precognition, prophecy, astro projection and others as well."

As he talked, I kept waiting to hear him announce the big one. The one that if it were to fall into the hands of the wrong person or country, it would promise world dominance almost overnight. With the kind of power it would give, it would create a human monster like none we've ever known. In fact, so powerful would it make them, the only true comparison would be the Antichrist himself. But Nugent finished, never mentioning it, so I did.

"What about Mind Control?"

His face took on a strain and it was easy to see I had hit a raw nerve.

"Look," he said rising to his feet. "I really must be getting back."

"Not that easy, Professor," I said. "Not until you've answered the question. What about Mind Control?"

He sighed and threw up his hands again. "All right. It's not yet perfected, but what we're working on would allow the injected individual the power of mind control for up to a week without the worry of synapse depletion. At the end of that time a repeat injection would be required."

I said it just under my breath, "Holy shit! And what about the cloning requirement? Would the person to be controlled need to be injected?"

"It won't be necessary in this case. You see, every human being, whether they realize it or not, has a sixth sense, a universal mind of sorts. It's enigmatic, I admit, but they have it. It's just that very few are able to develop it for use. And it seems that while they are unable to use it, they are in fact unconsciously susceptible to one that can, at least to one with a boosted clairvoyant psyche...which is what the serum creates."

Joe looked at me and there was concern on his face, maybe fear. Looking back to Nugent he asked.

"When will this serum be ready?"

The professor shrugged. "We're close. A few days, perhaps."

Nugent glanced at his watch and almost yelled. "My God, look at the time. I must return to the lab. By now they are all over the place looking for me."

"What do they do, make you check in on the hour?" I asked jokingly.

"Yes!" There was panic in his voice.

He moved to the door and stopped. Turning to face us he said quietly. "I will leave it unlocked. And please, if they catch you, do not say I helped you. Natalie would have me killed."

Then he was gone, easing the door closed behind him. It clicked shut and at first, we stood there staring. If they were out there looking for him then they would be around any minute to check on us. We had to move fast. Pronto we scrambled to the bedside for our shoes-they were gone! My jaws tightened.

I looked at Joe, my face a twisted mass of anger.

"Those sons-of-bitches. Can you believe that? The commie bastards stole my shoes."

He stood there looking at me, speechless, his mouth open. I threw up my hands. "You know what?" I added, "I'd lay odds they're on their way right now to some Siberian farmer. He'll probably wear them to clean his barn in. This is it Joey, the last…"

He cut me off by placing a hand over my mouth.

"Look Alfie, I realize you're upset. But try and remember, this is not Buckingham palace, and we are not Charles and Andrew. These people do not like us. These people want to KILL us. I would like very much to get the hell out of here, O.K.?"

I nodded and he let go.

Shaking his head he moved to the door and eased it open just a crack. Surveying the area carefully, he gave the high sign it was clear, and we moved out into the hallway.

All was quiet. We had only a minimal knowledge of the layout of the house, but it was enough to get us out.

The hallway would open into the large dining room where we had eaten, then pick up again on the other side. In that far hallway we would find the entrance to the study with the hidden elevator.

Stopping just short of the dining room entrance, we listened with our backs tight against the wall. There was nothing to hear. The house was quiet, uncomfortably so; the kind of quiet you get at a funeral parlor. The only thing missing were the deceased. I frowned at myself; what the hell was I saying?

Joe glanced back at me and whispered.

"You ready to cross?"

"Let's do it," I told him.

It was Murphy's' perfect timing again. Halfway into the room we heard the muffled sound of voices drifting up the far hallway. A frantic search showed one exit close enough to get to before they reached us. It was a door leading into the kitchen.

Scrambling, we made it only by the skin of our teeth. When there the door closed just as they entered the dining room. There were three and they were in a hurry. It took no effort in guessing their destination.

Glancing around we saw that the kitchen was much larger than normal. In fact, it looked more like one you'd find in a restaurant than a domestic home. Knowing what we did about what was going on in the tunnels, we understood why. This kitchen cooked for a lot of people.

Pots and pans hung from the ceiling and there was a huge walk-in freezer at one end of the room.

Giant metal shelves scaled the entire length of one wall and held countless cases of canned goods. Near the sink, on a butcher-block counter we found a container of knives, and after picking one out, I turned to Joe.

"I've got a hunch, pal. Let's find the basement."

He looked at me from the corner of his eye but didn't waste time asking questions.

There were three doors that exited from the kitchen. The one we had come through, another to the outside and a third up a narrow stairway to what was probably the servants' quarters. Voice low, I told Joe.

"There is probably a basement entrance from the outside somewhere. I think it's worth the risk."

He nodded his approval, so I cracked the back door and peered around. Things were clear so we slipped out.

The sky was a beautiful blue and a warm afternoon sun wrapped around us. It was bright and we squinted as our eyes adjusted.

Hugging the wall, we moved along the backside of the house to the first corner. Peeking around I saw no one. Then suddenly a guard with a shotgun came around at the far end heading in our direction. Jerking back, I whispered to Joe what I saw, and he nodded in silence. I knew what to do; we had done it before. It was risky, but always effective.

Waiting until the guard was just about ready to round our comer, I stepped out like someone who had lost their way. Immediately his startled eyes came on me and Joe came around with a haymaker. It was a perfect knock out. Rocky Balboa would have been proud. My want came true. I would now have a gun in my hand.

Joe took the shotgun, and I pulled the man's handgun from the shoulder rig...a nickel-plated 357. It wasn't my Beretta, but I liked the feel of it anyway.

After dragging the body close to the wall we moved on. We were now headed up the side that would bring us to the front of the house. We were paralleling the free end of the garage.

At the corner I crouched low and took a peek around. Another guard stood braced against the house, near the front door. He was staring idly out over the huge front lawn, looking bored and inattentive. But there was no way of taking him out without using a gun, so we pulled back and thought things out. At this point we had no desire to alert anyone. A needless shot to take out one man would bring all the others running. And much to my disappointment, the entrance to the basement we sought was nowhere to be found. There was nothing left now but to go back the way we had come.

Joe nudged me with his elbow and whispered, pointing to a garage window.

"Maybe it's in there."

Looking from him to the window I made a happy face.

"Yeah Joey," I whispered back, "just maybe it is."

The window was open, so he set the shotgun down and cupped his hands. I climbed up and in, then helped him.

Inside we stood motionless a minute and let our eyes adjust to the semi darkness. There were three overhead doors with windows, but their light added very little in helping us see.

The garage housed only one car-Joe's Corvette. After smiling at me he stroked the hood tenderly and made the motion of a kiss.

A quick check showed the keys were still in the ignition and for a fleeting second the thought of making a run for it crossed our minds. But bottom line if we did that, we knew what would happen to all those people in the basement-Billy had made that clear. Within minutes of our escape the place would go up in a violent explosion.

It's strange, growing up I had always been taught it was wrong to hate, and I tried not to. But now it seemed so easy...and right.

We found the basement entrance near a door leading back into the house. It was our big bonanza and I wanted to shout out loud. I had a good feeling inside, like just maybe we were going to get out of this thing after all, especially if my hunch turned out positive.

The entrance to the basement was a metal door covering a cement stairway. Pulling it open we saw the light switch on the wall just a few steps down. While entering, two men came running past the row of garage door windows and we ducked. It was apparent the body of the guard Joe had cold cocked had been discovered. They knew now we were outside somewhere.

Descending into the basement, we closed the metal lid behind us then hit the switch. The darkness exploded into light and once again we had to wait for our eyes to adjust. While they made their transition, Joe asked.

"So tell me Alfie, what is this hunch you were talking about?"

Within seconds the black spots vanished, and I stood staring over the basement area. It was a sea of discarded crap. Just to the left, a small section had been converted to a wine cellar and several rows of wide, wooden shelves held countless bottles of wine.

Boxes, furniture, tools and everything else imaginable stood stacked against rough, cinder block walls. Above our heads, 4 by 6 joists constituted the ceiling and in a sporadic fashion an array of assorted junk hung from hammered spikes.

The floor beneath our feet was rough cement painted burgundy.

Impatient, Joe grabbed my shoulder.

"Alfie, will you tell me what the hell we're going down here?"

As I explained, I began searching frantically behind the countless boxes.

"Look, Joey. I doubt Billy is stupid enough to build this house with only one entrance and exit to the tunnels. She may want to keep other people trapped down there, but not herself. I'm sure, should the worst happen. I'm positive she had another exit built somewhere, one that only she herself knows about. And I'm willing to bet your reputation, worthless as it may be, that it's right down here somewhere, right under our noses."

He made a face that said I just might be right, then moved farther to the left and began looking, too. We searched anxiously, knocking over boxes, casting things aside and strewing junk everywhere. It was a door for which we searched and if it existed, it would be expertly hidden. Relentlessly, we moved in tornado fashion, frantically looking under or behind anything large enough to hide an entranceway but came up with zilch.

Pausing, I put my hands on my hips and looked around. Nothing but cinder block, wood beams and junk. It just didn't figure.

I gave thought to the elevator ride we had taken the day that we arrived. We had descended at least fifteen or twenty feet. From the basement ceiling to the floor it was 8, maybe 10 feet, which meant we still needed to go down another ten or so, give or take a foot.

Frowning, I sighed. If I were wanting to safely hide an emergency escape route that I wanted no one else to know about, where would I put it and how could I conceal it? I'd want it to be small.

Snapping my fingers suddenly, I looked at Joe. "Ten feet, maybe fifteen." I said. He looked at me.

"What?"

"A ladder Joey, a small hole, a scuttle; one just big enough to crawl out of and easy to conceal. If it's not in the walls then it has to be in the damn floor."

He scowled at me. "The floor! How the hell can it be in the floor Alfie, it's made of concrete."

I looked at him feeling stupid. He had a point. Biting nervously at my lip, I glanced around again.

"I don't know," I said puzzled. "Shit!" I wiped sweat from my forehead.

Then I blurted it out, "The wine!"

"What?"

"The wine, Joey!"

He started to say something but stopped. Above our heads we heard the muffled sound of garage doors opening and the voices of a dozen men scurrying across the floor. They knew we were here…and to them we were fish in a barrel.

# CHAPTER ELEVEN

Clutching the shotgun tightly, Joe positioned himself behind a stack of boxes offering a clear view of the stairway. I in turn devoted my full attention to the wine shelves.

Time was running out and I madly searched for a lever or button, any kind of mechanism one might use to open a secret compartment. Somewhere beneath this shelving was an opening…there had to be!

Above us we could hear the clear chatter of the men and it was no chore realizing there were more than what we cared to think about.

As I scoured the shelving, my thoughts wandered. Is this how it was to end? We were to die here buried in some shallow unmarked grave deep in the woods, or worse, our bodies cast into an unfinished tunnel atop the cold earth?

Beads of sweat formed on my brow. Above us, the voices fell silent and we knew they were ready. Frowning, I swiped my forehead with the back of my hand while at the same time groping the shelves in frantic search. I knew full well there was simply no more time, yet, despite Murphy's determination to stick it to me, I hoped for the best while anticipating the worst. Desperation brought a curse to my lips and that was the ticket. Just like in the movies, the heroes are rescued at the last minute. When I pushed hard against the last section of shelving, it gave way and I nearly lost my balance.

Damn, that was it. I couldn't stop the big smile that showed up on my face. The section creaked as I rotated it outward to an almost 90-degree angle. And when I brought it to a slow jerky stop, the wine bottles rattled gently. Looking down, I found myself staring into a round gaping hole with ladder attached.

Bathed in a shadowy haze created by the basement lights, it descended straight downward, gradually disappearing in a dense blackness.

After a quick prayer of thankfulness, I yelled for Joe to get his butt over to where I stood. Then stepping onto the rung, I smiled and told Murphy to go step into a cow pattie.

With Joe right behind me, we descended down into the awaiting darkness. Unlike the tunnels, we had toured with Billy, there were no lights here, only that which poured in through the opening. I'd have traded all the shoes I owned for a sing flashlight.

Just as Joe pulled the shelving back into place, we heard the metal door to the basement being flung open and a stampede of feet clamber down the stairway.

They would search but they wouldn't find us. Joe and I both would have enjoyed seeing the look on their faces when they turned up empty handed, for we were sure none knew of the secret passageway.

We stood in blackness as dark as the inside of a sealed coffin. With arms extended I could touch the walls on either side. I couldn't see them but could easily tell they were unfinished, nothing but cold, hard earth.

It was absolute blackness. For the first time in our lives we would experience the horror of losing our eyesight. There would be no seeing as we made our way, only feeling.

We contemplated waiting until the pack above us left, then simply climbing back out into the light. But a guard, we were sure, would be placed at the basement entrance while the others searched the grounds like a school of hunger-starved piranha. And for sure, the moment Billy heard the story, she'd know where we had disappeared to and place permanent guards in the basement. They would have us shot long before we even had the shelving removed from the top of the hole. So like it or not, we were locked in.

Beneath our bare feet, the tunnel floor was damp and cold, but that was the smallest of our worries. We had little idea of which direction to go. Billy had said these unfinished tunnels traveled on for miles.

We knew too, that they would constitute an endless maze, making it nearly impossible to maintain a sense of direction. And I wondered what might lay in them? Would there be traps? Open shafts perhaps, deep and seemingly endless, a horrifying fall to the death, manmade snares originally set for those who came hunting the runaway slaves.

My mind's eye envisioned the layout of the house above, forming a mental image of where the elevator shaft might be in relation to the basement. It was probably somewhere to the right of where we now stood. If we followed along the wall, bearing always to the right, it just might lead us to the lighted tunnels…and the Bordenwells.

Taking the lead with Joe close behind, I began inching my way along. My right hand maintained contact with the wall while the left groped the darkness ahead. Each step was slow and deliberate, always setting the leading foot down with a careful easiness. If there were open pits I wanted to sense them before I took the next step.

The temperature was fifteen or twenty degrees cooler here, stealing away precious body heat. And in only a few short minutes, our exposed feet ached from the cold. Had we been dressed for it being under the earth would have made for good natural air-conditioning and comfortable traveling.

The tunnel made a turn to the left and I guessed we were travelling toward the far end of the house. We both knew the lighted tunnels wear nearby; the trick was choosing the correct turns leading to them.

There was another turn, this one back to the right, then another left again. Then yet another turned to the left.

We travelled what seemed a long distance before the next change. Here, the tunnels came to a 'Y'. Feeling with my hands, I could tell the bifurcation was narrow and that both channels cut away sharply.

I told Joe what I'd found. "Okay pal," I said into the darkness. "Your guess. Which way?"

It took little effort in knowing what ran through his mind. If we chose the wrong fork, it would probably lead us away from the house and into a maze with no way out. The other might lead to where we wanted to go…maybe.

"Come on pal," I said eagerly, "it's your call. If I'm destined to die with no shoes on my feet, it's going to be your fault."

While Joe thought, my stomach growled and I realized I was hungry. It was growing colder too and I turned up the collar of the coveralls.

In the silence of the darkness I could hear Joe's breathing and it sounded calm and easy. For me it was different. A little voice coerced me to return to the ladder before it was too late; that even now we might have come too far and taken too many turns to find it again.

Leaning against the wall, I stuck my hands in my pockets for warmth. While waiting for Joe's decision, my mind drifted back for a memory long ago while working as an Indianapolis Firefighter.

We had been toned out to a three-alarm fire at a huge downtown apartment complex. Fifteen people were reported trapped on the fifth floor with flames climbing out of several windows. Charged hoses sprawled the ground like a pit of wet snakes and red lights streaked the buildings. As the first company in we were ordered to front a rescue. Even as we donned air packs in preparation, one of the trapped victims hurtled themselves out of a window rather than endure the agonizing pain of burning to death. Helplessly we watched his screaming body tumble to the earth below, his life ending in a red splattering.

Aerial ladders were scaling the walls like the seize of the Alamo. Black smoke rolled heavy from the windows of the fire floor and from time to time as the wind shifted we'd catch a glimpse of a head gasping for air.

Like the deadly smoke, time was a sworn enemy, a ruthless adversary. But it was the fire itself that truly challenges us, destructive and aggressive, a mindless killer forcing a race; with the winning prize being that of human life.

Rushing to my assigned aerial, I scrambled up the narrow ladder, slowed by the cumbersome gear I wore and weight of the breathing apparatus on my back.

Above, the dark smoke spiraling from the window waited patiently, wanting me, but I knew what to expect.

Once inside, I'd find a no-man's land, a deadly world filled with poisonous gases and zero vision; there would be no seeing, only feeling your way. And the only air fit enough to breath would come from the heavy tank on my back, and when it was gone, if I wasn't near an exit, it meant I too would become a victim.

As I scrambled up the narrow rungs, I could hear my regulator open and close vigorously. I was breathing far too hard and ordered myself to slow down.

Inside somewhere, the seat of the raging fire roared and rumbled like a hungry dragon waiting in its dark burned out world for a team of daring and foolish heroes to hunt it down and kill it.

A window to my far right exploded from the hot gases and sent fragments falling below.

Reaching the top of the ladder, I felt the hot smoke engulf me like the fog of death. Alone and a hundred feet in the air the ladder swayed, reminding me of the fatal consequence should I make a single mistake.

Standing on the very tip, I strained to see into the menacing cloud of heat and gases, but visibility was zero. My breathing remained loud and sweat ran like a river over my face beneath the air mask.

The wind shifted and I could scarcely see what appeared to be the outline of an arm. It lay motionless hanging just out of the window. Carefully, I moved closer and with my face only inches away, guessed the body to be that of a woman.

If she was breathing I couldn't tell so I shook her, and she moaned. Using great caution, I maneuvered her onto the ladder and began a slow decent down. Once at the bottom, I turned her over to the Paramedics who began quick and aggressive treatment. She responded almost immediately to the oxygen they gave her, and I knew she'd be fine.

Turning to climb once again I heard a cry out after me, so I stopped and look down at her. Nearly drowned by the roar of the engine her voice was muffled but I heard the fear. It was intertwined with pleading on a face covered with soot and smoke and as tears streamed through the black film she cried out to me, "My children, get my children, they're by the window!"

Suddenly, Joe was shaking my shoulder and I realized the darkness around me was not hot smoke.

"What did you do, fall asleep?" He asked.

"No, just thinking." I said into the blackness. Clearing my head I asked him. "Well how about it, which way?"

"To the right, Alfie. The way I see it, if you don't know which way to go-go the right way."

I agreed with him, and we inched on.

Frequently, we stopped to listen, straining to hear sound, any sound. And constantly we searched for even a remote flicker of light.

The absolute darkness was eerie and the idea of these tunnels being over a century old demanded special caution. Who knew what might lay in our path…perhaps rusty old relics to slice open our vulnerable feet or hanging items to fall down upon us?

And what about a cave-in? No doubt the finished tunnels had been reinforced to prevent such a mishap. But these channels, on the other hand, had not been touched for over a hundred and forty years, a hundred and forty years of wearing and eroding. And what of the traps set for those Southern hunters who had come tracking those poor slaves who had risked all for the taste of freedom? Would such dangers still exist?

Suddenly, my mind shifted to the Bordenwells. They were so close, perhaps only a few hundred yards away…but in which direction? If we failed here, lost in these tunnels, their lives would remain as it is until the day of their deaths. They would stay prisoners, a family of human guinea pigs destined for more suffering at the hand of a cold, sadistic, inhuman bitch. The bible says we reap what we sow, and I wanted to be there when Billy reaped hers.

So much needed to be done, I thought. Things like getting the Bordenwell family back together and taking possession of the formula, then turning it and Billy over to proper authorities. And finally, collecting our two hundred grand from good old James W. and last but not least-get the hell out of this business.

I remembered what Nugent had told us. That Natalie was both a soviet agent and working for our government at the same time, and it was all top secret. That alone brought up several good questions. Questions like who in the hell would we turn to even if we did get our hands on the formula? Who would believe us anyway and what would the CIA and new Russian government do if they found out we even knew about it?

We had stumbled into something much bigger than white slavery. And to date, we had only one friend we could turn to, Jay Jenkins. But even he might refuse to help us when he discovered what it all added up to. If he did, I couldn't blame him.

Nothing, it seemed, stood in our favor. Here we were prisoners in a house belonging to a Russian agent, lost in the horrid blackness of century old tunnels, out gunned, outnumbered, candidates for the gauntlet, caught up on the wrong side of two governments, cold, hungry and shoeless.

Regardless of how you shuffled the deck Billy held all the trump cards. To say the least things looked bleak. I patted the 357 in my pocket and for the first time thought of a Murphy law I liked...'A Smith and Wesson beats four aces.'

The tunnel made a sharp turn to the right and just as I rounded the corner my foot kicked something lying in the pathway. It made a faint rattling noise then fell quiet. I jumped back, stepping on Joe's foot. It caused him to yell into the darkness.

Not moving, I froze, expecting something horrible to follow, but nothing happened. Remaining motionless I waited for my heart to quiet down then told Joe what occurred. He had heard it too.

"What do you think it is Alfie?" He murmured quietly.

"I don't know," I whispered back, "but whatever it is I think it's laying across the pathway wall to wall."

"Can we step over it?"

"How in the hell do I know."

"Well, feel it and see."

"Bull shit, you feel it and see!"

"You're in the lead, Alfie." He insisted.

I mumbled under my breath. "Okay, you big wuss. Hand me your shotgun."

Groping through the darkness I felt it then took it from his hands. Leaning forward I slowly swept the barrel across the tunnel from wall to wall, zigzagging downward. About knee level the barrel struck something leaning against the left side of the wall.

"Tell ya what." I told Joe, handing back the shotgun. "You start feeling down the wall to the right and I'll feel down the left. If you make contact with something stop and let me know. I don't have to tell you to move slow and easy."

"You've got that right Alfie." He whispered.

Hands in place we began working down. The walled earth remained cold and hard as we cautiously patted toward the floor. About knee level my hands touched the thing I had struck with the barrel of the shotgun. Stopping immediately, I informed Joe.

"Listen pal," I told him. "I'm going to finish feeling it out. Why don't you back away, just in case."

"Okay buddy but be careful." I heard him shuffle backwards a few feet then stop.

Delicately I continued.

It felt like the top of a small, rounded stone. Walking my fingers easily down I felt two holes about an inch apart; they were Perfectly opposite each other and a little larger than my fingers. Moving down a little further I suddenly caught my breath and jumped to my feet.

"Son-of-a-bitch!"

I couldn't see him, but Joe jumped too.

"What the hell is it?" He exclaimed.

My voice was high, "It's a man...bones. Human remains."

There was a moment of silence as it registered, then Joe laughed lightly. "He's dead, Alfie! He can't bite you."

"I know that you ass. It's just not what I expected, that's all." I put a hand to my chest and told my heart to be still.

Following a moment of silence we stepped over the remains and continued on. I couldn't see it, but I knew Joe was still grinning. We covered several feet before either one of us spoke. Finally Joe asked in a whisper.

"Who do you think he was Alfie?"

"Hard to tell. Maybe an old bounty hunter, or a slave who never made it out. Who knows."

"Or maybe," Joe added, "an escapee from Billy's chamber of horrors."

Joe may have been more right than he believed. These old tunnels would be the only hope of escape the prisoners down here would have; maybe the remains were those of one of her unfortunate human guinea pigs. A smart one who had made it out and found a way into the old network—only to end up dying in this very spot after days of searching for light and slowly starving to death.

Just who the person was would forever remain a mystery. However, one thing that was not a mystery though, was that Joe Hardon and Alex Stone had no intention of joining him.

# CHAPTER TWELVE

The darkness was endless. That we might never see light again was becoming a frightful possibility. They say you don't miss something until it's taken away. And I vowed if we made it out of this alive, I would cherish my sight forever.

Time passed in segments unknown. Seconds, minutes and hours did not exist in this eternal abyss. Here, hope and prayer served as our eyes.

Even Joe was silent, lost within his own thoughts, bringing to life sweet visions with which to chase away the fear and despair that fought hard to take possession of his mind.

Turn after turn, the tunnels wound their way through the blackness far beneath the lighted earth above us. Up there, I thought, the sun would be shining, covering the world with its golden warmth. And there would be streetlamps, flashlights and candles; all one would ever need to make a world of sustained light.

I thought about the ladder that could lead us back up to all of it. Where was it now? We had long lost count of the rights and the lefts we had taken. There had been too many turns, too many 'Y's'. To find it now would be a miracle. I heard it the same time Joe did, and we stopped almost together.

"Alfie, did you hear that?"

"Yeah."

Though the darkness had stolen our sight, in return, it had given us a keener sense of hearing. Something was there in front of us, waiting. It had growled a low, deep warning, then went silent.

Joe lowered the shotgun level with his hip, while I eased the 357 out of my pocket. The thing growled again, this time slightly louder. I guessed it to be ten, maybe fifteen feet straight ahead. What could it be? The possibilities ran rampant. A wild dog perhaps, one who had wandered in through some opening far away and lost the way out. A Bear? Possible. They were not uncommon in New York State; one could have wandered down from the Adirondack Mountains. Maybe it was a wolf or, even worse, a pack of wolves!

My heart pounded as a shivering thought filled my head. If whatever it was decided to attack us, how would we defend ourselves? Never before had we fought an adversary totally blind. If this were a man we could anticipate its move, know how to fight it. But what stood in the darkness ahead was not human, and without the aid of vision, the danger increased greatly. Whatever it was, it stood its ground with firm determination. I could only hope the creature had no more desire to attack us then we did it. Yet, like it or not, this would have to be a standoff, for we needed to continue down the very path which it blocked. Whatever it was, neither Joe nor I had any desire to kill it, only to move around it.

Whispering, I asked him, "What do you think?"

"I don't know Alfie. For certain we have to get past it."

My head nodded in the darkness.

"Yeah, but..."

There was no seeing it. How we knew I don't know. Perhaps we sensed it, or heard a slight rustling, or felt the faintest feel of air movement. It lunged through the darkness with a grace and power that promised battle. Instinctively we ducked, but on the way down it caught Joe mid chest. His shotgun went off and for a split second the blast brought light to the tunnel. Only for a fraction did my blurry eyes catch a glimpse of it. The thing was huge and covered with long hair. Snarling lips yielded a fleeting sight of sharp canine teeth.

The huge size of the thing easily toppled Joe and together their combined weight smashed hard onto the cold ground. Fierce and aggressive, it snarled viciously, determined to kill the human predator that dared infringe upon its territory. A wild animal over the edge, its razor-sharp teeth snapped and tore at the flesh on Joe's arms. Despite the blindness, I could envision the scene. Helplessly he covered his face, fighting frantically to protect his throat. In desperation he screamed for my help, his voice frantic in the darkness.

"Alfie get it the hell off me. Shoot the sun of a bitch."

A mere second of decision seemed a lingering eternity for me. My thumb pulled back the hammer of the 357...but where was my target? What if the bullet struck Joe? Or passed through the animals' body and into him? His cries for help grew louder and more frenzied. If I did nothing this beast would surely kill him, yet, if I dared take a wild shot, I myself might become his killer.

Fear and indecision gripped me like a ton of stones. The snarling animal continued to bite and rip with fierce determination. Their bodies rocked and arched repeatedly while locked in their grisly battle of man and animal. Joe would die if I didn't do something immediately! Then I remembered...in the kitchen, the knife! I had poked it through the upper pocket of the coveralls to serve as a sheath.

Reaching up I groped for it and came away with it gripped in my palm. Fingers tight around the handle I raised it far over my head and at the same time, dropped the 357 to the ground. With my free hand I reached out into the darkness.

Though they thrashed wildly in their struggle, I groped until I clutched a fist of fur. Bringing the knife down in a powerful arch it sank to the handle with a sickening sound. The beast yelped into the darkness, and I could feel its head turn to snap at the thing that had caused it pain. But I gave it no time to bite, for again and again, the knife arched and stabbed into the animals' body. It was a repeated frenzy of needless effort, motivated by the adrenaline that blocked the senses and supplied the strength needed to win the battle.

Over and over the blade arched and stabbed until finally, my breath coming fast, it dawned on me the fight was over, and the animal lay dead.

Slowly I regained my composure and climbed to my feet. Reaching down I helped Joe to his.

The right arm of his coveralls had been torn to shreds and I could feel his blood drip onto my hands as I held him steady.

Leaning him against the tunnel, wall I used the knife and cut off one leg of my coveralls. Ripping the long section into two wide strips, I wrapped them tightly around the bleeding arm then tied them off. I couldn't see, so I spiraled it down the entire length just to be sure. Sighing I shook my head and asked him.

"You bleeding anywhere else, hotshot?"

His voice sounded like the same old Joe. "Nothing worth mentioning, Alfie, thanks."

"Forget it, pal," I told him.

Searching through the darkness he found my shoulder and rested a hand on it. "Alfie, are you ready to get out of this place?"

"What do you mean? I've been ready!"

"That's good," he said cheerfully. "Look down the tunnel."

Turning, I caught my breath. In through three tiny holes bright rays of light shot toward us like beams from a flashlight. To us they were beams from heaven. The blast from Joe's' shotgun had obviously ripped through a wall separating the two tunnels. A wall we may never have otherwise found.

The very beast that had tried to kill him had shown us the way out.

Retrieving the knife and guns, we stepped hastily over the dead animals' carcass and moved toward the rays of light.

We came to another Y on the way and discovered the light emitted from the channel veering to the right. Even as tiny as the holes were the light was blinding at first, so we stood waiting until our eyes adjusted.

From the point of bifurcation, we had only traveled twenty feet before reaching the wall. It consisted of a typical sixteen-inch spaced wall framing lined with soft fiberglass insulation. Hurriedly we ripped most of it away. The only thing separating us now was a sheet of paneling nailed to the two-by-four framework.

From the lighted tunnel side, it would be impossible to tell this passageway was here.

Using the knife, I enlarged one of the three holes and peered through. The hallway was vacant.

Diligently we listened but heard no sound. Our hands scoured the framework searching for a handle or latch but found none. Apparently, what we had discovered was an old channel of tunnel Billy had never intended to use; so she had it framed in and paneled over.

The only way out now was to rip away the sheet of paneling; it would make noise and neither of us liked that idea, but there was no other alternative short of returning into the darkness.

Locating what I thought might be the edge of the paneling I inserted the knife blade and began prying. The blade flexed with each attempt, and nothing gave. Joe waited patiently while leaned against the wall. As I moved from area to area he asked.

"Alfie, do you suppose they heard the shotgun when it went off?"

Moving farther to the left I inserted the blade in a crack and answered, "I don't know. It would seem odd that they didn't."

"Yeah, I know. It's funny," he continued. "That dog or wolf or whatever it was, must have been here because it could hear and smell people on the other side. It had probably gotten lost in these tunnels somehow and this was as close as it could come to finding a way out. Hell, who knows how long the poor animal had been locked up in here."

"Probably weeks Joey" I told him, "the thing must have been starving. I mean, even after the first bite it kept coming back for more of you. Any animal in its right mind would have turned and ran after the first taste."

"That's funny Alfie. When we get out of here maybe you should forget about the Hawaiian job and become a stand-up comic."

I started to say something back but there was a snap and the blade broke. I swore under my breath and told Joe what had happened.

"Fine," he said, "now it's my turn."

Moving to the framework he felt with his hands then turned sideways and stepped back.

"As soon as I'm through follow me in and be ready with the 357."

Then he lunged forward with his shoulder, and I heard the thin sheet of paneling rip. Bright light poured into the blackness, and I could see down the dark tunnel even to where the dead animal lay.

Stepping into the bright light I held the pistol ready. Joe had nearly fallen but recovered quickly. There was no one around and I wondered why.

Side by side we moved quickly down the brightly lit tunnel, eyes and ears alert.

Why was no one here? Were they all above ground still searching for us-or was this a trap?

I glanced up at the movie cameras and wondered if they were all watching us right now, laughing. Perhaps even now Billy was readying the explosives with which to destroy everything, especially us.

Where were the Bordenwells? The thick metal door behind which they were locked had to be nearby. There, I knew, we would at least encounter one guard.

Each time the tunnel took a turn we slowed to peer around the corner. There were as many twists and turns here as there had been in the darker, untouched ones.

We moved swiftly, knowing we had little time.

The spray of bullets came from behind us. One ripped through the cuff of my sleeve, and another whizzed past my ear. Several more tore into the wall to the right.

Turning as he ran, Joe fired from the hip and the shotgun bellowed deafeningly through the narrow hallway. The man who had fired went down and we rounded a corner on the run. There was another man waiting but Joe fired first. He too went down, his body slamming hard into the wall where the tunnel made a 't'.

Stepping over him we turned left and came upon the big metal door. There was no guard now. Kneeling on one knee, I readied the

357 while Joe pulled the heavy bar out of the way and opened the door wide.

I don't know why, but I expected to see a dozen heavily armed men waiting with pointed guns. But all was clear except for those imprisoned within their cells. We searched the walls for hanging keys but found none, then I had an idea. Returning to the dead man at the 't' I gave him a quick frisking and smiled. With a soft jingle I pulled what we wanted from his pocket.

Back at the cell area, Joe moved to the door and stood ready with the shotgun as I moved hurriedly from cell to cell looking for the Bordenwells.

Crying and pleading came from all those who were able, and hands groped through the bars, grabbing for the keys that could free them.

Next to the last cell I found what I was looking for. They were together. Elizabeth and Bradley had both come to the front to see what all the excitement was about. Emily sat on the edge of a metal bunk staring blankly at the floor. When I inserted the key, she looked up slowly, her face expressionless.

Inside I moved quickly to where she sat and knelt in front of her.

"Mrs. Bordenwell." She glared into my eyes with a fixed stare. "Mrs. Bordenwell, your husband has sent us to bring you and the children home. We're here to help you. Do you understand?"

She continued to stare, unresponsive. Grabbing her shoulders, I shook her slightly. "Mrs. Bordenwell."

She won't answer you, Mister."

I looked up. Elizabeth had come to stand near my side. Staring into my face she asked, "Did my daddy really send you?"

Smiling, I replied, "You bet he did, sweetheart. He really misses you. Think you can help me get your mom to her feet?"

"Yes."

Looking over at Bradley I said, "How about you Bradley? Think you're up to helping us?"

Not speaking, he nodded then came over.

Working together, we pulled Emily to her feet and walked out into the hallway to where Joe waited.

When we were at his side, he smiled and gave the kids a wink. Then he asked with a motion of his head. "What about the others, Alfie?"

Glancing over my shoulder I looked back into the cell area. Arms were extended from the bars and faces pressed against them trying for a glimpse of what we were doing. I knew what had to be done. I just didn't know how to do it. We were their only chance; beyond us they had no hope.

If we left them behind and escaped, this would become their grave, forever buried beneath the rubble and earth of a violent explosion.

Yet if we tried to escape with all of them with us, probably none of us would make it out. Turning them loose to fend for themselves was out too. They would never find their way to safety by themselves. "Damn it!" I said to myself. Walking back into the cell area I held up my hands.

"Everybody, quiet." There were a few moments of continued crying and pleading while the more alert worked to hush them. Soon they all fell silent, and every eye was on me.

"My name is Alex; my friend is Joe. We are Private Investigators who have come for the Bordenwells. But we are going to help you too."

Those who were able cheered and whistled and sent up a round of applause while others blessed us and broke into tears of joy. There was warmth in my heart, a good feeling, one that comes from knowing you truly helped someone in need, and it was greatly appreciated.

Going from cell to cell I unlocked the doors, turning them loose.

One by one they collected where Joe stood until finally thirty-seven people had gathered waiting for our direction and guidance.

After teaming the strong with the weak we moved on in search for a way out. Joe took the lead while I brought up the rear.

The moving was slow and cumbersome. We really weren't sure how to get out and even if we found the elevator, would it be safe to use for fear of setting off the explosion that would kill us all? But like it or not, everything considered it appeared to be the only way in and out of the tunnels. It was probably used frequently during working hours so would hopefully be safe.

Two guards suddenly rounded the corner in front of Joe, and he screamed for everyone to get down. People scrambled to the floor while others pulled those whom were drugged down with them. An Uzi erupted but went over everyone's head. Joe's' shotgun exploded and I fired twice with the 357.

The hallway echoed with the gunfire and the smell of smoke was strong. One guard went down, and the other fell to the floor grabbing his leg. His gun fell from his hand and Joe was on top of him in seconds with the barrel of the shotgun pointing at close range.

Yelling for everyone to stay down I worked my way through the crowd to Joe's side.

Kneeling, I told the guard.

"You got one chance. Where is the elevator or some other exit leading up to the house?"

He stared at me a few seconds then said something in Russian. Pulling back the hammer of the 357 I pressed the barrel into the guy's chest.

"Okay, if that's the way you want it." His eyes grew big around and he spoke out quickly.

"No, wait."

Pulling the gun free, I said, "Talk fast."

"Next Left. You will see the door."

"Is it wired?"

"No, not until night."

Grinning I told him, "then good night to you."

He wasn't sure what I meant, but it didn't matter. I brought the butt of the gun down against his skull and he went out like a baby.

Hustling everyone back on their feet we moved to the left and there it was. Joe pushed the button and in a few seconds the doors opened. The elevator was small, so I told him to take the Bordenwells and two others, then send it back down for five more. I would control things here.

So we loaded Emily, Elizabeth, Bradley and two other children. The elevator doors closed, and I let out a sigh.

Anxiously I waited; we were so close!

What concerned me now was how we were going to get everyone out safely. A crowd this big made for perfect targets. With just the Bordenwells we could have squeezed into the corvette, it could easily outrun anything that might chase after us.

The elevator seemed slow in coming back but I knew Joe had to position everyone in safe places.

Scanning the tunnels, I remained alert. So far, we had encountered four guards. The night we arrived there had been many more-where were they? Where was the lab Billy had taken us into that first night? And, too, where was the room with the gauntlet? We hadn't passed either on our way here.

I heard the elevator coming down and readied five more people. But at this point I trusted no one so with the 357 pointed I waited for the doors to open. When they did Billy smiled. She was leaning against the back of the elevator with arms folded.

"Well, Mr. Stone," she said the words with irritating calmness, "you've proven yourself quite a challenge. I've obviously underestimated you. You may pull the trigger if you wish, but if you do, your partner dies just as instantly. So please, give me the gun and I'll have these people returned to their cells. Then we can all go upstairs for coffee and some dinner."

I've a better idea Billy," I said smiling back. "Why don't you and I return to the surface and make a trade."

She threw back her head and laughed.

"Obviously you've underestimated me as I have you. Do you honestly believe I would allow such a thing? I can assure you that if we return to the house with that gun in your hand and not mine, Mr. Hardon will die the moment the doors open. Please remember I am not an American. In Russia it is an honor to die for the cause of the Mother Land."

For a long time, I studied her face. She was not bluffing. Behind me down the hallway, armed guards were closing in on the run. I could hear the clatter of their feet.

Shaking my head, I handed over the gun and stepped into the elevator. Billy yelled something in Russian to the approaching men and the doors closed. On the way to the surface I leaned my head against the wall and said, "shit" aloud.

Billy laughed. "Yes, Mr. Stone," she said, "I think shit is a most appropriate word for your situation".

# CHAPTER THIRTEEN

When the doors opened four guards were waiting. Following behind Billy, I was led to the dining room where Joe and the others sat waiting. Priveman was dressing Joe's arm and when I passed by he gave me a look that told me he was sorry. Shrugging my understanding, I pulled up a chair beside him and sat. Billy took her spot at the head of the table, and we waited. Looking from Joe to me, she shook her head.

"Whatever am I going to do with you two? Do you realize how close you've come to completely ruining this project?"

"Not close enough." Joe told her coldly. She looked at Priveman. "How serious is the arm, Doctor?" Priveman glanced her way then came back to Joe, speaking as he worked. "He has several lacerations, multiple puncture wounds, and some minor edema. But I believe in time he will be fine."

"Will it require suturing?"

"No, I don't believe so."

"Good." She said grinning. "For tonight, following dinner, he shall run the gauntlet."

The doctor in Priveman came out harshly. "Natalie please, he needs rest. The man has been through a traumatic experience."

"So have we, Doctor. It will be tonight. End of discussion!" She glanced at the watch on her arm. "It is now 3:20. Dinner will be at six, the gauntlet at eight."

Turning to the guards, she motioned with her hand." Return these gentlemen to their room and the others to the holding cell. See to it Mr. Hardon and Mr. Stone get clean coveralls."

Rising from her chair she gave Joe a pensive grin.

"I strongly suggest you get some rest. The gauntlet, to say the least, can be somewhat...exhausting. And, as food for thought, I might as well tell you, no one has yet made it out alive."

Two of the guards marched the Bordenwells and the other two children past us and as they went by, Elizabeth looked at me. "Thank you for trying." She said quickly.

The words came from that of a little girl, but for some reason my mind brought to memory the books I had seen in her room the day we inspected it with her father. She was a little girl yes, but one I guessed to be well advanced in her years. Then they were gone, disappearing behind a door that closed with the sound of finality.

Back in our own room we stretched out on the bed, then both yawned almost at the same instant. We were fatigued. Joe looked over at me and said apologetically. "They were waiting for us Alfie. If I'd have made a move, they would have shot the kids."

"That's all-right Joey," I said scowling, "I did something far worse than you." Wrinkles showed on his forehead.

"What?"

"I had my sites on Billy and didn't pull the trigger. I could have decorated the walls of the elevator with her brains."

"Why didn't you?"

I looked over at him.

"Because the bitch hasn't told me where she hid my shoes yet."

Joe laughed and rolled over on his side. His back to me, he muttered, "if that gauntlet is everything she says it is, we had better get some rest."

Still looking at him I shook my head. He could sleep anywhere, any time. Lacing my fingers, I placed my hands behind my head and stared at the ceiling.

The time was nearing. We had about four and a half hours until the gauntlet. I tried remembering what it looked like the night Billy had shown us. There had been four compartments and countless lines and hoses connected to the thing, their purpose the good Lord only knew. I recalled also the metal catwalk and tiered seating with the strange binocular looking devices.

GAUNTLET. I said the word under my breath. The Apache Indian used a gauntlet to mark the brave of a man. But Billy, I was sure, had not designed the thing for that reason. In some way, and at this point I had no idea how, this gauntlet would tie into the development of the Mindtalk formula.

Billy stated no one yet had made it out alive and that was not comforting. Over and over in my mind I tried recalling every detail I could about what we had seen during that short visit. Yawning I closed my eyes. I called Murphy a Dick-weed then shortly after fell asleep.

The door being opened startled me awake. There were three guards, one of which was carrying two sets of coveralls in his hand. He set them on the dresser near the door and turned to look at us.

"These are from Ms. Robinson. You have exactly one-half hour before dinner, so get ready." Then they were gone.

We rose slowly, our minds groggy with the need for more sleep. After showering we slipped into the clean coveralls, talking as we dressed.

At best, things looked grim. And not having to say it there was an uneasiness in both of us, an obvious fear of the unknown. We discussed Billy's food for thought; the fact that no one had ever successfully ran the gauntlet and lived to tell the story.

In my mind there were memories concerning the experience with Godzilla. Man and animal had actually communicated verbally, or at least a close facsimile. I was sure that Gorilla's level of understanding was limited critically by his level of training; but never the less he and I had actually carried on a conversation. And my furry friend had clearly proven his closeness to human emotions through the cloning effects of the serum. If man and animal were so able to communicate because of it I thought, then how exactly would it be between two human beings? Come 8:00 p.m., I was sure, that answer would come.

Dinner would have been a fitting tribute to any dying man's request for a last meal. Steak and Lobster, red wine and Black Forest Cake for dessert. Billy had called for the best in tableware too. The finest of China and Silver spaciously dressed a white cloth trimmed in gold. And the company was all here as well...that is, all but one. Slowly my eyes circled the table, and I took them all in. Billy, Dixie, Priveman, Phieffer, Mandagon, Barkin...but no Nugent. His chair sat empty.

I thought of the last thing he had said to us before leaving our room earlier and felt sadness. Taking into account his visit had been an act of human compassion, I hoped against the worst, but somehow knew better. Like breakfast earlier, these people were not given to overwhelming conversation at mealtime. Dinner was all but over before anyone said a word. Billy was the icebreaker.

"So," she chimed following a sip of wine, "did we rest well gentlemen?"

We nodded without speaking.

"I sincerely hope so. Especially you Mr. Hardon." Rising gracefully from her chair she walked to where Joe sat, speaking as she moved. Her eyes sparkled and drank in his body as she approached. "For you see," she went on, "what lies ahead for you in particular, Mr. Hardon, will require great endurance."

Having reached his chair she stood behind it, continuing to talk. Her hands fell softly on his shoulders and she began massaging them gently.

"Endurance, Mr. Hardon, will mean the difference between life or death for you, but perhaps..." slowly her right hand slid beneath the coveralls to his bare chest, "perhaps it will require more endurance than you can give."

Every eye was on them now, the room a giant vacuum of silent disbelief. Dixie's face showed displeasure as she glared from across the table. Lost within her own carnal thoughts Billy's hand began kneading the chest muscles beneath it. Her eyes had that look a woman gets when she's considering saying yes. Reaching out, Joe picked up his wineglass and took a long sip. The moment he set it down his hand came up and clamped over Billy's, squeezing hard. Holding it at bay he told her.

"Billy, unless you play dirty, I'll lay odds I'm the first to win out over your gauntlet."

She stood silent, liking the pain Joe was causing her and at the same time calculating his chances. When he let her go, she slipped her hand free, rubbing it gently between her fingers. Returning to her chair she sat and stared at him with a licentious glare, her breasts rising and falling noticeably.

Billy's eyes were broadcasting her desire for a man she wanted but wasn't sure she could have. Joe was the defiance she had never before encountered. No other man, I was willing to bet, had ever turned her away. Now suddenly, here he was; the true challenge, the worthy opponent, the ultimate test of the sexes. Bringing her breathing under control she said finally.

"It will take more than cockiness to win out over the Gauntlet, Mr. Hardon."

Shrugging, Joe grinned. "Whatever it takes, I've got it."

"*Do* you now?" She grinned slightly. "Let me get this straight, you're confident you possess all those things necessary for a successful run; patience, perseverance, strength, stamina, a cool head under pressure, and most importantly impeccable self-control?"

"You got it lady." Joe replied.

Her grin turned sinister. "Why don't we just see!" Billy clapped her hands and the kitchen door opened. A guard came through with Elizabeth and Bradley following behind. Emily was not with them. There was noticeable fear in the children's eyes. Taken to Billy's side the youngsters stared quickly around the table then lowered their eyes to the floor and kept them there. Inside, fear for them both gripped like a vise. Billy was capable of anything and we knew there would be little we could do should she decide to harm them.

Rising from the table she pulled her chair to the center of the room, then motioned for Elizabeth to be brought over. Her little hands were tied behind the chair's high back while Bradley was placed at the wall near the kitchen door. Looking at Joe, Billy smiled.

"Self-control, Mr. Hardon? Let us see how much you really do have." Moving her eyes she looked at Barkin and Mandegon. "She's all yours."

Our eyes watched Billy return to the table and stand out of the way. My heart pounded. This couldn't be happening. No one was this inhumane.

Mandegon went to the boy and Barkin ambled to the chair where Elizabeth sat bound. The little girl watched him approach and on the verge of tears she pleaded, "Please don't hurt me." Barkin gave her a twisted grin, went around behind the chair and stood silent.

"Webster, Mr. Hardon," Billy spoke tip, "defines perseverance as meaning, 'to not give in, to endure." Glancing at Mandegon, she nodded.

Slowly, Mandegon's hand went into his coat pocket and came out holding a knife. It was a short blade, subdued, two-edged commando type with sharp point, used for silent assassinations. We knew the technique. A stab to the kidneys followed with a ripping twist and or a slash to the jugular while holding a hand over the victim's mouth. I looked at Joe. Surely this was just a bluff; Bradley was just a little boy. Billy looked to Joe. There was coldness in her eyes, a daring, maybe even wanting.

"You will remain in your chair, Mr. Hardon. If you leave it, and believe me you will want to, then the boy's throat will be cut. Is that clear?"

Joe looked at her. His eyes told her yes, but no words came from his mouth.

Looking this time to Barkin, Billy nodded again.

A sick twisted smile came to his face and he looked flagrantly at Joe.

His hands were huge. One alone could nearly cover the little girl's face. Provokingly he placed both on top of Elizabeth's head and began stroking her hair. Frozen in fear, she did not move. A lone tear streamed down her cheek and ran onto a quivering lip.

Barkin slowly slid his right hand down to her tiny neck and encircled it. He squeezed tight enough to make her eyes bulge and turn her face red, then let up.

Joe's teeth were gritted, his knuckles white from gripping the seat of his chair. Billy watched him closely, amused by the hatred and torment Barkin's sick act was bringing him.

Barkin let the tips of his fingers play at the neckline of the little girl's coveralls. His eyes were alive with the sick thrill of what he was doing. Without realizing, he was caught up in the twisted perversion of his imbalanced lust. It was all so sick and never had I felt such a desire to kill a man. His big fingers began inching their way slowly down her front inside the coveralls.

Around the room there were various reactions on the faces of those present. Dixie looked on with a curious fixation. Phieffer and Priveman were looking away, not wanting to watch. Little Bradley's eyes were on his sister, and there was hate in them, accompanied by a cold contempt for the man making her cry.

Tears descended the girl's cheeks, but they were silent. She was a brave little sweetheart and her parents could be proud of her. Tension mounted and appalling hatred shrouded us like a heavy blanket. Barkin's hand was now all the way inside Elizabeth's' coveralls. Tears welled in my eyes as I helplessly sat-by. I wanted to charge Barkin, to jump him, to kill the son of a bitch. But to do so would surely get Bradley murdered.

Suddenly, blatantly, and without warning Joe burst into laughter.

Surprised and shocked, all in the room turned to look at him.

Snapping up a wine bottle from the table he poured himself a drink. The bottleneck clanged against the glass rim and the room had grown so quiet we could hear the liquid swirl in. Everything stopped. Bewildered eyes were glued to him. Glass in his hand, he took a sip then turned in his chair to look at Barkin.

A burst of laughter exploded again and this time continued until he was laughing so hard that it seemed he was unable to control it. No one, including myself, could figure out what the hell was going on with him.

I began to wonder if maybe the horror of what was happening had caused him to slip off the deep end. I'd seen it in Viet Nam, post-traumatic stress they called it.

Grasping his stomach Joe fell from his chair onto the floor, laughing so hard he bordered the edge of hysteria.

My partner, my best friend, had finally tripped out. He was cashing in his ticket to lolly land.

Billy spoke out but I doubt he heard her.

"Please Mr. Hardon, do control yourself." There was confusion on her face, an expression that told of her growing uneasiness.

Still laughing Joe climbed to his feet and looked at Billy from across the table. Raising a hand in gesture he said as best he could.

"You," he laughed, catching his breath and continuing, "you call this a test?" A savage burst of laughter brought him to his knees and he was unable to speak. Billy called out to me.

"Do something with him, will you?" Turning my palms to the ceiling, I shrugged. Holding onto the table Joe climbed back to his feet. Grinning, he raised a hand again and tried speaking one more time.

"Let me show you" he gulped for a breath, "what entertainment is." Again he laughed.

Mesmerized by his bizarre behavior, we watched him stagger to Elizabeth's side and stand almost at attention beside her chair, struggling noticeably to squelch his laughter. Reaching up over his head he raised the half-filled wineglass that was in his hand. "A toast." Everyone's eyes followed the wineglass up.

That's when he said. "A toast to Mr. Barkin," and brought his elbow down hard, smashing it into Barkin's face. Blood splattered and the man with the big hands toppled backwards, crashing hard to the floor, unconscious.

Joe's warning went to Bradley the same instant he threw the wine glass in his hand, "Run Bradley." Mandegon ducked clear of the flying object, and it shattered noisily against the wall.

Bradley dashed quickly for his sister's side. Mandegon's hand reached out for him, but he was too slow. Armed guards began moving in on Joe, but Billy stopped them. Under my breath I called Joey a crazy bastard and grinned. Like I'd said before, he knew his psychology.

Not only had he left his place at the table against Billy's warning, put Barkin on the floor unconscious, left everyone in the room glued to their chairs and Billy speechless; he had most of all, at least for now, put an end to this insanity.

I admired his genius, but silently inside my head I recited another Murphy truth, 'no good deed goes unpunished.'

Still near the kitchen door Mandegon stood silent, his eyes fastened on Joe. They were demented eyes, burning with a psychopathic arousal. But to Joe it didn't matter; he was staring back, and he was no longer laughing.

No one moved as heads turned on Billy, wondering what was to happen now. For a long while she said nothing. The room was quiet.

Through the kitchen door came the soft hum of an electric appliance motor, one of the guards cleared his throat and Bradley sniffled. Outside dusk had come and gone and now darkness lay gathered at the windows.

Barkin stirred on the floor, a soft moan coming from his blood-covered face.

It was Joe who broke the stare with Mandegon. Turning away he untied Elizabeth's hands and immediately the two children embraced.

Leaving her spot at the table, Billy walked slowly to where Joe stood, her boot heels clicking against the waxed, hardwood floor. Stopping in front of him she folded her arms and let a faint smile show. There was admiration in her eyes.

"Are you always this resourceful, Mr. Hardon?"

"Usually more so. Today's a bad day."

Looking over her shoulder at Mandegon, then back at Joe, she said.

"It is my feeling he would like very much to have his way with you."

Not taking his eyes from hers, Joe replied.

"I could give you a long list of people who feel that way."

Looking sultry she quipped, "Does this list constitute male and female?"

"That's a personal question."

"I'm a nosy person."

"I don't like nosy people. They get in my way."

"Like me, you mean?"

"You're what I'd call a classic example, yes."

Unfolding her arms she stuck her hands in her pockets.

"Tell me, Mr. Hardon, if you could have any last three wishes in the world, what would they be?"

Joe thought a few seconds, then grinned.

"First, to have the Bordenwell children and their mother returned to their home. Secondly, feel the grip of my.45 in my hand." He paused, dropping the grin.

"And thirdly? " Billy coaxed.

"Thirdly," he said soberly, "to pull the trigger with the barrel resting against your head."

"My," she laughed briefly, "you certainly can be hostile."

"I guess you've rubbed off on me." Joe said.

"I consider that a compliment."

"Don't."

Billy pursed her lips. "I do wish you could have been born one of us, Mr. Hardon. You would have made an excellent comrade."

Joe shook his head. "No way. I care too much for people."

Breaking his silence Mandegon spoke from his position near the wall. For the first time there was recognizable anger in his voice.

"This is shit, Billee, I want this Mon. I want to kill him with any bare hands." She looked at him.

"Patience Carlo. All in due time."

Glancing at her watch, she added. "Right now, it's time for the evening's entertainment. While calling to her guards she stared firmly into Joe's eyes.

"The time has come to prove you are everything you say."

Barkin groaned again and rolled onto his belly, pulling himself sluggishly to his knees. Blood dripped from his nose and a large pool of it lay beneath him. Billy made a motion with her head and two of the guards moved to his side to help him up.

Eyes still on Joe, Billy smiled wryly.

"Best of luck, Mr. Hardon."

Turning then she walked away, speaking over her shoulder.

"Take them to the Gauntlet."

# CHAPTER FOURTEEN

The room hadn't changed. Big as death the gauntlet stood uncompromising and eerie.

Menacing beneath soft fluorescent lighting it brought to mind the Nazi war machine and its frenetic attempt at exterminating an entire human race.

We were taken just inside the door and placed in two folding chairs set side by side.

There were three guards, one with an Uzi and two with shotguns. Taking no chances they kept their distance, watching us with cold eyes that stared out from faces of hardened stone. No words were spoken between us, but then, why should there be? What was there to say?

The gauntlet sat just to our right, even more monstrous from our sitting positions.

There was no way of putting a finger on how I felt; apprehension, fear, self-doubt. Hell, maybe one, maybe all of them.

Looking over at Joe I saw a face of positive determination. If he possessed anything other than confidence no one would ever know.

If it all, I thought, were to end here, then at least my life would conclude on one strong irrefutable note...I died alongside one hell of a friend.

Time passed slowly, but within minutes the company began to arrive.

Priveman was first, carrying his little black Doctor's bag. Then Phieffer and Mandegon arrived.

Wearing a long white lab coat, Dr. Bondsfield sashayed in with exuberance, and behind him came Dixie. Then three others we'd never seen before, they too dressed in white lab coats. Barkin strolled in last. He was holding an ice pack over his nose and already his eyes were turning black. If looks could kill, Joe would have been shot, stabbed, strangled and, with a little coaxing from Mandegon, buttaMized. But Barkin never said a word as he filed past, he did however, flash Joe the middle finger.

Each of them took a place on the tiered seating beside a pair of the strange binoculars. They had no more than sat down when Billy came in, followed by two more guards.

She went straight to the honored guests where she approached Mandegon and whispered something in his ear. He looked around Billy and down at Joe, then back again. As an afterthought, Billy patted his shoulder turned away and ambled over to stand smugly in front of us. Arms folded she let a grin show at the corners of her mouth.

"Well, gentlemen. The time has come, the day of reckoning as it were. And as you can see," she motioned toward those sitting in the tiered seating, "you have an avid cheering section."

Glancing their way, we found them all staring at us.

Billy continued.

"Allow me to explain what is about to happen. You see, a certain section of the gauntlet is undertaken in darkness. That way, we are positively assured that only telepathic communication can be used between the two subjects involved. Please note that each seat has its own set of infrared glasses, the best money can buy. They, of course, will allow our guests to see through the darkness as the runners go through their paces.

You will both be injected with the serum. One will go into the gauntlet while the other remains upon the catwalk with me…and my armed guards of course. Each compartment of the gauntlet will present a different problem, which will require team effort to overcome. You, Mr. Stone, will be on the catwalk with me, while your partner here," she swept Joe with her eyes, "will serve as the runner."

Looking at me again she said. "During the blackout phase, you will serve as his eyes by wearing a pair of the infrared glasses like the rest of us, giving telepathic direction to him as needed. If you make an incorrect judgment on your partner's behalf, you may very well become the cause of his death. While on the other hand, should he fail to do exactly as you say, he himself may become the means to his own end."

Glancing over her shoulder, she glanced up into the tiered seating. "Dr. Priveman, would you come down and do the honors please?"

Rising from his seat, the good Doctor shuffled past the three men we had never seen before and climbed slowly down to where we sat.

At my side, he kneeled on one leg and set his black bag on the floor in front of him. Glass bottles jingled softly, followed with the sound of him unzipping the case. His hand went in and came out holding a 10cc syringe. Here we go again, I thought.

While he readied my arm with the rubber tubing and alcohol prep, Billy looked at us.

"Do either of you have any questions before we begin?"

Joe stopped watching Priveman and looked up at her.

"Yeah," he said, "I have a two-part question."

"Very well, ask away."

"First, I'd like to know why the Bordenwells are here? Was it fate or where they targeted?" The question seemed to take Billy back a bit. "And for part two," Joe went on, "where did you hide Alfie's shoes?"

Her brow twisted into befuddlement.

Ignoring her, Joe looked over at me and grinned.

"See. And you didn't think I cared!"

Billy shook her head and went on to answer his questions.

"We have discovered the serum works best on individuals who are artistic and educated, those who see things more for their natural beauty than materialistic value. The ideal subject is someone in control of their life and with a high level of self-esteem. Someone happy with who they are and reasonably free of social and psychological problems. Mrs. Borderwell met these standards perfectly. In addition, her children provided invaluable data concerning the serum's effectiveness between family members…genetics." She paused and sighed softly. "I will admit, though, they have caused us a great deal of headache thus far."

Priveman punctured the vein and I flinched. This time, there was a noticeable pinch. As he slowly pushed the plunger on the syringe, I told Billy.

"Hey, I have a question too."

"Yes."

"Where is Nugent?"

"Oh, you need not worry, Mr. Stone. The helpful Professor will be along directly."

Finished with me, Priveman moved to Joe.

Like before, I felt a strange sensation inside, then the feeling of leaving my body and a few seconds of feeling light-headed. I had barely returned to normal when Billy spun on her heels and traipsed down the catwalk over the Gauntlet.

"Bring Mr. Stone." She said without turning around.

Two guards grabbed my arms and pulled me from the chair. Prodded by a gun barrel in the middle of my back, I was directed to an aluminum ladder, which I climbed right behind Billy.

At the top, I paused long enough to glance back at Joe. His face looked strained and I knew he was experiencing the strange reaction of the serum. Silently wishing him God's speed, I turned and stepped onto the medal walkway.

I followed Billy to the midpoint location where she positioned herself in front of what was obviously the control center for the gauntlet.

She struck a round center key on a large computer console and it clicked and clattered. Then somewhere beyond the wall to our back, I heard some sort of machinery and motors  start up.

The control center wrapped around her in a half moon fashion, consisting of TV monitor, keyboard, microphone and speakers. There were numerous gauges and switches and it reminded me of the instrument panel in a small aircraft. She smiled as I stood beside her taking it all in.

"Well, what do you think? Ever seen anything like it?"

"Once," I said studying it, trying to figure out how it all worked, "in a Star wars movie."

Her smile widened with pride.

"I can assure you, Mr. Stone, you will find no science fiction from here."

Leaning over the panel, she glanced down at Priveman.

"Is he ready, Doctor?"

"Ready, Natalie."

"Splendid," she said excitedly, "let the festivities begin. Guards, take our contestant to the top of the first chamber."

One of the three stone-faced men rolled a ladder platform to the gauntlet, while the other two pulled Joe to his feet. Like me, he had experienced the strange reaction of the serum but recovered quickly.

Once on top, a heavy pyramid of cement was chained to Joe's ankle by way of a thick shackle held in place by a combination lock. There was approximately two feet of chain, and it rattled noisily as they secured it.

The chamber was narrow, about six feet wide. Just enough width to keep a man from spreading his arms and touching both sides.

Her voice filled with enthusiasm; Billy called down to Joe as soon as they were finished. Bordered by the armed guards, he looked up at her in silence.

"At your feet, Mr. Harden, you will notice a hatchway door with a sliding bolt." Joe looked down, then back at her, and nodded.

From our elevated position on the catwalk we had a clear view of everything.

"This is the program." She continued. "You will be placed into the chamber where your partner will furnish you with the lock's combination to free yourself. Keep in mind, however, that, once we bolt the hatch behind you, the chamber becomes entirely soundproof, except of course for external speakers. In other words, we can hear you, but you will hear nothing. Your only chance of being set free will come through telepathy sent from your partner…and oh yes, I nearly forgot. Look down into the chamber." She clicked madly at the keyboard in front of her, then stopped and smiled. The huge Plexiglas room began filling with water.

"You have two minutes before it fills." She said with a pernicious grin, "Might I suggest you put your newly arrived 'skills' to a trial run?"

Immediately Joe looked up and we stared. He spoke no words, but I heard him inside my head, just as I had With Godzilla.

"Oh shit, Alfie."

"Oh shit is right, pal." I said back in thought.

Surprised, he grinned at me and immediately bantered back clearly, his lips not moving. "Damn! It is true. It does work."

"It works, Joey."

Shaking his head at me, he sent up the thought, "I hate to think it Alfie, but we're in a world of shit."

The water swirled and bubbled as the chamber filled. Time was running out and there was nothing we could do but wait for the worst. I thought about Joe. Could he make it?

"I'll make it, Alfie." Smiling, I remembered he could read my every thought. "Hell," I told him back, "Now I can't even think about calling you a dirty name without you knowing it." Grinning, he winked affectionately.

I heard footsteps clamber down the metal walkway toward us and turned to see who it was. Dixie Barnibin approached, obviously eager to join us.

"Have you been cloned?" Billy asked with a quick side-glance. Moving close beside me she stopped and nodded, "Yes".

Peering down at Joe I sent him the thought, "I wonder what this is all about?"

Dixie didn't give him time to answer. In thought form that only the three of us could hear she said.

"Worry not gentlemen. Think of me as your mind reading overseer, a silent eaves dropper, if you will".

Then turning to Joe, she shot a thought that surprised us both.

"Mr. Hardon." Joe looked up at her. "Do you by chance realize Natalie has a thing for you? She would like very much to seduce you."

Joe grinned mockingly… "No, do you think?"

Smiling back she said. "Now honestly, hasn't the thought of making love to her crossed your mind as well? She is beautiful."

Shaking his head slowly, he replied.

"NO-WAY-IN-HADES!"

"Really!" Dixie chimed. "I'm speechless. Do you not find her attractive?" She folded her arms across her chest. "I mean, she is quite beautiful." Dixie looked at Billy briefly then went back to Joe. "A lot of men would give all they have to spend one night with her."

"A lot of women too!" The thought popped into my head before I could stop it. Bringing her face around, Dixie studied me along while before replying.

"Yes, that is true. And yes, I am one of them."

"So you are lesbians?" I asked in thoughts.

"We prefer the word 'lovers'."

"Call it what you like," Joe broke in silently from the top of the chamber, "I prefer the word dykes."

Ignoring his remark, Dixie slowly reached over and cradled my hand gently into hers. It took me by surprise.

A pair of big green eyes widened as she looked brazenly into mine and her soft lips parted slowly. They were full lips, glossy, shaping the sexy form of her mouth. Beneath the fluorescent lighting, her red hair cascaded to her shoulders, falling classically over one eye. Her gaze was powerful, pulling me into her. There was no doubt she was beautiful!

I was beginning to feel as though I was back in Indianapolis, in the warehouse-my palms were a little sweaty.

"And what do you think, Alfie?" She said the words in sensual thought. "Am I just a dyke to you, too?"

I looked down at the hand resting on mine then back into her eyes. She was so beautiful. My words took her by surprise.

"A spade's a spade, Dix."

She went silent. Her mouth closed. Those green eyes never left mine and she never let go of my hand.

"Quite true, Alfie. A spade is a spade. But spades are not always your only trump. I like men too. Especially your kind; strong and intelligent, capable of conversation beyond fast cars and sexual conquests. Men with IQs higher than the length of their penis. The kind who know how to mix gentle with strong... when a woman is in need of both. Later, should the opportunity present itself, I'd..."

Without even realizing she had interrupted, Billy cut her short.

"There!" She said out loud while punching a final key on the computer. "We're ready."

The water had stopped flowing now and the chamber was filled to within a foot from the top.

"Mr. Hardon," Billy said looking down at him " We will drop you into the water where you will sink to the bottom. The depth has been adjusted according to your height so that when fully stretched, your head will be only inches from the surface…and oxygen. If Mr. Stone fails to give you the correct combination, or you panic, you will die oily inches from safety. Are You ready?"

Joe gave her a big grin.

"READY? Hell, I' excited about it!"

"The moment you're under the water, I will give Mr. Stone the combination; For this experiment, we shall leave the lighting on. This first step of the gauntlet is designed to test an individual's ability to receive telepathy while under mild to moderate stress. I have all the confidence in the world that you will succeed."

Reaching down she hit a switch and we heard the mellow squawk external speakers come on around the room.

"There," she said sprightly, "now we're ready." Nodding at the guards beside Joe, she gave a whimsical chuckle.

"Drop him."

Setting Joe on the edge of the hatch, they lowered the cement pyramid into the water then let it go. It pulled him cruelly through the hole and I saw him take a final gulp of air before he went under.

The clear plexi glass gave us all a view of what was happening. The heavy piece of cement pulled him down rapidly. It struck the bottom before he did, and it came across the speakers as a muffled thud.

While the heavy pyramid remained on the bottom, Joe's weightless body floated upward the length of the chain. Just as Billy had said, his head was only inches from the surface.

If it hadn't been so serious a predicament, I would have found it amusing. Joe, confident now that the serum worked, floated leisurely in the water with his arms folded over his chest, tapping his fingers against his arm, mockingly.

Grinning and shaking her head, Billy turned to me and whispered the combination into my ear. She then placed a pen between my lips. "Please hold it there until he's freed himself."

Looking at Joe I repeated the combination in thought form. 10 to the right once, 6 twice to the left, back to the right stopping on 5.

Pulling himself down by the chain, Joe grabbed the padlock. Through the speakers we could hear the bubbles that emitted from his mouth and streamed to the surface above. His hair floated in thin long strands. As he worked the combination, I could hear him thinking to himself.

"Come on, Hardon, keep your cool. You've got plenty of time. Ten. Got it! Now twice left, that's it take it easy and slow, six once, six twice, good! One number left. Damn my lungs are beginning to burn. Bullshit, forget the pain. Concentrate. Easy now, you're coming up to it, calm, that's it, slow, Bingo!" He snapped the lock open, pulled the shackle free and swam to the surface.

Sighing, I smiled lightly and sent him the thought, "Way to go, partner." Then removed the pen from between my teeth.

Two of the guards reached down and pulled Joe out. He looked like a drowned rat, but at least he was a live rat. Billy looked at him and smiled approvingly.

"Well done, Mr. Hardon. But to borrow from a cliché, it is one down and three to go."

There was a narrow walkway leading to the top of the next compartment and that's where they took him.

Unlike the first, this one was much wider, twenty feet or so. In addition, there were two top hatchway entrances, one at each end, both with a ladder leading down to the floor inside. And this one had been plumbed with tight rows of piping running full length across the inside ceiling. The floor was tiled in two colors, black and white.

One of the guards opened the hatch nearest us and motioned at Joe with his gun barrel.

"Wait!" Billy yelled down. "Have Mr. Hardon remove his c coveralls. I want this phase ran in the nude."

Looking up, Joe glanced my way then over to Billy, giving her a boyish grin.

"Can't resist, can you? You've gotta know!"

Slowly, he unzipped the coveralls then worked them free of his shoulders. Once clear, he let them drop in a pile around his ankles. Holding out his hands, he smiled wide for Billy.

"Well?"

Cupping her chin between thumb and finger, Billy nodded.

"I must admit, you're everything I had imagined."

"Good," he told her, "Now do I get a scenario for this run?"

"Your scenario. Of course."

She cleared her throat. "Notice the dark and light tile on the floor? Each is an 18-inch square and can be electrically charged, individually or collectively, with whatever amount of current I so desire and in any pattern I wish. In this case, I will charge all of the dark tile only. Your job will be to step on the light, non-charged tile, working your way to the safety of the ladder on the opposite side of the chamber. Should you make a mistake and step on a dark one, the current will be such as to instantly blow your feet into mush and at the same time fry your insides black." She hesitated a second then went on. "And for added measure, I have randomly selected some of the light tile and turned them into 18-inch hot plates; just hot enough to boil water or, more appropriately, burn your feet. So should you step on one of them, your feet will cook like a fish on a hot grill."

Joe smiled. "I like it, ingenious."

Billy continued.

"The idea is that you sense the heat before you step down and relay this to Mr. Stone. He in turn will re-direct your step. Hence, the two-way conversation insures us the serum is working properly."

"Sounds too easy so let me guess." Joe yelled up to her. "The lights will be out, and it'll be darker than the inside of your heart down here. Only Alfie will be able to see the pattern of light and dark tile, right?"

"Correct, Mr. Hardon. He will be directing your every step. And to make it at least somewhat challenging for a man of your capabilities, the piping at the top of the chamber will be dripping down droplets of hot scolding water. Should you linger, the pain will be excruciating and perhaps too much to bear. Then again, if you hurry and get hasty… well, you know the consequence. This phase of the run is designed to test extrasensory powers while under severe stress and pain."

Stretching out her arm, she motioned toward the opened hatch. "Now if you will be so kind, Mr. Hardon. When you've reach the bottom rung, remain on the ladder until Mr. Stone is ready. Got it?"

"Nooooooo problem!" Joe said cooly as he stepped onto the ladder and descended down.

He appeared calm to do all those looking on, but Dixie and I could hear his true and only thought… "Oh shit."

Turning, Billy spoke to those sitting in the tiered seats.

"Observers, please put on your infrared devices." Immediately, they turned to do as told and she fumbled with keys on the computer board again while giving me directions.

"As mentioned, Mr. Stone, there are two colors of square tile on the floor, light and dark. The dark ones have been electrified to 1000 volts. You must keep him on the light tile only. Remember. however, I have heated some of the light tile as well, and those only he can tell you about.

By use of these," she quit typing long enough to hand me a pair of the infrared glasses. "You will be able to see his every step as you guide him through the darkness across the patterned floor. I can assure you, there is no room for error. One mistake, you will turn him into a very dead, well-cooked human shish-ka-bob"

Joe was at the bottom of the ladder now resting on the last rung, waiting.

After giving glasses to Dixie and putting on a pair herself, Billy hit 'enter' on the keyboard and immediately the room went dark.

Our glasses turned the blackness into an eerie world of crimson. But Billy was right. I could easily see Joe and readily placed once again into a world of sightlessness. Only this time, it was one offering no second chances, no time for resting or thinking. It would mean moving quickly and carefully. And clearly, there would be no room for error. Within seconds, Joe's thoughts came into my head.

"Hey pal, it's darker than the inside of an Australian dock rat's ass down here. Why don't you march me right across so I can climb out and get the lights turned back on."

"I'm ready if you are, Joey."

"Let's do it; you're wearing the headlights."

My eyes studied the floor. Billy had made it difficult. There was no discernible pattern whatsoever to the tile.

The colors were scattered sporadically and would require Joe to make both long and short steps as he made his way across.

"Okay, Joey " I began "Put your right foot against the outside of the ladder rail and slide it straight down to the floor; there's a light square there." He did it and sighed.

"Now, we are going to turn around and put the ladder to your back. Turning on the ball of your right foot, spin around easy and place the left foot directly in front of the right; you've got two light tiles in a row." He began moving slowly. "That's it, slow and easy…and down. Good boy. Now you are facing the right direction at least.

"It's hotter than hell down here, Alfie."

"No sweat, big boy. We'll be out in a heartbeat. Now, listen. You've got to keep your balance, whatever you do. There's a light square straight in front of you just to the right of a dark one. Lift up your right foot and move it in front of the left, but don't touch the floor." My eyes strained through the glasses. "That's it, now move it to the right until I say stop. When I do, set only the toes down first. You've got to feel closely for radiating heat, got it?"

"Yeah."

"Good. Keep going. Keep going. Stop! Now, lower the toes, easy."

"Feel any heat?"

"No, I don't think so."

"Beautiful, set your foot down and rest."

Sweat had accumulated on my forehead, and I wiped at it with the back of my hand. Over the speakers, we began hearing a strange noise, crackling. It sounded somewhat like static but different somehow. Ignoring it, I turned my attention back to Joe.

"OK pal, ready to move on?"

"Yeah… oh shit, ouch, damn it. Yeow! Get me the hell out of this spot."

"What's the matter?"

"I'm being burned to death. Billy's hot water is running…damn is stings. Get me out of here Alfie, fast. It's burning me to death."

Through the infrared glasses I watched him twitch and jerk from the pain of the hot water as it dripped repeatedly onto his naked skin. There was nothing he could do to protect himself. Mercilessly, it fell steadily, striking him everywhere. Though I read his thoughts clearly, he had said the words out loud and they had come over the speakers. Now I knew what that crackling noise had been. It was the constant fall of water splashing down on a hot burner. The audience in the tiered seats were now learning forward, obviously caught up with the live show before their eyes. I wondered what their real interest was, the ability of the formula or the cheap thrill of seeing a human being struggle against the odds, caught between that thin line separating life and death.

"All right, Joey. There's a good tile just one tile up from your right foot.  You'll have to stretch. Remember, using only your toes to touch, pick up your right foot and move it straight ahead until I say stop. Then like before, lower it easy, toes first. Now lift. Fine, keep going, good, almost there, stretch it out, keep your balance…keep your balance."

"Alfie, this hot water is burning the shit out of Me."

"I know buddy, I can feel your pain. Hang in there. Your foot's almost there. Just a little more, easy does it. Stop! Lower your toes, that's it, good, keep going…"

"Shit Alfie, I think it's a hot tile." I saw him begin to sway, losing his balance. I screamed out verbally, "No, damn you. Keep your balance. Bring your foot back." Wildly his arms began making big circles as he fought to regain his balance. "Beside the other foot, Joe. Bring your foot down tight beside the other one. There's room damn it, do it." His thoughts screamed at me.

"I'm trying, you dumb ass."

"Don't try, do it." Then his foot was there and after a couple of recovering jerks, he stood balanced.

Some of those in the tiered seats applauded but he didn't' hear them. I sighed out loud and wiped sweat from my brow again.

"That was close, Alfie," he said twitching, "Sorry for the dumb ass thing."

"Quiet all right pal, considering the pressure you're under."

"Man, you should hear it in here, Alfie…damn…ouch…it sounds like a million French fries boiling in a giant batch of hot grease. She's got water falling everywhere."

"I know it pal, we can hear it over the speakers."

"I can't take much more of it, get…ouch!…me out soon, I'm beginning to feel like a lobster."

I watched him twitch endlessly as the scalding drops splattered down non-stop.

I knew his body couldn't keep taking this kind of punishment. Sooner or later, he would grow shocky, become weak and slowly lethargic, eventually to the point of losing consciousness. Yet we had no choice. We moved on slowly, tedious step after tedious step. And everywhere, the hot water dripped from the piping above. Joe cursed in his thoughts, screamed obscenities in his mind and moved in every possible position to try and find relief from the stinging droplets. But it was no use. There was nothing he could do but cry out in his thoughts and somehow, beyond human understanding, endure the pain that pounded his brain for relief.

The distance from ladder to ladder was little more than twenty feet, but to Joe it seemed an endless trek.

There was no time to linger. Sweat flowed from his body like running water, pooling dangerously at his feet. To linger too long would mean his own body fluids creating a watery contact to one of the electrified tiles. And deadly too were the pools of falling water beginning to accumulate across the floor.

We lost track of time as we inched his way along. Each step, and each agonizing drop of burning water, weakened him. Through the red of the glasses, I could see the hundreds of burn welts over his body. Heat inside the Plexiglas box grew intense and began fogging the sides, limiting my vision. The constant fall of water soddened his hair and it lay flat against his head.

As time pressed on his foremost thought screamed like a neon sign in a world of darkness; the pain was too agonizing, too unbearable. He wanted to run, to say the hell with it and take his chances-a run for the ladder was worth the risk of electrocution. And in a way I understood-but we both knew the odds.

My heart and sympathy went out to him as I concentrated on his every step. Then almost to the ladder the water stopped falling; the crackling speakers fell silent.

Joe took two more steps and his hands grasped the ladder rails.

In great pain and unspeakably relieved, he stepped free of the electrified floor and climbed to the surface, to the waiting guards.

As quickly as the lights had gone out, they came on again. I sighed out loud and pulled off the infrared glasses. Bright light brought dark spots to my eyes, but they cleared rapidly. Billy leaned her elbows on the control panel and stared admiringly at Joe.

"Very well done, Mr. Hardon. I am indeed impressed. Only two to go. Are you up to it?"

In all his naked glory, Joe stood tall and flashed a smile.

"Let's do it."

# CHAPTER FIFTEEN

Joe was a sad-looking thing. His hair lay soaked and dripping, and red burn welts and tiny blisters covered his entire body. Now he stood shivering from the cooler air outside the hot chamber.

Billy's eyes drank in what she saw; a man who had endured unbelievable torture, a remarkable example of self-control and determination, a confident individual with a seemingly unbreakable spirit.

Her stare spoke of a private carnality; an erotic desire and lecherous wanting. I couldn't hear her thoughts but they were there, locked behind the deep blue eyes exemplifying her impeccable loveliness.

She was a Black Widow spider, an alluring beauty in search of that special mate. A woman in need of sexual satisfaction, and once her wanton needs were fulfilled she would kill her unsuspecting lover.

But Joe would not succumb to her feminine wiles and it frustrated her as much as it created admiration. And now, while staring at his naked form she smiled almost benevolently.

"Mr. Hardon. You have been through a great deal, perhaps more than most men could endure. In fact, you've already made it farther than anyone before you. I believe a rest is in order. And a rest is what the next chamber shall provide."

She called out to the guards standing at his side.

"Take him to the next section."

Again, a catwalk provided the way.

I looked over at Billy. "You are going to let him put coveralls back on, aren't you? He's freezing."

Her answer was pointed and she didn't look at me. "No."

I called her a bitch in my mind and to my surprise, Dixie agreed with me. Looking over at me, she grinned.

The last two chambers were connected, separated by a Plexiglas wall with a narrow doorway between the two.

The chamber on which they stood was the smaller one, little wider than an arm span. A single hatchway door with ladder leading down offered the only way in or out, except for the inner door that allowed access to the adjacent chamber. And that chamber, a 12 ft. by 12 ft. room, had no exit of its own.

As Billy had mentioned, now seemed a time of rest. Inside the little chamber sat a folding lounge chair with small end table. On the table sat an empty glass and a pitcher.

Skeptical, I shook my head. Joe looked my way and shrugged. Our one agreed thought was 'What the hell was she up to?' it took only a minute longer to find out.

A guard came through the door of the gauntlet room and with him was Nugent. The professor's face showed fear and he looked weary.

Escorted to the top of the chamber where Joe now stood, they stopped and turned to face Billy. Her face sober, she looked to Nugent and spoke coldly.

"What is there to say, Professor? You broke a cardinal rule. These gentlemen are marauders. Outsiders who would destroy all that we have strived for, yet you aided them in an attempted escape. Clearly, you understand the consequence?" She paused to let Nugent reply but he remained silent.

Joe took a step forward and the guards grabbed his arms. Speaking as they held him, he told Billy.

"Damn it, you can't kill him simply because he cares for people. He didn't sell us information, he only left a door unlocked, nothing more."

"Spare me the bleeding-heart rubbish, Mr. Hardon." She joined her hands as if praying and touched her fingers to her lips, thinking.

"Let us say you had escaped. Upon returning the Bordenwell family, would you have simply went about your life, business as usual and not mentioned this project, its location, and the 'inhuman atrocities' that go on here?" She paused and frowned, glaring out over the rim of her glasses. "We all know the answer, don't we? You would have done whatever was necessary to end our research."

"Not research," Joe yelled up, "human experimentation!"

"Call it what you will. The fact is, we who manage the world must upon occasion do things necessary to insure long range survival of the human race."

"Human race my ass." You don't give one little iota about people. You're a sick wench on a power kick and love every damn minute of it."

She took her bottom lip between her teeth and stared in a moment in thought.

"I suppose, Mr. Hardon, I shall never understand how you display such superior maleness, and yet you are so weak-minded."

"It's easy, Billy. I've got a heart."

"So, we shall see."

She turned to the guard with Nugent. "Take the good professor and secure him."

Forced onto the ladder, Nugent reluctantly climbed down, his mind filled with one thought-his life was about over. Two guards followed after him.

Once at the bottom, they pushed him through the narrow doorway into the larger chamber. Then dragged him to the far side where he was fastened to the wall with chains and leg irons bolted to the thick Plexiglas.

In our thoughts, Joe and I called Billy some very exclusive names. Dixie smiled and chimed amusingly in silence.

"Gentleman, please. That's my lover you're talking about."

Looking her way, I sent the unheard words. "Given the opportunity, she'll be your dead lover!"

The amused face disappeared.

Nugent made no attempt to try and free himself from the chains that held him imprisoned.

Abandoned and helpless, he stood there alone. Silent and with head hung, he stared ponderingly at the floor of the chamber. There was no escaping his fate and he knew it.

Joe turned to face me and was about to send up a thought when Billy turned to those sitting in the tiered seating.

"With the exception of Mr. Barkin and Mr. Mandagon, I would like for everyone else to leave the room."

Looking surprised, they mumbled angrily among themselves. General Phieffer stood in protest, aggravated she thought him not important enough to remain.

"Ms. Robinson, I must object. I represent the interest of the United States Government here."

Billy smiled openly.

"General, I know damn good and well who you represent, and I fully understand your need to protest. But I have spoken, now go protest somewhere else."

There was no other way to explain the look on the general's face except wholly pissed. Turning angrily on the balls of his feet he marched from the bleachers and out of the room. The others followed sullenly behind.

Looking at Joe I threw out the silent thought, 'this must be one hell of a last phase.' Nodding in silence he made a worried face.

When the last of the others were gone, both Barkin and Mandegon rose to their feet. Barkin climbed to the catwalk with us while Mandegon made his way to the top of the chamber to stand next to Joe. Looking up he stared at Billy.

The smile on her face gave away the nearly uncontrollable excitement she fought to contain. Her voice had changed somehow, edged with the fervor of pure power, the feeling of playing God, deciding who will live and who will die.

Leaning once again on the console, she laced her fingers and smiled at Joe.

"Now for your last and final scenario, Mr. Hardon. As you can see there are two chambers left. The smaller of the two belongs to you. Please note the chair in which to relax and sugared iced tea for nourishment in the pitcher. The larger chamber, on the other hand, belongs to Carlo. It too will provide him relaxation...his personal brand."

Looking at Joe, Mandegon smiled.

Joe shook his head. "You're one sick faggot, Mandegon. You don't even deserve the right to be called gay. You're and embarassment to their community."

Seemingly unaffected by the remark he turned calmly back Billy, who told Joe. "Mr. Hardon. The idea is that you will remain within your own chamber, enjoying the fruits thereof. Carlo meanwhile shall remain in his, doing the same. It's quite simple really. You see, the longer you remain in your own domain, the longer the professor lives. Put simply, if you cross into the other chamber, Nugent will die instantly by Carlo's hand. Then Carlo will concentrate fully upon you. Understand?"

"I have a better idea," Joe told her. "Why don't we just let Nugent go, then Faggot man can give me his full attention right away."

"No, for two reasons Mr. Hardon. First, the good professor has been very naughty and must be punished. Secondly, remember we are running experiments here. The principle of this last phase is to test animal reaction and loyalty to master when ordered to act aggressively toward a human being. The idea is..."

"The idea is military." Joe cut in. "The Government with this formula could turn an entire animal kingdom against its imposing enemies. Hell, you wouldn't have to lift a finger or fire a single shot."

"Precisely, Mr. Hardon."

Not taking her eyes from Joe she yelled to Priveman waiting outside the door of the room.

"Bring in Godzilla, Doctor."

Priveman walked through the door pulling the big gorilla by a chain attached to a thick leather collar. They crossed the room, climbed the ladder platform, then made their way to the others.

"Has the animal been cloned, Doctor?"

"He has."

"And you, Carlo?"

He nodded a silent yes.

"Splendid." She said. Looking at Joe again she asked cheerfully. "Ready, Mr. Hardon?"

"I was born ready."

Sweeping his nakedness, she replied.

"Yes, I can see you were."

Glancing at Mandegon she told him. "You may begin. Take Godzilla and go."

Mandegon stepped onto the ladder and started down, ordering the Gorilla to follow. Priveman freed the chain on the collar and the ape did as he was ordered, descending behind the big Jamaican.

"Now, Mr. Hardon," Billy ordered, "please climb down to your chamber and enjoy the treats awaiting you there."

Giving me one long last look, Joe hopped onto the ladder and climbed down.

Mandegon crossed into the large chamber and walked over to Nugent. In his hand he held the same knife he pulled on little Bradley.

Godzilla ambled just inside and sat Indian style on the floor in front of the doorway.

Joe went straight to the chair and sat, then poured himself a glass of the iced tea. He drank it hastily. His hands were shaking, and I knew why; he was in dire need of the sugared energy.

I caught but a fragment of a thought from him that ended abruptly when he went suddenly silent and began whistling. The Marine Corp Hymn. I had picked up only three words; tea, pitcher, son of a bitch. I thought it strange but knew how dangerously fatigued his mind had become.

Billy hit a switch on the console and followed with an adjustment of the microphone in front of her. With it in place, she spoke calmly into it.

"Okay Carlo, you may begin."

He nodded and turned to face Nugent. Joe rose from the chair and stood looking through the Plexiglas to the right of the doorway.

Mandegon used the knife to cut open the front of Nugent's lab coat and shirt, exposing his bare chest. Uncovered, it heaved in fear, rising and falling frantically, anticipating the pain that was about to follow. In sick gesture, which he enjoyed, Mandegon tauntingly ran the back of his hand down the side of the professor's face. Nugent jerked his head away, humiliated by the sordid action. Grinning, Mandegon sunk the knife blade and cut a long furlough down Nugent's chest. The professor's scream filled the chamber and blood raced to the surface to roll down and pool at the belt line. Joe started through the door, but Billy yelled into the microphone.

"Do it Mr. Hardon, and he dies."

Stopping at the threshold he looked up through the Plexiglas roof and pointed a finger.

"You cold-hearted bitch. You know damn good and well, even if I don't go in, he'll die anyway."

"Probably, but I might reconsider, after all he is valuable to us. At this point, it could go either way, I haven't decided yet-only time will tell. Still, if you wish to rush my decision and get him murdered, then by all means, enter through the doorway."

Joe teetered, his thoughts privately wrestling the frustration and indecision sweeping his mind. Swearing under his breath he returned to the Plexiglas wall and stood silent but began whistling the Marine Corps Hymn again.

A smile on his lips, Mandegon continued. This time his free hand went into Nugent trousers to his crotch. Humiliated, the professor jerked to get free. The chains rattled as he struggled but it was of no use. Mandegon continued to smile, sending a thought to Joe for the first time.

"See what it is you are missing Hardon. Come on mon, don't you wish this was you? Why don't you come here to help him? I am waiting for you."

With the hand holding the knife, Mandegon went to the throat and applied light pressure. Nugent stopped struggling and stood terrifyingly still. "Perhaps Hardon," Mandegon continued. "I will cut his throat now."

Joe went wild! In a fit of rage his hand snapped up the glass pitcher of iced tea from the table and at the same time kicked over the chair with his foot. It tumbled over, slamming noisily into the Plexiglas wall.

Whirling around he stepped to the doorway and yelled out loud for all to hear, pointing with the big pitcher in his hand.

"That's right Mandegon, you faggot bastard. Cut the poor soul's throat. Go on kill him!" To emphasize he raised his hand and slammed the pitcher of tea to the floor. The glass exploded into pieces across the doorway and the tinted liquid flowed over the floor of both chambers.

"You're not even a faggot man, Mandegon," Joe yelled, "You're a faggot baby. Anybody can cut the throat of a chained man. In my estimation, if you kill him, you're a bigger cunt than your boss."

Mandegon screamed the word..."NO!"

The knife came away from Nugent's throat and his hand free of the trousers. Reeling around he pointed with the knife, his face a twisted poison.

"COME! You think you are so bad. I show you, who is bad."

Joe tormented him. "You couldn't show me shit, Faggot baby."

Billy spoke into the microphone to Mandegon, her voice accented with authority and yet highlighted with the exhilaration of an escalating confrontation.

"Carlo, stop it. He's only trying to anger you. He's using psychology."

There was cold silence as both men stared. In our thoughts we could hear Mandegon mulling over what Billy had said but eyes his remained locked on Joe.

Godzilla had changed his position and now sat huddled in a corner watching and listening to all that was going on. I wondered how much he really understood?

Joe prodded again.

"That's right Mandegon, I'm using psychology. I'm trying to psyche you up, because I think without it, you're afraid of me. Look at you, I'm naked and exposed, tired and weak, burned and blistered. You're fully dressed with shirt, pants, and shoes. You're such a faggot wimp you need all the help you can get."

Mandegon shook the poisoned expression and replaced it with a demented grin.

Doubling up his fists, he raised them and said, "All I need are these to kill you mon."

I let my breath out silently; the man was pure Psycho.

Laughing, Joe bantered.

"All right, let's see. Take off your clothes like me. We'll make it a fight to the death, man against man, bare flesh against  flesh, naked muscle against naked muscle."

There was excitement in Mandegon's eyes and a challenge in his voice as he spoke.

"Never have I wanted to kill any Mon so much. And never have I wanted to be with someone as much as I do you."

Slowly, Mandegon removed his clothes, a piece at a time, until finally he stood naked in the chamber. His eyes never once left Joe.

Billy spoke to him again through the microphone.

"Carlo please. This is not what I planned. We must run the experiment as agreed." He was ignoring her and she put pleading in her tone.

"Please, Carlo! You have Mr. Hardon for yourself, but after the experiment."

For the first time in minutes, he broke his stare with Joe to look up at her through the plexi glass wall.

Softly, as if speaking to a child, Billy told him. "You know how important this experiment is. So much depends on it!"

Silently, he nodded and pulled his eyes away. Looking at Godzilla he snapped a command to the ape still huddling in the corner… "Come here to me!"

The gorilla hesitated slightly but did as ordered. At his side, Mandegon stroked the ape's head in acknowledgment of his obedience. Then taking his hand, he turned him so that they both were facing Nugent. Again, he spoke in thought to the gorilla.

"This Mon he is bad. He would hurt those who care for you. He must be killed. You remember what killed is?"

The gorilla looked into his eyes a few seconds then shook his head only once. We all watched with uncertainty. Nugent, still helplessly bound in the chains, spoke verbally to Godzilla, his voice desperate.

"Please Godzilla. He is the bad man not me. He says he cares for you, but I love you. Can you remember what I taught you about love?" Godzilla looked at Nugent a second and again shook his head once.

"Damn it Carlo, he's confusing the animal. Get on with it!" Billy shouted into the microphone.

She was angry and directed that anger to Nugent "Damn you Professor, what the hell have you done? That sense was not to be taught to these animals. You just may have blown everything we've worked for."

Looking up at her from his bonds, Nugent told her. "Yes Natalie I may have blown it, as you say. And if I have, than at least I can go to my death knowing I at least did one thing right."

"Damn you to hell," she hissed into the microphone.

"Yes Natalie, and I deserve it."

"Order him now Carlo." There was pure hatred in her words.

Mandegon placed his knife in the ape's hand, wrapping the animal's fingers tight around it. "Godzilla, do you remember where and how I taught you to stick it to make da kill?" Again, came a single nod. "You must do it NOW!"

Obviously unsure, the gorilla looked confusingly from the knife to Mandegon then into Nugent's face. Throwing in his ante too, Joe called out to Godzilla in thought.

"Hey Godzilla, look over here at me, by the door." The big ape turned his head and looked over his shoulder to where Joe was standing. He made a funny face and remained staring, waiting for this stranger to speak. But I didn't give Joe time.

"Godzilla. Up here, it's me, remember?" He looked around now unsure of who was speaking to him. "Up here, above, high, overhead, on top, beside Natalie and Dixie."

That gave it away. His head turned to look up through the Plexiglas roof. Trying not to be noticed, I bent my arm at the elbow and waved. Upon acknowledgement, Godzilla nodded his head repeatedly. I wasn't sure, but I thought he was happy to see me. I talked to him. "Hey, that man near the door behind you, he's a good…"

That was all I got out. Dixie turned to me and said out loud, "If you utter another thought, I'll have Natalie order you shot. Understood?"

Falling silent, I made a face.

Billy spoke into the microphone immediately. "Mr. Hardon, if you speak even one more thought to that animal, your partner will be shot on the spot, is that clear?" Frowning, Joe gave a nod.

Mandegon turned to the gorilla. "It is now time. Kill him!"

We stood silent, holding our breath. The ape gripped the knife tightly. Joe's mouth opened to speak but he caught himself. Everyone watched with eyes glued to the chamber.

The moment of truth had come. Godzilla's hairy shoulder moved. Nugent screamed "NO!" as the dark blade came up beneath his rib cage, tearing through the soft flesh and ripping into his heart.

Mandegon practically yelled it… "again!" Godzilla pulled the knife free and stabbed it a second time into Nugent's body. "And again!" And the knife slashed for the third time; but the funny looking professor never felt it. He was dead.

For a minute all was still, with no sound in the room except for our breathing. Shock, disbelief, joy, sadness, shame, it was all here in a mixed array of emotions.

Godzilla was the one who broke the almost hypnotic spell. He scampered off to his corner and sat quietly, the bloody knife still clutched in his hand. Mandegon turned slowly to face Joe.

"Now, Hardon. It's time to fight."

Joe looked from Nugent's lifeless body to Mandegon. On his face was an expression even strange to me.

Mindful of the scattered glass fragments, he moved carefully into the large chamber and stood unbending.

"No, Mandegon," he said coldly, "It's time to die."

# CHAPTER SIXTEEN

Nugent's lifeless body hung slumped in the irons where he had died. And sitting alone in the corner still clutching the knife that took his life, Godzilla glared at him, knowing that somehow, he had done wrong.

I could feel his guilt and confusion and wanted to console him. But for now, that was but a secondary worry.

In mutual want, Joe and Mandegon stood only a few feet from one another, each waiting for whatever it was that would start their battle to the death.

There would be no way out, no compromise, only one would climb the ladder to the surface. If it were Mandegon, he would be hailed a hero, and if it were Joe, they would kill him anyway.

For us, there was nothing left but to play a final hand here and now. I was sure Joe was thinking the same thing, but because of all who had been cloned he could not relay such thoughts. Our only chance was to trust in the other, to rely upon our long running friendship and years of working together.

Like the lightning that flashed across the sky the night we arrived, Mandegon's foot left the floor with astonishing speed.

Like a Boxer's deadly roundhouse, only using his leg, his foot came around and snapped brutally against the side of Joe's face. The power behind it was incredible and sent Joe wheeling across the chamber, slamming him hard into the Plexiglas wall.

The place vibrated from impact and the harsh sound echoed through the speakers.

Like a ball of rubber Joe's body rebounded and toppled to the floor. For a moment he didn't move, and I held my breath.

I recalled Mandegon's rap sheet; Master, Fifth Degree Black belt. He would be deadly, a professional killer always in Possession of his favorite weapons.

Joe would need to fight like he had never fought before.

Mandegon stood ready, waiting ardently for Joe to rise.

In the corner, Godzilla watched with question in his eyes and twice he looked up at me as if to ask, why? I wasn't sure he'd understand but I told him anyway. That man himself was the real animal, far more cruel and barbaric than his own kind ever dreamed of being.

Joe moaned and began moving. Shaking his head, he pulled himself to his knees then climbed to his feet.

There was a small cut on his right cheek that trickled blood.

Mandegon's foot was a blur, his speed lethal. Again his foot came up slamming into Joe's head, sending him flying like a child performing a crude cartwheel. One more time he struck the wall of the chamber, this time crumpling into a corner.

My thoughts shot out, mixed with concern and anger. "Damn it, Joe! What the hell are you doing? This guy has a black belt, watch him!" Mandegon turned only briefly to look up at me and grin arrogantly. Again, Joe pulled himself to his feet, bantering my remark in his thoughts.

"What are you talking about Alfie? This guy doesn't have a belt, he's bare-assed."

"Very funny." I said, not amused. Mandegon executed an incredibly fast front snap kick and Joe pivoted to avoid the blow, but didn't make it. The impact caught him under the nose, spinning him around and knocking him hard into the wall once again. Bright red blood splattered the glass, and the shock of the collision stunned him.

Helplessly I watched as he staggered three steps backward, turned, then rose sluggishly to his knees. Haggard and fatigued he remained in the kneeling position for several minutes, staring blankly at the floor, his head hung. Again my thoughts went out to him.

"Damn it, Joe! What the hell are you trying to prove? Man, you're not Rocky Balboa, you can't take this kind of beating, you've got to stay on the move."

His reply surprised me. "Trust... Alfie...can hand...problem." His thoughts were coming into my head like an old skipping record. Running my fingers through my hair, I puzzled for a second, then it dawned. Dixie and I both spoke the very instant we turned to look at one another.

"Synapse depletion!"

The serum was beginning to wear off and the idea pleased me. We would all be on equal ground again. With no more mind reading there would be no more advantages, and that would be the edge Joe needed. That he was by far more resilient then the man he fought, there was no doubt. The trouble had been Mandegon's ability to clearly anticipate his every move.

When this capability ran out, so would his advantage.

Flippantly, Mandegon taunted Joe.

"Who is the pussy now, Hardon? I'm going to kill you, but I would like to have been your lover first."

Joe used the wall to help pull himself to his feet. Looking at the big Jamaican he forced a smile through the curtain of blood now covering his face.

"Don't let a couple of lucky kicks go to your head, faggot boy. You're still first choice for pussy of the gauntlet." Mandegon let a strange noise escape his throat, then came around with a double spinning back kick. This time, Joe moved quickly enough and avoided both strikes. I told him good job, but he never replied, he couldn't hear me anymore.

Looking from the corner of my eye I glanced at Dixie and called her a little tittied sleaze; she never replied either.

Smugly I turned back to the chamber and nodded to myself.

The serum had definitely worn off; all mind reading was now over. The time had come for the fat lady to sing.

Mandegon tried another kick but missed. Slowly the two circled within the chamber, their eyes locked in hate.

Mandegon the malefactor, the transgressor of evil, moved with grace and poise, a skilled killer, a murderer who loved what he did. On his face was an expression of heightened involvement, a man caught up in the challenge of life-or-death combat.

There was the look of confidence too. He was sure of himself; positive he couldn't be beaten. He was the fighter who had always been the victor, the winner; the one hailed the best. Never had he lost, nor felt the pangs of defeat. But never had he fought Joe Hardon.

Mandegon struck again, an incredibly powerful sidekick. It struck Joe center chest and sent him sailing through the air.

If we had been in Hollywood on a movie location, I would have called it a perfect stunt. Joe's flying body hurtled dead center through the doorway back into the smaller chamber. Noisily he crashed into the far wall plunging to the floor.

The entire gauntlet shook sending a resonant clatter across the speakers.

This time Joe didn't stay down. Grimacing painfully to his feet.

"That was your last kick faggot," he told Mandegon. "Stay where you are. Because if you come in here, I'm going to rip off those Jamaican balls and stuff them down your fairy throat."

Mandegon stood silent, perhaps stunned, surprised any man would dare be so brazen toward him following the beating he had just given them, but Joe continued the taunting.

"You're nothing but a low-class ass reamer scared of his own shadow. In fact, you're so yellow you had to get a Gorilla to do your killing." Joe smirked, then laughed annoyingly. "Mandegon, you call me a pussy; YOU take orders from a WOMAN!"

Mandegon's facial expression changed like a kaleidoscope of evil, twisting slowly into dark, psychopathic anger. But Joe persisted, dangerously heckling the man already intent on killing him.

"You can't even think for yourself. It's my guess Billy has to dress you in the morning then spoon feed you breakfast from a baby jar?

Tell me, does she wipe your little bottom after you've gone to the bathroom? You're the biggest of all pussies, Mandegon. Even little Bradley Bordenwell is more of a man than you."

Mandegon exploded. Violent rage flushed his face as it twisted into a malignant madness. Screaming out Joe's name he raced furiously through the doorway after him.

Temper enraged; the angered Jamaican ignored the broken class fragments scattered over the threshold.

Through the speakers we could hear the razor-edged pieces crush beneath his bare feet as he ran. Nodding my admiration, I now knew why Joe had begun humming the Marine Corps Hymn right after he had broken the pitcher.

Its breaking had been pre-planning and his own thoughts would have given away his strategy.

The sharp fragments sliced Mandegon's feet profusely, but it didn't stop him; the pain was overcome by his obsessive determination to kill.

Immediately through the doorway he grabbed Joe, and the hands of both men went to the throat of the other. At least now there would be no more karate, only man against man. No more fancy kicks to imbalance the scale.

Teeth gritted and muscles bulged as each strained for every ounce of strength with which to kill the other. Mandegon's feet flowed with blood, covering the floor with red liquid.

I could feel myself grow tense as I watched this final battle. Mandegon was the bigger man, but Joe Hardon was no rookie.

Groans and rasping breaths came howling through the speakers as the two struggled for their lives. Joe, I thought, was either one lucky man or twice as crafty as I had given him credit for.

The last kick Mandegon executed had sent him flying safely over the broken glass pieces, clear of its disabling danger. Could he have aligned himself so perfectly and at the same time anticipated the sidekick that would send him sailing?

Maybe, after all, he was shrewd enough to distract Mandegon, and then anger him sufficiently to come charging blindly over the broken rubble.

The flowing blood from Mandegon's mutilated feet pooled with the spilled tea making the floor inherently slippery.

Joe's feet went out from under him, and the entangled bodies of both men toppled, slamming hard to the floor. The sound vibrated through the speakers like a load of bricks. Mandegon freed a hand from Joe's throat and threw a punch to his face. It connected and we heard the smacking sound.

Then Joe returned with one of his own and for a while it became hit for hit, blow for blow, with the sickening sound of each strike pouring from the speakers for all to hear.

Blood and sweat covered the bodies of both men, making them slick and almost impossible to grip. Constantly they lost their hold on one another and scrambled frantically to regain it.

Then Joe broke free and scrambled to his feet, moving quickly to the end of the narrow room. Mandegon rose in pursuit, now limping noticeably.

In a flash he was in the corner with Joe, and it became a volley of hit for hit once again. Mandegon was fast. His years of martial arts training clearly gave him an edge, and his fists moved with blurring speed. Left and right his iron hands bludgeoned Joe's face and body. Though I knew he couldn't hear me I yelled for Joe to get away, get out of reach.

Mandegon threw a solid right then he came back with an elbow to the face. Joe's head crashed into the glass wall and the power of the impact dropped him to his knees at Mandegon's feet.

Mandegon immediately brought up his knee catching Joe under the jaw. His head snapped back, smashing again into the Plexiglas wall, then he fell forward, catching himself on his hands and knees.

Shaking his head to stay conscious, Joe remained in that position. He was stunned, weak and slipping into shock. Blood rolled from his face onto the floor. Mandegon watched him closely, towering high above, poised ready and arrogant.

Not looking up Joe spoke to Mandegon, his voice flippant.

"Well, queer bait, I'll bet you're getting excited seeing me in this pose, aren't you?" He paused, then added. "Tell you what. I'll move a little farther away so you can get a good look at what you'll never have."

There on his hands and knees Joe began inching his way through the doorway leading into the larger chamber. Mandegon watched his movement with close attention; then without warning moved to his side and brought up his leg and smashed the heel of his foot hard into Joe's back.

Joe collapsed in a cry of agony then lay silent across the threshold of the doorway.

Mandegon, despite his blood soddened feet, was now caught up in the thrill of victory. He began an endless and unmerciful parry of kicking. Repeatedly his feet wailed out wherever he could find an opening. Joe moaned at each blow and his cries moved over the speakers in despondent tones that tapered gradually, ending finally in silence.

Mandegon's face was twisted. He was out of control, caught up in the need to kill and lust for winning. The beating he gave Joe seemed endless, each kick was felt in my heart and as I watched tears welled in my eyes. I wanted more than anything to stop it but knew I couldn't. Mandegon kicked until he grew tired or perhaps began coming to his senses. As if coming out of a daze his kicks grew fewer and fewer until finally he stopped altogether.

Joe had ceased moving long ago and we on the catwalk stood speechless. An emptiness clung to my soul as I wiped away tears with the sleeve of my coveralls. I hated Mandegon now, like I had never felt hate before.

Turning, the big Jamaican looked up at Billy. Running sweat and splattered blood covered his ebony body from head to toe. Heat within the chamber had soaked his hair and it lay glistening, tight against his scalp.

A small grin began to grow at the corners of his mouth, spreading into a large smile and finally into a burst of laughter. Billy did not return the smile but gave her nod of congratulations and spoke into the microphone.

"Well done, Carlo. Once again, you've outperformed yourself. Although Mr. Hardon proved a very worthy opponent and has made it farther than any other before him, it appears he was not all he had claimed to be. But then again, how could we ever expect him to win against someone like you? After all, you have been a four-time world karate champion."

Joe remained motionless. It now appeared I was on my own and needed to do something fast. Silently I sized up the situation.

To the left, Billy stood alone at the console. To my right, almost touching my shoulder, was Dixie. And just behind her, Barkin. To his right there was one guard clutching a shotgun, obviously enjoying the show.

On top of the gauntlet stood two more guards, with a third near the entrance door of the gauntlet room itself.

If, I reasoned, I took Barkin out fast enough, there might be a chance of getting to the guy with the shotgun before he caught on.

Carefully I judged the striking distance to Barkin. If Murphy kept his nose out of it and my calculations were correct, I was close enough for an elbow strike to the face. Then Joe moaned. It came across the speakers as total surprise. Disbelieving, Mandegon looked down at him.

Positioned half on his side with arms folded beneath him, Joe stirred slightly and moaned a second time. Mandegon glanced up at Billy then back to Joe again. Then lowering himself into a squatting position he reached out and stroked Joe's hair almost tenderly.

Then he rose, stepped over his body and limped into the other chamber, this time careful to avoid the broken glass.

Blood from his feet left red prints on the floor behind him and I had to admit, the sight pleased me.

Crossing to where Godzilla sat huddled, Mandegon reached down and pulled the knife free from the ape's hands. The animal stared at him, as if unsure that giving up the knife had been the correct thing to do. But Mandegon ignored the look and turned rudely away to hobble back to where Joe lay.

At his side again, he kneeled on his knees to take the weight off his mangled feet.

Switching the knife from his left to his right hand, he clutched a fist of Joe's hair and arched his head back, exposing his throat.

Leaning down he kissed Joe on the lips then pulled the knife out to the side for a strong swing. That's when Joe rolled over and yelled it for all to hear.

"Kiss this you son-of-a-bitch." His right hand came up clutching the broken handle of the tea pitcher. A large, jagged fragment protruded from it and Joe thrust it powerfully into Mandegon's throat. It tore fiercely through the muscle and severed both the carotid artery and windpipe. For only a second there was enough air to allow a short-lived scream. And although his mouth remained open, Mandegon made no further sound. He dropped the knife from his hand and clutched at the sharp instrument now lodged deeply and fatally in his throat. Bulging eyes told of his shock and disbelief.

Clumsily he rose to his feet, staggered backward, and braced himself against the wall of the chamber to turn and look up at Billy. Noiselessly his mouth moved as if trying to speak, then he slid down the wall and fell over dead.

With great effort Joe pulled himself to his knees, then to his feet. Using the wall for balance he looked up at Billy.

Like Mandegon, his body was covered head to toe with blood and sweat. Scores of burn welts showed themselves where there was no blood, and his eyes were partially swollen shut. I wasn't sure, but I thought his nose might have been broken and there were three noticeable lacerations on his face, one under the right eye, on the right cheek, and in the middle of the forehead. Fatigue had taken its toll and he had little strength with which to hold himself up. But despite his condition he smiled for Billy.

"Poor Carlo! And just when he thought it was safe to get back into the chamber." Billy shook her head while grinning.

"Tell me Mr. Hardon, was it you who wrote the definition to the word, resourceful?"

Joe dropped the smile and folded his arms. Still leaning against the Plexiglas wall he told her.

"I don't do much writing, never was very good at it. I do, however, have a trademark on survival."

"Yes, obviously," Billy said, "but let us not gloat, just yet. Perhaps Mr. Barkin would like to come down now and sample that trademark."

"No way in Hell!" The words came out before I even realized what I had said. Forgetting about Joe for a time, everyone turned their eyes on me and for a second, I was as surprised as they were. Billy frowned.

"What did you say?"

"I said, No way in Hell. Joe has had enough of the fun; it's my turn. I want Barkin!"

My eyes went to his and we stared.

Billy laughed lightly. "Well why don't we just ask S.B., what he would prefer."

Barkin's face was sober. He looked from me down into the chamber.

"First I want to finish him off. Then," he said looking back at me, "I'll take care of him."

Billy turned to the microphone and spoke provokingly.

"Well Mr. Hardon, it appears Mr. Barkin would like a try at you. If I send him down, think you can handle him?"

With a nod Joe told her. "So far Billy, you've tried to drown me, fry me, boil me, and lastly have me beaten to death-all of which I survived. Now, thinking I might be frightened, you're going to send down little peckered S.B., spare me, I can't wait."

I looked at Barkin and let him see the grin on my face. He was turning red with anger, and I wondered if Joe ever knew when to shut up.

Then Joe added looking up with a grin, "You know Billy, before you send little pee-pee down here, you got to ask yourself one simple question, can you afford to lose any more help?"

# CHAPTER SEVENTEEN

s Barkin descended the ladder another Murphy law burst into my head. 'Friends come and go but enemies accumulate.' As of late Joe had certainly acquired his share and now if I didn't do something fast this one would end his life.

Under normal circumstance Joe would have a more than average chance at winning against Barkin, but not now. By far too fatigued and badly hurt, he would be lucky to last even a few scant minutes. In desperation I tried reasoning with Billy.

"Damn it, you can't be serious about this. Barkin is fresh and fully dressed. You know good and well Joe doesn't stand a chance."

Never taking her eyes from the chamber she told me indifferently.

"Worry not Mr. Stone. If S.B. wins you will be permitted the opportunity of avenging your partner. Now please be silent and let us watch."

Angrily I looked away and reevaluated my situation.

With Barkin gone, that left only Billy, Dixie and one guard on the catwalk with me. He was too far away to reach without moving a considerable distance, but if he were to become distracted, I might have a chance at getting to him.

Joe had moved into the large chamber and stood waiting against the far wall near Nugent's hanging body.

Having reached the end of the ladder Barkin stepped onto the chamber floor where he paused a moment to stare down at Mandegon.

His face without expression, there was no telling what he was thinking or feeling. He lauded but a short time before stepping over the body.

Godzilla remained secluded in his corner, watching it all through puzzled eyes. I wondered how much he really understood and how it was all affecting him.

Like Mandegon, Barkin was a big man. His shoulders flanked the doorjambs and the broken glass beneath his shoes crushed easily from the weight of his heavy body.

Bending down he picked up the knife Mandegon had held, then slowly milked the handle in his hand. He raised his eyes to Joe. They were cold, iced over with a cruel hardness.

The guard to my right stood watching intently. I wondered if now was the time to make my move? The room was quiet, the speakers silent. On top of the chamber the two guards had squatted in an effort to make themselves more comfortable and get a better view of what was about to happen.

The guard at the door had remained where he was, although he probably wanted very much to move within seeing distance.

Dixie was still close, nearly touching my shoulder and like the others she too was caught up in this travesty of inhumane brutality.

Joe had certainly told Bordenwell correctly when he said we would be entering into a sewer of psychopaths and perverts. And even truer was the statement that where we were going would be a slice of hell itself.

Barkin moved into the large chamber, stooping through the doorway to do so. Knife tight in his right hand he worked the fingers of his left, gesturing for Joe to approach. This was it!

Taking a deep breath Joe glanced up at me then did just that, moving toward him slow and cautious. God, I couldn't believe what was happening; Joe was too far-gone and stood no chance at all.

Watchful of each other they moved in a small circle. Barkin slashed out with the knife but missed. Eyes fused, they moved with a concentrated grace. Again, Barkin slashed but missed; Joe blocked it and landed a roundhouse over Barkin's right eye. The big man staggered backward but recovered quickly.

Angered, he lashed out with four consecutive swings of the knife, landing a cut on the fourth. The muscle on Joe's upper chest sliced open and he gritted his teeth against the pain. Barkin leaped and the bulk of his weight took Joe to the floor.

Falling hard, they rolled twice, coming to rest against Nugent's slumped knees. The chains that held the dead professor rattled loudly and the sound clambered out through the speakers.

Barkin's strength was fresh, his untapped energy more than Joe's exhausted condition could bear. In seconds he was astride Joe's waist, thrusting the knife blade downward. Only by grace did Joe catch his wrist.

In a last futile attempt, Joe's free hand went to the big man's throat and squeezed. Barkin gasped and his eyes bulged, but he managed a punch to Joe's head, a hard left, followed with another and yet another after that.

They were jolting blows that Joe couldn't stop. Like chunks of iron Barkin's fists flew, landing hard, rendering Joe increasingly weaker.

No man could take that kind of punishment and live; especially Joe, after what he had already been through.

In my temples I could feel the pounding of my heart and it went well with the sickness wallowing in the pit of my stomach. A tiny bead of wetness dropped from my eye, streaking its way down my cheek and into my mouth. I could taste the salt.

Helplessly I watched, wishing it were me down there.

Gallantly Joe struggled. They were noble and frantic attempts at warding off this mountain of a man slowly beating his already frail body to the very brink of death.

And although capable of much more than we give it credit, the human body can endure only so much before it reaches the limit and crosses to the world on the other side.

Having been hurt too much, Joe reached that limit. His struggling ended at last. Arms giving way he collapsed into a numbed, zombie-like state.

Barkin's fists ceased their relentless pounding. For Big Joe Hardon, the fight was over. As another bead of wetness stormed my cheek I pleaded silently for God to help us.

Powerless and vulnerable Joe now lay staring up at the man above him. And although dazed from the hard blows, he lay with honor, waiting with dignity for the final fall of the knife.

Grinning, Barkin raised it over his head, slowly, teasingly, agonizingly prolonging the horror that was to befall the only true friend I ever had.

I screamed "NO!" but the words echoed against deaf ears. Barkin widened his grin and told Joe. "Kiss your ass goodbye smart mouth, I'm sending you to hell."

When Godzilla's giant hand wrapped around Barkin's wrist it startled him. Surprise on his face, he looked first at the hairy hand gripping like iron, then into the ape's eyes. Brazenly he yelled at the animal.

"What the hell do you think you're doing, you stupid shit? Let go of my arm!"

Godzilla didn't budge. He made a funny face at Barkin then looked up over his shoulder at me. Our eyes met and I wished for the first time the serum had not worn off.

For what seemed an eternity we stared in silence, and I knew in his heart the big gorilla was pleading for direction.

The room was silent, testimony to the shock and disbelief on our faces. Every eye was on Godzilla. Beads of sweat covered my forehead. Something needed to be done. But what?

Slowly Billy turned her head to look at me and I yelled, "Screw it!"

Ramming her with my shoulder I shoved her away from the microphone and yelled into it.

"Help Mr. Hardon, Godzilla. Help him!"

The guard with the shotgun was behind me in seconds and smashed the butt brutally against my head.

The blow brought an explosion of stars and sent me to the catwalk floor where I laid for several seconds as the room swirled and blackness fought to take me away.

I heard Godzilla scream angrily from within the chamber...he was one pissed monkey.

With both hairy hands now wrapped about Barkin's arm he held him leisurely at bay. Barkin struggled with gritted teeth to free himself but in vain.

Composure regained, Billy covered the mike with her hand and yelled down to the guard at the door.

"Quickly, go get the tranquilizer gun."

Immediately he turned and bolted away.

Barkin quit struggling and now stared up at Billy for help.

No one moved, unsure of what to do. Slowly I climbed to my feet. The guard stood right behind me now, the gun barrel at my back. He didn't know it, but that was just where I wanted him.

How long it would take for the tranquilizer gun to arrive I didn't know, but at least for right now things were at a stalemate.

As a ploy to stall, Billy spoke into the microphone, putting so much tenderness in her tone I thought I was going to be sick.

"Godzilla, what are you doing? You know it is us who love you. We are your family. You must let go of Mr. Barkin's arm and return to your corner. Do you understand?"

Godzilla did not move. His dark eyes remained on Billy a long time, deciphering her words. He made another funny face followed with a few strange noises, which to him was probably an attempt to talk.

What exactly he said, we would never understand as words, but in action he made their meaning perfectly clear. With ease, he pulled Barkin's arm across his knee and we heard the loud snap of bone as it broke.

Barkin's scream came through the speakers as music to my ears.

To Godzilla, this big man with the knife was but a lightweight toy. Pulling him free of Joe he sent him crashing hard into the wall, where he bounced back and fell flaccid to the floor.

Angrily, Billy covered the mike and yelled under her breath, "Where the hell is that gun?"

Godzilla turned his attention to Joe.

Gently he pulled him into a sitting position then sat holding him in his arms. While rocking him tenderly, he stared remorsefully at Nugent's hanging body. And even from my elevated position on the catwalk, I could see the ape was crying.

Then the door to the gauntlet room burst open and everyone turned to look. I made my move.

Spinning quickly around I knocked the barrel of the shotgun free of my back and at the same time came up with a left hook. It caught the guard under the jaw, and he went down to stay.

Diving to the floor of the walkway I swept up the shotgun and pumped a round into the chamber. Lying on my side I fired without really aiming, confident I wouldn't miss at such close range. The shotgun kicked in my hands and sent a thunderous roar through the room.

One of the two guards went toppling backwards off the chamber while the other pulled his Uzi around to fire on me. He was too slow, my second shot took him in the chest, and he spun around, falling motionless, half on and half off the edge of the chamber.

Scrambling to my feet I fired a third shot at the guard with the tranquilizer gun but missed. He dashed behind the gauntlet, and I could see him clearly as he ran its full length, moving to the far end for safety.

Billy made a dash for me, hoping to grab the shotgun. I swung the butt and caught her under the chin. Her head snapped and she tumbled backwards to the catwalk floor. On her way down I wished the bitch sweet dreams then turned to see Dixie running for the ladder. Pulling my sights on her I eased the trigger but couldn't bring myself to fire. In seconds she was down and scrambling through the doorway out of sight.

Climbing over the rail of the catwalk I jumped onto the top of the gauntlet and ran to the far end after the remaining guard. Once there he fired up with a tranquilizer bullet but missed. It was his mistake. I pumped the shotgun and fired down. The close range of the slug hit so hard he slammed to the floor in a sitting position then fell onto his back, dead before he quit moving.

In a short time, I knew more guards would be on their way. We had no time to lose. Moving to the chamber entrance, I yelled down to Joe.

"Hey hotshot, think you can you make it up the ladder?" Not very convincingly he yelled up.

"Nooooooo Problem, Alfie."

Maneuvering slowly into a kneeling position, Joe looked into Godzilla's eyes and placed a thankful hand on the ape's shoulder.

"Thanks friend, I owe you."

Putting a hairy hand back on Joe's shoulder Godzilla puckered his lips and kissed him on the lips.

Startled at first, Joe slowly grinned then turned and started up the ladder.

Turning away, Godzilla scampered off to Nugent's hanging body where he sat to stare in silence.

Painfully Joe climbed back into his coveralls then picked up the Uzi belonging to the dead guard.

Eyes alert we climbed free of the gauntlet and made our way to the door.

The hall looked clear, so we stepped out, ready for action. Nothing happened. The way to our left would lead in a direction we had never been. To the right somewhere would be the holding cells with the Bordenwells. That was the way we went.

Joe moved slowly, fatigue taking its toll. Twice he stumbled and I helped him back to his feet.

The corridors remained quiet, and we encountered no guards. That surprised us since we were expecting the sound of pounding footsteps making their way toward us, their hands full of automatic weapons.

Time passed slowly as we struggled to maintain a good pace through the long corridors. Joe limped as we moved, and I helped him along with an arm around his waist.

When we finally found the holding area, we encountered our first opposition. One lone man stood ready at the entrance. He spotted us only seconds before Joe cut loose with the Uzi. The spray of bullets peppered his body, and he danced the steps of death before sprawling face first to the floor.

Throwing the long bar aside we pulled open the door and I rushed in. As before, Joe stood watch.

The keys hung on the peg near the entrance, and I grabbed them quickly, moving to the Bordenwell' s cell.

The others once again pressed themselves to the bars to watch, only this time there were smiles and faces of eager anticipation. They knew there would be no need for begging, I would free them too.

As I turned the key in the lock the speakers in the hallway ceiling squealed and Billy's voice came over them. Hesitating momentarily, I listened as she spoke.

"Congratulations gentleman. No one else could have been this successful. I can't tell you how impressed I am, or how depressed. As of now, and all because of you, this project is terminated. Allow me though, if you will, to have the last laugh. In exactly four minutes, twenty-six seconds, there will be an explosion and you will all be buried alive. Don't bother with the elevator, it's locked out and you are all locked in." She paused a few seconds then added.

"As for you, my dear Mr. Hardon, in parting, I should like to say how sad it is we were not offered the opportunity of sharing a night together. To borrow from your American slang...I would have screwed your socks off. Good-by."

The speakers tweaked a second and went silent.

Quickly I finished freeing the Bordenwells, then yelled at Joe to start counting the minutes. Scrambling like a mad man I opened all the other cells and bunched everyone together. Joe pulled the dead guard's watch from his arm and began the count.

Again, I paired the strong with the weak and the moment it was done, we moved out.

With the elevator shut down we had but one chance to survive...race for the old tunnels and get in as far as we could before the explosion.

As we moved, I calculated our chances.

Counting Joe and myself there were thirty-nine of us, men, women and children alike. Some of which were drugged or otherwise disabled. We had about two and a half minutes left by the time we started down the hallway in search of the opening Joe and I had made earlier.

And like before, those tunnels would be dark and cold and especially scary to the children. They would run on for miles, twist and turn in an incomprehensible maze and this time, following the explosion; there would be no known exits to give us hope. There would be no food, no water and no warmth. So, the way I figured it, at best our odds of making it were 10 to 1-against us! I just love that fucking Murphy.

# CHAPTER EIGHTEEN

On our way to the tunnels, I stuck my head in a couple different rooms and came up with various paraphernalia that might prove helpful once we became trapped.

I collected two flashlights, a penlight, two blankets, a roll of paper toweling and a hand radio with nine channels. Just who the frequencies would contact, if anyone at all, I didn't know. But until we tried, it was at least a glitter of hope.

After stuffing everything in a large clear trash bag I swung it over my shoulder and maintained watch at the end of the moving crowd. I had hoped to come upon the lab Billy had taken us to, the one with all the technicians, that I might warn them of their impending doom, but we never came across it.

By the time we found the ripped section of tunnel, we had one minute, and twenty-six seconds left until detonation. Screaming for everyone to hurry, I turned to search the corridor and to my surprise saw Godzilla bounding his way toward us. The sight of him made me smile and I realized how fond of him I had become. He reached me just as the last person disappeared through the crude opening.

Scurrying to my side he gave me a big hug then made a comical face. I squeezed him back then grabbed his hand and pulled him into the tunnel where I yelled once again for everyone to hurry.

Joe took the lead with one of the flashlights and I brought up the rear with the other.

Time was running out too fast. When the explosion took place a large section of the unfinished tunnels would cave-in along with those that had been reconstructed. It took little brains to realize the importance of getting in as far as we could.

Trying to move a party of thirty-nine people and one Gorilla in a hurry was no easy chore. Our breathing was loud and many in the party chattered nervously in an attempt at easing their fear.

Others, especially the smaller children cried from being frightened. Often there was stumbling, followed by several more tripping over them, and amid the sound of hustling feet slapping against the hard dirt, we heard the soft murmur of several more praying.

Just as countless slaves a hundred and forty plus years earlier had walked these very tunnels for freedom, we too looked to them as our saving grace.

When the explosion happened, it shook the earth like a rambling thunder. In the breadth of a second, dirt and debris came shooting up the narrow tunnel and into the crowd like a spray of wild bullets. Many screamed and all of us threw our bodies to the tunnel floor. All around us the ground rumbled, and dirt fell like a hard hammering rain. Whether we had made it in far enough, we did not know. The dust and fine dirt clogged our nostrils and filled our mouths with the taste of stale earth. The sensation of not being able to breathe magnified the closeness of death. Everywhere the walls and ceiling crumbled like flour, pouring over us like the cold dirt from a caretaker's spade. Relentlessly it fell; growing heavy as it literally buried us alive.

The children cried; their screams nearly muffled by the thunderous roar of the shaking earth. Black was this massive grave and horrid was our style of execution. All of us prayed, for all of us knew prayer was our only chance. Seconds passed into minutes and the minutes seemed as hours. An endless eternity the earth rumbled, and dirt fell, burying us beneath its coldness and weight. Tightly I clutched the light in my hands, protecting it beneath my body.

Above the roar of the quaking earth and cries of horrified people I tried yelling up to Joe but there was no reply. Down the tunnel from where the house use to be, there came one more muffled explosion and it seemed to be the penny to balance the scale. The earth beneath us shuttered one final time...then fell silent.

No one moved. In a mixture of fear and what seemed to be answered prayer, we held our breath, listening with hope in our hearts. The tunnels were silent, and except for an occasional fall of dirt or childish whimper, a spooky silence prevailed.

In my mind I envisioned the sight where the house had once been. Now there would be a giant hole filled with the debris of twisted and deformed things, scattered fires would burn rapidly and beneath the tons of weight would lay the lifeless bodies of innocent people...and all because of one woman.

Pulling the flashlight free, the light beam appeared dull as it stabbed through the thick cloud of floating dust. Moving to my feet I coughed to clear my throat of the dirt that choked me. Then I spoke sharply.

"Everybody! Listen. Is anyone hurt?"

There was no definite reply, only mumbles of thankfulness and I took that as a good sign.

"I want you to sit up slowly, do not stand, sit only."

Immediately they began moving, coughing and wheezing while pulling themselves into sitting positions. There were moans and groans and I could hear the sound of them brushing dirt from their bodies. I yelled once again to Joe and this time he answered.

"I'm here, Alfie."

A sigh of relief escaped from my lips.

"Good, how you doing?"

His voice was strained and weak as he spoke through the darkness.

"Actually, I feel like I've been hit by a MACK truck. I could use a shower, a hand full of band aids and a big steak. Otherwise, I'm Okay."

"Hang in there, pal." I told him as convincingly as I could. "We'll be out of here in a short-short. How do the tunnels look ahead?"

Through the fog of floating dirt, I could see the beam from his light streak the area.

"Looks OK. We've got a lot of piled dirt in the passageway, but nothing we can't climb over."

Sighing again, I shouted up to him. "Looks like we got lucky."

Turning back to the crowd I spoke again.

"All right folks, it's time to get underway. Everyone, move slowly to your feet. Check yourselves and let me know if you hurt anywhere."

Immediately, they began moving, working as a team by helping one another up. I was happy to see that since this would not be the place or time to argue. With no misgiving, if any of es were to survive, we would need to work together.

There was only one direction we could go, straight ahead. And what lay in wait for us was anybody's guess. There might and might not be a way out.

A lot of years had passed since the tunnels had been used; the Civil War was many decades gone.

The wild animal Joe and I had killed earlier came to mind. Somewhere down that long string of darkness it had found a way in. The good Lord willing, that entrance would be our exit.

There turned out to be several injuries; a couple of cut heads with minor bleeding, some bruises, a broken hand, a sprained ankle from someone falling on it, and much to everyone's shock, one fatality. One of the older men never made it up.

Kneeling beside him I felt for a pulse and found none. There were no outward signs of injury, so I guessed him as having had a heart attack during the cave-in.

With thirty-eight others and Godzilla to worry about I had no choice but to leave him lay. So, after getting everyone doctored and paired off, we turned into the dark tunnels and began our hopeful trek toward freedom.

For several hundred feet we met with remnants of the explosion. Partial cave-ins or mounds of piled dirt blocked our way regularly, forcing us to move around, over, or dig enough to allow passage past.

In one long, drawn-out file we etched our way. And as before, these dark, hollow halls turned and twisted, often branching in two different directions. When they did, Joe marked the tunnel we took by digging a small hole in the wall at shoulder level where the tunnel began. It was our way of assuring we didn't travel down the same path more than once.

Switching through the nine channels on the portable radio, I called out for help as we moved along. "Mayday, Mayday. Breaker, Breaker. Is anybody out there?"

The set crackled with static, and I tried adjusting the squelch, but it did no good, no one replied. Time and time again I tried but never an answer. Perhaps we were down too far with too much earth between us, or maybe the radio possessed its own frequency for private use only. Then again maybe it just wasn't working or was transmitting but not receiving. Hell, it could have been anything. I shook my head in hopeless despair and called Murphy an S.O.B.

At least the flashlights worked, and they were certainly a blessing. To play it safe I left mine off for the most part, turning it on only occasionally to check the crowd.

Before moving out, I had positioned Mrs. Bordenwell in front of me that I might assist her as needed. For the most part she navigated on her own and appeared to be slowly coming out from under whatever effect the serum or drugs they had given her had caused. In front of her was Elizabeth and then Bradley. And beyond them the long line seemed to amble forever.

Behind me, Godzilla made the last link, his hand holding tightly to the back pocket of my coveralls. As we moved steadily through the darkness I thought about the others.

There were nine children total, the Bordenwells included. Six appeared to be with one or both of their parents and none appeared younger than Bradley. The sexes seemed equally mixed although it did look as though more women had been adversely affected by the serum than men. Ages varied from Bradley to senior citizen. Some of them limped, others appeared nearly blind and some, like Mrs. Bordenwell, effected from drug effect or even showed signs of retardation.

Theirs had certainly been a life of torture and degradation. What was it Joe called it, Billy's chamber of horrors? How it must have been. And how dark and have seemed while locked in their dungeon of hell. How could such a thing happen in our country? We claimed to be the most Christian nation in the world, a leader, and an example to follow. So why would a government whose basic belief states that in God they trust, sanction such a project and allow a cold, sadistic Russian agent to head it?

Human suffrage, human bondage, experimentation, murder, the list was endless. And for what? To hold key to world dominance? It's said you can't fight City Hall may be so, but when, or if, we made it out of here alive I intended to pay them a visit, and before I was through, they'd at least know they'd been bit in the ass by a mad dog.

Joe kept tabs on the watch he took from the guard at the cell door and after the first two hours of travel he called for a rest.

Backs against the dirt wall for support we closed our eyes and relaxed. All were exhausted from the steady march, and understandingly so after having spent weeks, months and even years in jailed captivity.

Whether the thought crossed any of their minds or not I didn't know, but depending on what lay ahead in our journey and how long it took, it was very possible that some would not make it out anyway.

We were thirty-eight people with no food or water. Warmth would be in limited quantity and when the batteries in the two flashlights went dead, we would be once again locked in a forbidding world of permanent darkness.

For now, though I had light and with it walked the line of sitting people, searching their tired faces and ensuring they were okay. Most were in poor to only fair condition. They were weak and lacked muscle tone from their long periods of inactivity. Most of the children lay on their side, curled in a ball with their head resting on an adult's lap. The adults themselves talked softly, mostly speaking of family and home and the things they would do as soon they were free. There was hope and excitement in their voices and I was happy for each, but of them all, Joe was my biggest concern.

He was cut and bruised, burned over nearly every area of his body, bleeding, weak and dangerously fatigued. His body had been pushed far beyond its limits and now, torn down and exposed to the cold temperature of the tunnels, he would become a prime target for fever and shock.

Having made my way to the front of the line, I moved to where he sat and plopped down beside him. His arms were stretched across his knees with his head resting on them. Putting a hand on his shoulder I kneeled at his side. Looking up he smiled; it was a forgery, and I knew it right away.

"What's up Alfie?"

"Nothing pal, just came to check on you. How you holding?"

"I'm all right. How are the others getting along?"

"They're fine, thankful to be resting."

"No doubt," he said turning to look their way, "They've been through a hell of a lot."

I shook my head and grinned at him warmly. With the back of my hand, I touched his forehead, and it was hot. Scanning his body with the light's beam I found that most of the cuts had stopped bleeding. The laceration over the right eye still seeped a little but soon it too would coagulate like the others.

The countless burn welts had worsened; turning into tiny blisters marked by noticeable swelling.

"You cold?" I asked soberly.

"No, I'm fine, really."

"You're sure?"

"Yes mother," he said forcing another smile. "I promise. Now help me up so we can get going. These folks would like to get home."

"Okay," I said pulling him to his feet. "But you take it easy."

He winked.

"You got it buddy, slow and easy."

Returning to the end of the column I ordered everyone up and ready to move. There was no grumbling as they climbed to their feet. Joe was right; they wanted very much to return home, to be with family and friends again.

As we ambled along my thoughts kept returning to Joe. That I should have remained in front and sent him to the rear crossed my mind. Back here the moving was slower and it would be easier on him. But what worried me about that was the idea of him growing progressively weaker and eventually with no one even realizing it, therefore leaving him behind, lost and separated from the rest of us. Already his skin was warm to the touch; fever was building inside his body. Sooner or later he would get the chills followed by sweating and finally unconsciousness. Locked here in these tunnels, lost in their dark corridors of cold, damp earth, his ultimate fate was obvious. If we did not find our way out reasonably soon and get him to a hospital, death would come for him and there would be no turning it back.

I thought too about the tunnels and what Billy had said about their stretching all the way to the city of Rome.

According to the map Joe and I used while following her to the house, we were just a few miles outside of a small town called Camden. And Camden, I remembered, was about twenty miles east of Rome.

At the speed we were moving, given the fact we had women, children, disabled adults and guided only by the beam of a flashlight, I estimated that at most we might average six to ten miles a day. Undoubtedly there would be an exit or two in between here and there somewhere and hopefully one of them would show itself. But if not then the remaining glimmer of promise would be that in three to four day's time we would be somewhere beneath the bustling city; providing we maintained our pace.

Like they say though, for every positive there's a negative. Back in the far side of my conscious thinking, I wondered if maybe we shouldn't have hung around the explosion sight hoping for discovery by the fire or police departments during their salvage and investigation efforts. It was possible I reasoned. But logic dictated we were one hell of a long way down with a lot of earth between them and us. All the screaming in the world wouldn't have come close to being heard. And all of the explosives planted by Billy, I was sure, had been strategically placed to ensure that such a miracle never happened.

No, I thought, to gamble on being discovered there would mean a slim to no chance at all of being found; thus we would have done little more than waste precious hours. Our best and probably only shot at getting out alive was to stay on the move and pray we stumbled on one of the old existing entrances.

Shaking my head I sighed...so it goes with life, you never know if you've made the right decision until it's all over or too late.

We traveled almost three more hours before discovering the first real change in the tunnel's monotonous pattern. We made a sharp 90 to the right and it led us into what turned out a large, square room.

The beam from my flashlight showed rotted remnants of what use to be bunk beds against one wall. There were the remains of two old chairs and a table with a rusted plate and cup still sitting on it.

Appropriately we seized the opportunity to sit everyone down for another much needed rest.

Moving to Joe's side again I gave him another check. His forehead felt hotter, he was sweating slightly and shivering just enough to notice. Leaving him temporarily I moved back to the rear of the sitting column for one of the two blankets I had brought along.

After tearing a hole in the middle of it I went back to Joe's side and slipped it over his head like a poncho. Fever was spreading like runaway fire. The blanket would help...but not for long.

# CHAPTER NINETEEN

Joe insisted he was well enough to move on. I wanted to argue but couldn't. To stay where we were would amount to slow suicide. We had to keep moving and pray we came upon an exit soon.

Before rustling everyone up I designated an area as a bathroom, then sat back while they took turns coming and going. I loaned the penlight to each and issued paper toweling as needed.

According to the watch on Joe's arm it was nearly 3:00 a.m. Most in the group were exhausted beyond their means and badly needing sleep. But until we were out, stopping for short periods only would be the law.

While waiting for the bathroom line to finish Elizabeth came over and sat beside me. At first she was silent, watching the traffic come and go. Then finally, looking sober, she asked.

"Mr. Stone, are we going to die?"

Setting the flashlight between us, I put an arm around her and flashed a reassuring smile.

"No way sweetheart," I said, "I'm too young and you're not old enough."

She giggled.

"I didn't know you had to be a certain age." She said.

"You do when you're with me, sweetheart. It's my number one rule when I'm on a case. When it comes to dying, no kids and no handsome, macho dudes like me."

Giggling again she pulled her knees to her chest and wrapped her arms around them.

"Well, I like being with you." She said softly. "You make me feel safe, and Bradley likes you too. He says you look just I like Indiana Jones."

Smiling, I glanced around her at Bradley and gave him the thumbs up sign. Grinning, he gave it back.

"Mr. Stone," Elizabeth continued, "do you think Mommy will be all right?"

Pausing a moment, I considered carefully how to answer.

"I think she's doing fine, all things considered."

"Yes." Elizabeth added, turning her head to look at her mother. "So do I. In the beginning I wouldn't have charged her to MasterCard. They nearly killed her, you know. We thought she was going to die. It scared us terribly."

"I'm sorry, Elizabeth. I'll bet it did."

"Tell me Mr. Stone, do you think our President knows about Billy Beast and this place?"

"Billy Beast?"

"Yes." Elizabeth exclaimed. "Miss Robinson, that's what we call her, Billy the Beast."

"An appropriate name." I said making a face. "Did you give it to her?"

"No, actually it was my brother, he really hates her. Hates her terribly."

"What about you?" I asked. "Do you hate her too?"

"Oh, I don't know. The Bible says its wrong to hate. And the word does have such harsh overtones."

I couldn't believe I was talking with an eleven-year-old girl.

"I think," she continued, "I despise her, that isn't quite as strong." She moved her legs into an Indian style position and rested her hands in her lap. "How about you Mr. Stone. Have you ever hated anyone?"

Suddenly I felt uncomfortable. Leave it to kids to make you shine the light on yourself.

"Yes, I guess I have." I said after a moment of thought.

"Billy, right?"

"The one and only." I said.

"Do you hate her bad enough to kill her?"

Surprise jumped on my face.

"What kind of a question is that coming from a little girl?"

"An honest one." She quipped matter-of-factly.

"Mother has taught us to be open and frank… first with ourselves then others. Her most favorite quote is from Shakespeare, 'Be true to thyself.' She has taught us a lot of things and spends a great deal of her time working with us, developing our minds and preparing us for the world. Bradley is still a little too young to truly appreciate her efforts but I'm not. It's because of mother I'm already taking college level courses and possess an IQ of 194. I already know how to fly, although I'm too young for my license, and believe it or not just this year I received scholarship offers from Yale, Harvard, and UCLA."

She stopped talking suddenly and I looked over at her. The light from the flashlight showed an embarrassed little face.

"I'm sorry Mr. Stone.," she said apologetically, looking into my face. "I didn't mean to sound like a braggart, I'm not really, it's just that you're so easy to talk to. Actually, sometimes I wish, I was just a plain old ordinary kid."

After giving her a hug of admiration, we fell silent, and I gave thought to her question about killing Billy.

My mind reflected back to the elevator and catwalk incidences. I had my opportunity to do her in twice, and never followed through on either one. Was that good or bad? Did I do right or wrong? Should I or shouldn't I have?

Wanting to think about something else I looked down at Elizabeth.

"So, what about your Dad little lady? Think he will be glad to see you?"

Her answer was abrupt.

"No."

"No!" I said surprised. "And why not?"

"It's simple, because he's not my Dad."

"Oh!" The expression on my face probably looked pretty stupid. I wanted to change the subject again but Elizabeth didn't.

"I know he's not my father, because I overheard him talking to mother one night. He was telling her how sorry he was he had to adopt Bradley and I, and how he never would have, had it not been something he was forced to do."

My forehead wrinkled a little. "How was he forced?"

She shrugged. "I really don't know. Probably mother threatened him."

"Threatened him?"

Elizabeth looked up at me, embarrassed a second time.

"You know," she said quietly.

"No, I don't know, really. What do you mean?"

"GROWN UPS!" She said exasperatingly. "What I mean is she probably threatened not to give him any unless he agreed, understand now?"

Again, surprise jumped on my face. I was speechless. This little girl with the high IQ certainly didn't mince her words.

Ready to change the subject herself now, which I was glad of, she asked.

"Is Joe going to be OK? Word in the Mole Hole was..."

I cut her off. "What do you mean, Mole Hole?"

"Us, silly. You, me, Bradley, the others." She rolled her eyes. "The prisoners...you know, Billy Beast's guinea pigs. We were the moles, and the cells where they kept us was the Mole Hole."

"Oh!" I said again, forcing a grin.

"Anyway," she went on. " Rumor had it he was a sure bet to complete the gauntlet, but by the looks of him I'm not sure he fared so well."

"Well," I told her with a wink, "trust me when I say, he kicked Billy the Beast right in the seat of the pants."

"Good and hard I hope?" She said, grinning.

"Good and hard." I echoed.

The line to the bathroom ended and it was time to get going. Climbing to my feet I helped Elizabeth up then put my hands on her shoulders.

"Elizabeth," I said, "Do you think you're grown up enough to handle some adult responsibility?"

In the shadowy light I could see her face, a smile come across it.

"Sure! Consider me your indentured servant"

"Well," I told her with a chuckle, "indentured servant isn't quite what I had in mind, but what I want you to do is pretty important."

She folded her arms. "I'm ready, just tell me what?"

"OK. I'd like you to take my place at the back of the line when we move out, remain back here with Joe. He needs help, or at least watched, and back here the line moves a little slower. If something were to happen, you could just yell up to me, and I'd come running. What do you think?"

"To quote Joe himself," she said cheerfully, "Nooooo Problem."

Relief in my voice I sighed. "Okay champette, here's the rule. Only use the flashlight once in a while to check the line, making sure everyone is all right. It's important we conserve its life as long as we can, got it?"

Elizabeth gave me a funny looking salute. "Yes sir."

I made it a point to remember this kid was only eleven.

When we finally started out, Joe was in the back holding onto Elizabeth's hand. Bradley led his mother and I was in front guiding the way. My new found friend with all the hair and funny face making had followed me up, remaining faithfully at my side.

Like Joe, I marked the entrances to all the new tunnels we came across. So far we had been lucky, stumbling onto only two we had already been down. For the most part we were making good time and moving. I hoped, toward the city of Rome.

We pushed on. Our tired bodies looked like a long line of graveyard zombies, every step mechanical, automatic. Brains numb from lack of sleep and food we marched rhythmically, our minds dazed. We were sleepwalkers, dreamers moving through a cold and dark void.

Silence prevailed as time passed in endless segments, each of us waiting, longing for the shake that would awaken us back to reality, praying it was all a dream.

When I saw it my reaction was slow at first, my mind almost too tired to register what I saw. Over my shoulder I yelled for everyone to stop then drew in a deep breath and looked at it one more time.

Snapping off the flashlight I let total darkness swallow us.

No larger than the size of a dime it was there, far down the tunnel. Could I be imagining things, was I feeling a slight breeze blowing toward us from its direction? Twice I closed and opened my eyes, but it remained. I whispered the word under my breath and it had a beautiful ring...daylight.

Wondering if our tedious marching had put Murphy to sleep, I turned in the darkness toward the waiting crowd. Several people at the front saw it too and had begun jabbering excitedly, but not wanting a wild stampede on my hands I hushed them up then turned the flashlight back on.

Shining it down the long line of tired bodies I spoke loud enough for all to hear.

"Everybody listen. I think I might be seeing what may be a way out but I can't be sure." Everyone in the line began mumbling with hope in their voices and I had to shout to quiet them down.

"Listen." I said again, my voice loud. "It may turn out to be nothing so keep your fingers crossed and pray. Just don't get despaired if it turns out bad news. I want everyone to sit and rest while I go and check it out. Remember, these tunnels are dangerous, so stay put until I get back. Does everyone understand?"

There was more mumbling as they acknowledged their understanding and moved half-reluctantly and half-gratefully, into sitting positions.

Turning, I moved away toward the distant speck of light. Godzilla clambered up beside me and took my hand. I could tell he was excited too.

The closer we drew the more aggressive he became, inching out ahead of me. Like an excited pup he sniffed the air his way and pulled me along behind.

The light grew brighter and the hole unmistakably larger as we steadily closed the gap. My heartbeat quickened and I couldn't stop it. I wanted to shout, to turn and yell for the others to come and and share this glorious moment. For finally, we were going to be free.

Within twenty feet of the opening, I could easily tell it was large enough for any one of us to crawl out.

A strong breeze swayed several small roots dangling at the center of the entrance and outside in the bright sunlight I could hear tree leaves chime against the wind.

Our steps wide, we quickened our pace. We were so close now the light hurt our eyes. A huge beautiful ray of yellow warmth poured in and lay like an almost perfect square on the dark ground just three or four feet inside. Millions of tiny particles floated freely within its beam. It was beautiful.

Then Godzilla's hand slipped from mine and he was gone, his animal scream piercing the darkness that filled the bottomless shaft into which he fell. Shrilling at first, his frightful cry faded gradually into horrifying silence. The flashlight dropped from my hand as I fought frantically to maintain balance on the edge of the shaft. As I teetered I saw the light tumble downward, end over end, into the bottomless hole.

Cold shock engulfed me as I finally regained my balance and stood motionless. Fear ran rampant in my mind. I could scarcely see the dark edge of the shaft, my toes overlapping it.

Cautiously I moved slowly backward until I knew it was safe, then slammed my back to the cold dirt wall and closed my eyes. My chest heaved and I waited for the pounding of my heart to stop. Sweat had formed on my brow and tears welled in my eyes as I slapped at the dirt with an angry hand. I cursed the human carelessness that had sent my animal friend plunging to his death.

Alone I waited there, hating myself for what had Just happened. I should have known better. I should have suspected. I was human, I...

"Damn!" I said the word out loud.

Slapping the dirt wall one more time with my palms I listened as the sound echoed down the tunnel.

Sick in my heart I turned away and made my way back to the others.

They would be waiting anxiously, wanting an explanation of what had happened and news concerning the way out.

What would I tell them? Nothing I decided, at least for the time being anyway.

Once there, I yelled down the line for Joe to come up with his flashlight. He was there in seconds and the sight of him alarmed me. His face and hair were soaked with sweat. Even beneath the poncho blanket he held tightly around himself he shook noticeably.

I told everyone to stay put and continue to rest while we returned to the area where Godzilla had fallen.

At the hole, I got down on my belly and crawled to the edge of the pit, shining the light into the open shaft. I saw nothing but the end of the beam shooting downward, dispersing into nothingness. The shaft opening was huge, nearly as wide as the tunnel floor, and just as far across.

To the right, enough edge remained to allow a slow careful inching across-if you kept your back to the wall and didn't panic.

Obviously a death trap for unwanted slave hunters, the pit had been placed just far enough into the darkness to throw off any suspicion an invader might have had.

Rolling onto my back I stared disheartened into the blackness above and sighed. Godzilla was gone.

Joe kneeled at my side and grasped my shoulder.

"You OK, Alfie?"

"Sure." I said giving his hand a pat. "I'm fine."

Climbing to my feet I surveyed the narrow ledge with the light. Crossing would be extremely dangerous, but with careful steps possible to do.

Side by side, Joe and I took the first trip together.

With it no wider than the length of our feet, we pressed hard to the wall and worked our side-steps carefully. Slowly, we moved along, inch by inch. We fixed our eyes straight ahead to help maintain balance. There was no room for error. One slip, one wrong step and death awaited.

Though it seemed an eternity we were across in seconds.

Excitedly we crawled through the big hole to the outdoors; the light was blinding. Taking a deep breath I listened for a moment to the birds singing in the trees around us, and smiled. It was good to be free. I imagined the feeling slaves must have felt when they stepped out of this very opening.

The sun felt warm on our skin and everything seemed so bright with color. I hated to go back in, but it needed to be done.

Leaving Joe in the warmth of the sun, I reentered and led the others back.

One by one I escorted the children across, then the handicapped. When I had all of them safely outside I then instructed the healthy adults to cross.

As each scurried through the opening to their first taste of freedom in a long time, there were mixed emotions. Some laughed hysterically, others cried and some kneeled to kiss the ground. Many prayed, thanking God for having sent us to them. Joe and I both felt like kin to Moses.

We were on a hillside amid a small group of trees that opened to a big alfalfa field. The golden wheat swayed to the breeze that pushed gently against it.

Just to the right of the exit stood the remains of an old stone farmhouse, no doubt Civil War era, and somewhere near by would be the residence of the farmer who owned it all. When we found him, he'd be a welcomed sight.

# CHAPTER TWENTY

In less than twenty-five minutes of crawling free we were rescued. It had taken only one phone call to local law enforcement and help was there in minutes; police cars, ambulances, and even a bus came screeching in.

Scrambling Paramedics did some triaging and initial treatment then placed us on the bus or ambulance according to need. In one long caravan we were rushed to a hospital in Rome where Joe, Mrs. Bordenwell and twelve others were immediately admitted and taken upstairs. I was more than thankful to see them go.

The rest of us were checked then released into custody of local authorities to be put up in a hotel pending questioning and arrival of family. I kept the Bordenwell children with me and while they waited patiently in hardwood chairs I spent nearly three hours at the Police station. Repeatedly I told detective tales that sounded more like a Mickey Spillane novel than truth.

And as if that were not enough cruel and unusual punishment, following my hectic bout with them I was turned over to the FBI, and as always they too worked in pairs.

The obvious senior agent was tall, nearly bald and sporting a nose that looked more like a killer ski slope at Vail. He was bossy, rude and arrogant. First impression was not a good one.

His partner, a little shorter and noticeably younger, had all his hair plus a well trimmed Gable looking mustache. Quiet mannered, he had an air that made you want to befriend him.

But being an ex-cop, I took into account the upcoming modes operandi -'nice guy-bad guy' routine.

It was easy to figure. Ski slope would ask the questions in an unfriendly, aggressive manner while his quiet partner stood in a corner taking notes, looking sympathetic and eventually asking me if I wanted a cup of coffee.

The room we were in was classic; cramped with an old wood table, two chairs and a dirty glass ashtray all centered in front of a two-way mirror. Cinder block walls in need of paint highlighted the atmosphere and added a roaring twenties chicanery.

The bossy one introduced himself as Fred Lewis and his partner as Dave Reeves. Reeves flashed his sympathetic smile and Lewis played Mr. Iron Mask. As I predicted, it was he who started the inquisition.

Trying to look superior he pulled up a chair opposite me while Reeves pulled out a note pad and pencil then stood silently in the corner.

With amusement I watched Lewis unfold a piece of paper then lay it on the tabletop in front of us. Glancing my way he manufactured a solemn face then smoothed the piece of paper with his hand.

"So, Mr...." Pausing, he glanced down at the paper, "Stone."

Slowly he raised his eyes back to mine.

"I know you've just been over this with local authorities, but we need to start from the beginning again."

I gave him a reluctant nod.

"The police say you were on a kidnapping case, originating in," again he looked at the piece of paper, "Lafayette, Indiana. Is that correct?"

"That is correct." I said yawning. Covering my mouth, I apologized.

He ignored me.

"And you traced your client's missing family here to New York, is that correct?"

"That too is correct." I told him.

"Now," he continued, "you say you and your partner were held hostage by one," he glanced at the paper a third time, "N. Billy

Robinson, who resided at the residence which was just this morning destroyed by explosion and fire. And that you managed a heroic escape, with thirty five others,"

"Thirty seven others," I said, "you misread the figure."

Coldly he raised his eyes to mine and after a brief staring contest, snapped up his piece of paper and climbed to his feet.

Leaning on the table I watched him while resting my chin in my hands. I knew that if he smoked, he'd pull out a pack of cigarettes and light up, then offer me one.

Slowly he paced the floor in front of me, his hands clipped behind his back. I followed him with my eyes and decided that from the side, his nose looked too dangerous to be a ski slope.

After what was probably a perfect sixty seconds of pacing he stopped and turned to face me. Reaching into his coat pocket he pulled out a pack of camel filters and I grinned.

After lighting one up, he extended the pack to me but I declined with the grin turning into a smile I couldn't stop.

"Something funny?" He asked.

"No," I said trying to sober my face. "I was just wondering if you ever go to the movies." He shook off a dumb expression then went on.

"So tell me, how exactly did you escape? And too, tell me about this gauntlet. And oh yes, I especially want to hear about the mind reading formula...you know," he looked at his partner and flashed a skeptical grin then back to me, "the one that enables you to talk to monkeys."

I thought about a Murphy Law that fit Lewis perfectly, 'No one's life, liberty, or property are safe while the Legislature is in session.'

Irritated, I leaned back in my chair. It squeaked and I thought of my office back in Indiana.

"First of all," I told him in a tone that expressed my displeasure, "N. Billy Robinson worked at the First National Bank here in the city. I have no doubt that she escaped the explosion unharmed. If she did, then the formula will be with her. A formula you had better bust your ass to get back. Without trying to sound melodramatic, I'll tell you this. That formula could totally disarm U.S. National Security. Have you checked with the bank to see if she returned there? While held captive a member of her staff informed us that she was in fact a Soviet agent in charge of a Soviet/American research project. I told all this to the police two hours ago. Out of curiosity, have you or they checked and put out an APB on her?" His face strained but he continued to listen.

"Secondly," I went on "I mentioned to the police another name, a woman who works for your very own organization, Dixie Barnibin. Just for the hell of it, have you bothered to confirm her position, and more importantly, her immediate whereabouts? I've a hunch she got away as well."

He opened his mouth to speak but I cut him off. "And last but not least, Mr. Lewis, I'm not a fiction writer with a vivid imagination, I'm a Private Investigator who use to be a cop, so stop treating me like some derelict from the slums. I'm wise to the nice guy, bad ass routine. I've used it myself, so give me the common courtesy of professional treatment, all right?"

His lips tightened while he looked at me with a focused stare. Following a few seconds of that he then sat back down and waved his hand.

"Okay Stone. Lets start again. I'm sorry if I insulted you, it's just that we're so use to working with the other half it becomes old habit."

"Apology accepted." I said. "Now lets get this over with, I'm very tired."

We talked on for nearly another hour. I explained everything I could in detail and by the time they released me their heads were spinning with skepticism. While it was critical they believed me; I couldn't blame them if they didn't.

Before leaving the station, I put through a person to person call to Mr. Bordenwell and gave him the good news.

There was relief in his voice but it didn't convince me. Maybe the comments Elizabeth made had planted a seed of suspicion. I certainly didn't want to read anything into it, but bottom line, the case still wasn't closed.

During our conversation he agreed to a bank draft in my name for the amount of twenty-five hundred and I told him to make the arrangements through First National Bank on Black River Boulevard. After hanging up the phone I stood pondering our conversation for a short time.

At first he had insisted I put his family on a plane and send them home immediately but when I explained the situation concerning the authorities, he calmed down and agreed to letting Joe and I bring them home personally the moment we were released. I was glad of that, since Billy was still at large somewhere. But due to my suspicious nature I wondered why he did not insist on coming to get them himself.

Lewis and Reeves took us to the bank to both confirm my identity since mine and Joe's clothes went up in the explosion. also knew it was to take a look around.

The Vice President told them Billy had left early yesterday morning and not returned or called since. Having heard about the explosion and fearing for his boss the Vice President asked about Billy with legitimate concern. Lewis told him several bodies had been recovered but none as yet identified.

After leaving the Bank Lewis rented a car for us through the bureau since I didn't have my driver's license. The police had verified I owned one and wrote out a temporary permit for the time being.

From the rental agency the kids and I went shopping for new clothes. I bought a new outfit for Joe too. From there we checked into the hotel the Police had set up and all took showers. It felt inspirational being clean again not to mention properly dressed with new shoes on my feet.

All of us agreed we were starving and went to a restaurant called El Chico's off of South James Street. I ordered my favorite, spaghetti. Elizabeth requested a seafood platter and Bradley, a cheeseburger, Coke, and fries.

While we ate we talked.

They were both intelligent children, with manners that impressed me. I asked Bradley how he felt about being free again and shyly he told me.

"I was actually scared at first, but when I saw you that night at the table, I knew we would be okay, you're Indiana Jones!"

Smiling I shook my head. "No Bradley," I said amused but flattered. "I'm just a normal guy like you and everyone else."

He shook his head and swallowed a bite of burger. "No you're not, you're Indiana Jones and Joe is Rambo."

While he popped a fry in his mouth I glanced at Elizabeth for help. She shrugged, liking the look on my face so I stuck my tongue out at her.

"Real mature, Indy," She told me.

Turning back to Bradley I said, "Indiana Jones and Rambo are movie characters, actors, not real people. They are make-believe. Kind of like cartoons only with real people."

Growing indignant, he looked away, exasperated. Then he asked.

"Would Indiana Jones have run away from Billy Beast and left us behind?"

Again I looked at Elizabeth. She shrugged again and this time added a smile. I ignored her and looked back to Bradley.

"No."

"And would Rambo have been afraid to fight the big black man?" He continued.

"No! but..."

"And together, would they have been tricky enough to get us all out of there safe, like you did?"

"Yes, but..."

Gesturing with his hands Bradley ended the conversation. "See."

We left the restaurant around five and drove back to the hospital.

The kid's mother was sleeping peacefully, so I left them quietly at her bedside and went next door to see Joe.

He was dozing too when I went in, so I slipped into a chair beside the bed and watched him sleep awhile.

He was snoring like an old Cavalry trooper. There was an IV in his arm and a nasal cannula in his nose. He looked peaceful though and it was a good feeling to know he was going to be fine.

Closing my eyes, I laid my head against the back of the chair and reflected over the past three days.

From a rainy, typical Monday morning at the office, to a top secret, American/Soviet project three states away. I had to admit the thought of the formula in the hands of the soviets made my skin crawl. Would they really use it? Perhaps the answer lay with Billy. Were they all like her?

Joe opened his eyes and turned his head to look at me. Smiling, he wet his lips and spoke softly. His words were weighted down by whatever drug they had given him to keep him quiet.

"Hey Alfie, how you doing?"

"Fine pal, how about you?"

"I feel great, they've got me sedated you know." He laughed weakly and added, "but it's some good shit." I smiled at him and he continued on.

"Hey, you know what?"

His words were really slow coming out.

"What?" I asked, grinning.

"I did something I've never done before."

"What's that, pal?" I asked.

"Tonight at supper I ate all my hospital food."

"Good, I'm glad you enjoyed it."

"I didn't say that." He chimed losing his smile. "It was terrible. In fact," he wet his lips again, "I think I'd rather fight Mandegon all over again then have to eat another bite."

"Well Mandegon's definitely out of the question, but you better have a serious talk with your tastebuds. They've got at least another day or two in here."

"I'll never survive it, Alfie," he said slowly wetting his lips again. "My system can't take it." Closing his eyes he mumbled, "First the gauntlet and now hospital food. I think..." He never finished the statement before he began snoring.

Rising from the chair I grinned down at him and patted his shoulder. "Right now what you need is sleep, not conversation". I pulled his blanket up around him and returned to Mrs. Bordenwell's room.

This time I found her sitting up in bed holding the children's hands. When I went through the door all three turned and watched me approach.

At the bedside Mrs. Bordenwell smiled for the first time. It was beautiful and her dimples were back. Reaching out with a shaky hand she spoke meaningfully, her words choppy, but based on how quickly she was recovering, I figured she'd be back full swing in little time. Taking her hand, I held it while she gave me a thank you that I knew came from the bottom of her heart.

"Mr. Stone. Thank you for save...ing my child-ren, and please thank you, your friend for me."

Patting her hand I smiled warmly.

"That's all right Emily, we were more than happy to help you."

She looked back to the kids and released  my hand. Their eyes were glued on one another and the love in each filled the room with a warmth we all felt.

The thought of the two hundred thousand-dollar check James Bordenwell would soon be writing thrilled me, but it would never match the joy of watching this.

Within half an hour a nurse had come by and suggested we go back to our hotel to get some rest. I had to agree; there was little we could do here short of dozing in an uncomfortable chair all night. Both Emily and Joe were in good hands now and would be watched closely.

Before leaving we stopped in to visit the others and they too were happy to see us. A policeman had been placed on guard near the nurse's station and nodded a goodnight when we passed on our way out. On the way to the hotel we stopped off at a convenience store and picked up some snacks: Chips, pretzels, cupcakes, coke and Pepsi.

As soon as we got to the room we switched on the TV and began a wild junk food frenzy. We had disagreed at first over what to watch; I wanted amateur boxing while Bradley wanted the cable movie. Elizabeth didn't care. Since the movie was 'Raiders of the Lost Ark' I let little Bradley have his way thinking why not, bottom line, Indiana Jones is a pretty cool kind of guy.

At 11:30 I tucked the kids in and switched off the light.

Alone in the quiet darkness I lay on my back thinking.

I wondered where Billy had gone? Was she on her way this very minute to the Soviet Union, carrying the formula with her? Probably; to her nothing would be more important.

And what of Dixie? What would she do, return to her job, business as usual, denying everything backed with bogus alibis? Surely not. The testimony of all of us would be proof enough for anyone's conviction. And General Phieffer, what would he do now? There was Priveman too and all the others on Billy's staff. What had become of them? It could be they were all dead, buried deep beneath the pile of rubble that used to be Billy's beautiful home and secret shop of horrors.

Rolling onto my side I fluffed my pillow.

The serum had really worked; placed in the hands of all mankind it would have benefit. Now though, it would mean nothing short of world chaos.

Closing my eyes I sighed. What did it matter anyway, for Joe and I it was all but over. Upon our return to Indiana, Bordenwell would write us each a hundred thousand-dollar check. That was a lot of money.

With proper investment a sum that large could lead to financial security for the rest of our lives. And that was what I'd do, invest it, then move to Hawaii and work a few years for the corporation in the paper. That is, if the job was still there. But Hawaii or not, as soon as we got back, out of this business was the first place I was going.

When the phone rang I jumped to a sitting position with my heart leaping from zero to sixty before the ring ended.

It took a while for it to dawn but I realized, finally, I had been asleep.

The room was hazy with early morning light and in my groggy mind I tried to guess the time.

Swinging my feet to the floor I switched on the lamp and glanced at the new watch I had bought, 5:52 a.m.

The ringing was persistent. It woke Elizabeth and Bradley and now they were sitting up in bed wondering what was going on.

Picking up the receiver I scratched my head, yawned then said hello in a tone made for a Marine Corps drill sergeant.

At the other end Lewis spoke calmly, his voice speaking my name almost in a question.

"Stone?"

"Yeah Lewis, it's me. What's up?"

"Sorry to bother you so early, but we've got some new developments in the case. You'll never guess who we've got in custody."

I stood to my feet.

"Who?"

He paused before telling me, "actually I'd rather not discuss it over the phone. Why don't you meet me at the police station half an hour, and I'll fill you in then, okay?"

"All right," I said sleepily.

"And oh, one more thing," he added.

"What?" I asked.

"I'm sending a uniformed officer over. He'll stay with the children while you're here. Make sure they understand to mind him. Under no circumstances are they to go outside, okay?"

"Yeah! What the hell is going on?"

"When you get here I'll explain. See you in half an hour."

He hung up and I stood staring at the phone for a minute. I didn't like the sound of things. Why were the children being put under guard instead of staying with me? And who in the hell did they have in custody?

"Who was that?"

Breaking my stare I glanced over at Elizabeth.

"Oh, that was Lewis, the FBI man I was with yesterday. He wants to talk to me."

"About what?"

"I'm not really sure Elizabeth. I've got to meet him at the police station in half an hour."

"Not again," she moaned. "I hate it there.

That was my chance of not alarming them.

"No problem, he said he was sending a policeman over to stay with you while I'm gone. I guess he must have heard you thinking."

"I'm glad of that," she said sighing.

"One thing," I added. "When the officer gets here, you mind him and do what he says, okay?"

"Sure."

"When I get back we'll all go to breakfast, what do ya say? Is it a deal?"

"A deal." Elizabeth smiled.

"Yeah Indy, it's a deal," Bradley chimed.

When I walked into the station Lewis and his partner met me at the front door. The place looked almost deserted.

I followed them down a hallway through a long dark room then down a set of stairs into the basement. We rounded a corner and there he sat in a swivel chair.

His head turned and when he saw me he laughed out loud, that is if Gorillas laugh. Leaping to the floor he scurried across the room fast as he could toward me.

Kneeling, I opened my arms and he ran straight into them. A happy smile on my face, I couldn't stop the wetness in my eyes.

Godzilla gave me a big Gorilla kiss on the lips and hugged me till I thought my neck would break. I never dreamed I'd ever see him again and knew now, I'd never let him go-ever.

When the greetings were finally over, I rose and looked him over. He seemed to be in fine shape for someone I thought was dead. Patting his head I turned to Lewis.

"Where did you find him?"

"Actually he found us. One of the Camden police officers spotted him along the highway about 4:00 a.m. this morning. Of all things, your hairy friend was actually waving him down. He's one smart critter."

Looking down at Godzilla, I smiled again.

"He is at that." Looking back to Lewis I asked. "So is he the person you said you had in custody?"

Lewis acknowledged with a nod.

"Yes, but not the development." With a look I didn't like he glanced from me to Reeves.

"Should we show him?"

Reeves nodded soberly and Lewis looked back to me. "Say good-by to your hairy friend for a while and lets take a ride."

It was a silent ride for the most part. I stared out the window. Things just didn't feel right, something was wrong and I knew it. Was it Joe?

"No," I thought, he was doing too well yesterday. The kids were with me, so it couldn't be them; Mrs. Bordenwell maybe?

Sighing I shook my head. All I wanted was to get Joe released, load up the kids and their mother, then return to Indiana officially and pick up our money. Then we could call the case officially closed; at least as far as we were concerned.

Hell, it was already out of our hands. From here on in it was FBI, and not A and J Security. As far as I was concerned, A and J security no longer existed anyway. From the moment we crawled out of those tunnels, that agency had dissolved.

There were Police cars and Officers all over the hospital grounds when we pulled to a stop. Now I knew why the station had been practically empty.

After throwing the shifter into park Lewis turned to me and I didn't like the look on his face.

"We had some trouble here last night. The only reason I'm showing you is because you were involved in the first place." He paused, looked out the window then stared back again. "And it turns out, you may be even more involved now."

I had no idea what he meant, but I did know it wasn't good.

We left the car and walked into the hospital to the elevators. Inside the car a feeling of near panic waved over me and I broke out in a cold sweat. Lewis pushed the button and the doors closed. The elevator jerked and we started for the third floor.

"Joe!" I said his name quietly under my breath. It couldn't be Joe! Son of a bitch, it couldn't be him. The elevator stopped and the doors opened to the Nurses station.

There in front of us on the floor, someone lay zipped in a body bag, the inside of the clear plastic covered with red.

I trailed Lewis silently down the hall to Joe's room.

At the door he stopped and put his hand on the knob. Looking at me he started to speak but changed his mind then turned and went in. I followed, my palms sweaty.

Inside I froze at the door, eyes fixed on Joe's bed. It was empty. Mouth open I stood speechless, heart pounding. Finally, looking at Lewis I took a deep breath and asked.

"Where is he?"

Lewis shrugged, worry lines around his eyes.

"We don't know."

# CHAPTER TWENTY ONE

His words created a horrible feeling like sinking in quicksand and no one around to hear your futile screams.

As fear for Joe mounted anger boiled and one word flashed like a neon sign... Billy!

I looked suddenly at Lewis.

"Mrs. Bordenwell?"

His face twisted sourly. "She's missing too."

"Shit! So now what?" I asked.

Shrugging, he shook his head.

"We're not sure. I've got one dead officer, no witnesses and no clues."

"What about a night nurse?"

"They're gone too!"

"Gone! Gone where?" I asked, knowing he couldn't give me the answer.

Lewis grimaced. "To Hell, to Heaven, to Lake Tahoe, I don't know. They've just disappeared along with your friend and Mrs. Bordenwell."

"So nobody saw anything?" Anger made my voice climb.

"Nothing." He echoed softly. "Actually we were hoping you might help shed a little light on things."

Running his hand down the back of his head he continued. "I mean, if it is by chance Robinson who did the abducting, where would she take them? During your captivity did you catch even a glimpse of where some other location might be?"

I stared at him a long time, the wheels in my head racing through memories.

Finally I told him, "Not one".

Walking to the bed I picked up the IV line that had been in Joe's arm. Beneath it on the white sheet lay a pool of blood.

It was obvious the thing had been ripped free. Whoever took him did it against his will and that told me they were strong, strong like a man and not feminine like a Billy. Even with him sedated I doubted she would have been capable.

Without me realizing Lewis had moved to my side. He put a hand on my shoulder and it startled me. I jumped and he apologized.

"Sorry."

"Forget it." I said.

"Look, Stone." there was caring in his tone. "If Robinson does have him, I think she'll try and contact you. If or when she does we want to be ready. Help us, and we'll get your friend back, I promise."

They were meaningful words backed with good intentions, but bottom line, Lewis had no idea how cruel and sadistic Billy really was. She was no doubt cold war idealistic and wise to every trick he would try to pull.

If he was right and she did contact me, it would be done privately some how and he would never know otherwise, unless I told him. And if I did, Joe no doubt would die immediately.

Lewis gave me a quiet ride back to the motel. When he let me out he peered out through the open window.

"We'll be by in half an hour to put a bug on the phone. If she should call in the mean time, contact us immediately, Okay?"

Not saying yes or no, I gave him a wave then turned and started toward the motel.

I was hungry and wanted to get something to eat. And no doubt the kids were feeling the same way by now.

Once again I gave thought to Billy.

She had the formula and its delivery to superiors would bring her a top position in her government; never again would she want for anything. So why in the hell would she hang around? And why, I wondered, would she take Joe and Mrs. Bordenwell?

When I reached the Motel door I stopped abruptly. It was slightly ajar and there was no sound from inside.

Turning I looked quickly back for Lewis but he was gone. My gut told me this was not a good thing and once again I had the want for a gun in my hand.

Stepping to the side I pressed back to the wall and listened closely. I heard nothing, so reaching around I pushed the door open. Again, nothing.

Around me the sun was warm and birds sung in the trees above us. Fifteen or twenty doors down a young couple were pulling suitcases from the trunk of their car.

Quickly I looked into the room, taking only a second. Things appeared untouched. Then following a deep breath I counted to three and took another look. Again nothing happened.

This was silly, I thought finally. If Billy wanted to kill me, I'd already be dead. They would have shot me the moment Lewis was out of sight.

Looking up into the blue sky I sighed, then turned and walked in.

The place was deserted, no kids, no cop. Everything was in its place except for the phone. It lay off the hook and in the emptiness of the room I could hear the steady tone. Walking over I cradled it then stood looking around. Where had they gone the patrol car was still out front?

A feeling of helplessness began washing over me like a shower of ice cold water then my eyes fell upon the bathroom door; it was closed. "So?" I said softly just under my breath, "Bathroom doors are often kept closed." But there was no convincing myself...there was something I would not like waiting behind it and I knew it.

Moving around the bed I made my way toward it. It looked big and as I drew near, I could feel the hairs on the back of my neck stand on end. I had no idea what I'd find but knew that something or someone was there.

Reaching out I held my hand motionless on the knob.

A little voice whispered inside my head, warning me, telling me to get out, to go for help. I knew I couldn't. Feebly, wishing I didn't have to, I turned the knob slowly.

A trickle of sweat raced its way down the middle of my back about the same time a small bead ran down into my right eye, making it sting. When the handle clicked I pushed the door open. I said 'shit' under my breath and turned my head away. There were no kids but I found the cop.

He was sitting on the stool his head laid back against the tank. Blood covered the front of his shirt from the huge slash in his throat and his open eyes stared blankly at the ceiling. Across his forehead his killer had left a calling card. He had carved the initials S. B. into the skin.

Sick as it was that wasn't all of it.

On the sink lay a syringe and needle with rubber tubing. On the mirror, finger painted in blood, was the word, 'inject.'

Grabbing the stuff off the sink I quickly left the room, pulling the door closed behind me. In my mind I knew I should have killed Billy while I had the chance. I cursed her and prayed for one more opportunity.

Crossing the room I sank into a chair near the bed. The front door was open and I could see outside.

It was a beautiful day, warm, with a soft easy breeze that added flavor to a world full of color.

I knew what the syringe held, the formula. Laughing to myself I shook my head. Billy was a persistent Bitch, used to winning and getting the last laugh...at any cost.

Working the tubing around my arm I used my teeth to help tighten it, then pumped my fist. The vein came alive big as life. One careful jab and I was in.

Slowly I pushed the plunger, dumping the serum into my body. Maybe it wasn't the serum at all, I thought. Maybe it was something deadly instead. Hell, I wouldn't know until it was too late anyway.

Cynically I shook my head. No, it wouldn't be anything like that. Billy would demand something a bit more colorful, a more dramatic finish. It would be the serum all right and it would lead me to Joe and her grand finale.

When the plunger bottomed out, I pulled the needle free and waited for the after effects.

As before my head began to spin and the feeling of leaving my body came around, only this time it seemed to last a bit longer. Then came the dizziness.

Outside in the parking lot the young couple from down the way walked into view holding hands. They stopped and kissed. Staring at them I blinked. Their bodies were now shrouded in colors...reds, greens, yellows and blues. Like vapors, the colored waves wiggled and danced brightly about them.

Although some distance away, in my head I knew what they were saying. He wanted to return to the room and make love, she wanted lunch first. Then they smiled at each other and walked out of sight.

Slowly I rose to my feet my heart pounding in my temples. My fingers were numb and I worked them while moving to the door to peer out.

A black BMW pulled to a stop at the office across the way and a well-dressed businessman got out. He too was shrouded in bright colors.

In my own head I heard the very thoughts in his. He was angry because his wife never secured the room and wondered if his credit card was over the limit. Looking back to the couple that had just passed, I shook my head. They remained illuminated.

Returning to the chair, I sat again, then laid my head back and closed my eyes. What the hell was going on? This reaction was not what I had experienced at Billy's house. And what was with the colors? Both times prior I had not experienced them nor had the adjustment period lasted as long. And most importantly never before had I been able to read the thoughts of those not cloned.

Suddenly I bolted upright, remembering the visit Nugent had paid us that day at the house. He had talked of an undeveloped serum-the mind control serum to be exact. Damn, that was what I had just injected!

Climbing to my feet I paced about the small motel room, my mind locked in bitter battle. I wasn't sure if I was excited or frightened or both.

So this was it, I thought. I was to experience the ultimate power, possess the weapon of weapons, become the guinea pig of the century. I put my face in my hands and sighed.

Hell, with such a serum in your veins never again could anyone talk against you without you knowing. You would always recognize honesty or deceit and know when someone meant to do you harm-even when their smile told otherwise. Such a power, if possessed by all, would change the world forever.

Walking to the open door I leaned against the jamb and stared up into the sky. Was this what the Bible meant when it talked about having the mind of Christ? Such a serum would force every human being to forever tell the truth, to be honest always one with another. That was the good side. Was there a bad side too? Did it also provide the power I feared most-the ability to force your will over that of another? I had to know!

Staring across the way I waited for the stranger worried about his credit card to return to his car. It only took a minute and he exited the motel office. Stepping quickly back into the shadows of the room I sent the thought for him to come to my room.

From where I stood I could see him clearly but he couldn't see me. Across the parking lot my open door would look like the entrance to a tunnel of darkness.

I watched as he hesitantly opened his car door, then pause. The buzzer squalled but he ignored it. He gave a quick glance in my direction, shook his head and started to get in. Again I sent him the thought to come to me, this time telling him it was the room with the open door.

Halfway in, he paused again. Then he suddenly climbed back out, shrugged with bewilderment and walked dubiously across the parking lot toward where I waited. His perplexed wife called out after him but he ignored her.

With total apathy he continued on, his face puzzled. At my door he stopped. I could see the confusion in his eyes.e There was fear too.

My skin crawled suddenly, making me feel as though I'd tampered with something sacred. For lack of not knowing what to do, I flashed a smile and asked if I could help him? Shaking his head he shrugged. Then returning a fabricated smile of his own apologized for bothering me and walked away.

I watched him cross the pavement and climb into his car. When it was out of sight I turned back into the room. Near panic shrouded my brain like a dark cloud. I had no idea what the hell to do next. Returning to the chair I sat, slumping in exasperation.

Placing a call to Lewis seemed like the most logical, but it took no brains knowing that such a move right now would mean certain death for Joe.

Where was he? Hell, was he even alive? And what about the kids and Mrs. Bordenwell? Had they been harmed? Were they all together? Why had they taken the night nurses too?

Slamming a white knuckled Fist against the arm of the chair I yelled "damn it!" Then I sighed.

The voice came into my head clear as a bell and I'd have sworn Joe was standing right in the room.

"Alfie?"

Bolting upright in the chair I blurted out. "Yeah?" then waited. There was a few seconds of silence then he was there again, in my head.

"Alfie. They have the kids and Mrs. Bordenwell and three nurses from the hospital. I'm to tell you where we are and you're to come here immediately, alone. If you tell anyone at all, they will start killing the others, one by one."

He started to send another thought but I lost him. Jumping to my feet I grabbed my head between my hands and forced myself to concentrate.

Angrily I yelled out Joe's name.

Instantly pain shot into my head as if a giant railroad spike and been driven through it. I cried out, falling to my knees. Somehow my skull became an empty void and in a mad frenzy bizarre noises rushed in, as if being sucked in by a giant whirlwind. All were familiar sounds but strange somehow.

Nonstop they filed in: the sound of squealing car belts, thousands of pounding hammers, the voices of the young couple again, she moaning frantically and he calling her baby, over and over. I yelled for them to get the hell out of my thoughts as more of the painful sounds crammed their way in.

Microseconds apart, every sound I'd ever heard since birth clambered in by the thousands, mixing and swirling, until there was no more room and I thought my head would explode like a melon dropped from the Empire State Building.

There were whistles and screaming and cars, plane engines and crying, static, and crackling, and thousands of conversations all at once.

The pain was unbearable and I clenched my teeth while covering my ears. My pulse raced wild and I could feel myself begin to hyperventilate.

Even my eyes ached. The pressure grew and grew inside my head and I knew my brain was literally swelling inside my skull. My body screamed for relief and droplets of blood now dripped from my nose onto the carpeting.

My eyes blurred and slowly I began losing consciousness. The noises grew in intensity and the sound of ringing bells joined the collaboration, deafening my ears. As if locked helplessly inside a giant tower with them, their magnification brought a piercing scream to my lips.

The room began to spin and I fell over slamming to the floor. My body twitched and darkness came. The sudden sensation of being catapulted through a wide, shadowy tunnel took place. Like a bullet from a gun, I shot through the blackness, end over end, my stomach flipping as if on a roller coaster ride.

I could feel my mouth open and the scream rise to my lips, but it couldn't get out.

Tears filled my eyes and my skin mottled from the incredible speed of my travel. Darkness, emptiness, nothingness, those were the words I thought as I streaked wildly through the long veil of darkness. Death! That was it! My God, I was tasting death!

Alone, I was on the road to hell. But then suddenly there were others shooting through the darkness with me, some behind and others flying past at even greater speeds, disappearing into the distant darkness far ahead.

Fear filled my head and I cried in my thoughts for God to save me.

Endlessly I tumbled, a human projectile shooting through the black of eternity. Ahead, I could catch a glimpse of something orange, something obscure; it flickered and moved. It grew nearer and giant in size and I could feel its incredible heat.

Mere seconds and I would be there. Bodies continued to shoot past and in my head I thought the words-'time for me will be no more.'

My scream made it out, stabbing through the darkness like a giant beam of light and out of my mouth came four words..."Dear God help me."

Then I awoke! I was lying on my back. The room was spinning like a runaway wheel. Frantically my hands gripped at the carpeting to slow me down. The mad, wild ride lasted several minutes and somewhere along the way I vomited into the air.

Around and around the room spun, trying to throw me free of the floor on which I lay. But desperately my hands clung to the carpeting-knowing my very life depended on their grip. My teeth gritted against the pain in my gut. And when I could hold on no more and my hands lost their grasp-the insane ride ended. As if someone had flipped a switch the spinning abruptly stopped and the room came to an immediate standstill...it was over.

For several seconds I lay motionless, feeling sick while staring at the ceiling. Then slowly I sat up and took a deep breath. My heart, racing like an engine, slowly eased. Looking myself over I discovered I was all intact and let out a long sigh.

Weak and fatigued I used the bed to help pull myself to my feet then slowly made my way to the bathroom door and opened it.

The dead policeman was still there, but ignoring him glanced into the mirror. Blood and vomit covered my face, so I dampened a wash cloth and wiped it off. When finished, I closed the door again and went to the bed where I stretched out to wait for my strength to return.

What the hell had happened to Me?

"Alfie."

It was Joe again. He was back.

Sitting up I threw my feet to the floor.

"I'm here pal." I said in thought. "Where are you?"

"Indiana, at the farmhouse. We're all here."

"Indiana!" I exclaimed.

"Yeah, by chartered aircraft. The same way you're going to get here. Billy has one waiting for you. Go to the airport and tell them your name is John Hancock. She says not to waste your time on the pilot, he knows nothing-only to take you to a private strip just north of the farmhouse. Remember, you're to tell no one. Got it?"

"I got it buddy."

"And one more thing, Alfie."

"What pal?"

"S.B. wants me to tell you your ass is his."

"Fine with me Joey." I said. "But one thing."

"What's that?"

"Ask the psycho bastard if I'm to take that literally?"

I heard Joe laugh and his thoughts faded away.

# CHAPTER TWENTY TWO

phoned the police station and asked Lewis to meet me at Billy's bank in half an hour, never mentioning anything else.

Then I went back into the bathroom and dutifully removed the dead officer's revolver. There was blood on the handle, so I wiped it off with a towel. The weapon was a Smith and Wesson, 38 special with two spare loaded cylinders. Total, that would give me eighteen rounds, two of which I personally ear marked... 1 for S.B. and 1 for Billy. The remainder would be for anyone who dared get in between us.

Also, just for GP, I stuck the dead officer's cuffs in my pocket.

Exactly fifteen minutes from hanging up with Lewis I left the motel and drove to the police station. By now he would be on his way to the bank and out of the way.

Hurrying inside I stopped at the front desk, acted cool, and told them I was there for the Gorilla. No questions asked, an old beer-bellied cop with a fat red nose led me to the basement and gladly turned him over.

He made an idle remark about how dirty apes were and behind his back Godzilla raised his arm and stuck up his middle finger. I laughed out loud and the fat cop looked back for a second then shrugged it away.

Exactly twenty-three minutes after leaving the station we were on the chartered plane flying over New York State, back toward Indiana. It would be a three or four hour flight so I tried catnapping. Eyes closed I thought about Joe, wondering how he was he doing and if Barkin had harmed him? I also wondered if Billy was with them? In my thoughts too I wondered why Joe hadn't contacted me since the motel.

The farther South we flew the darker the sky grew and the more turbulence we experienced. The plane bounced almost constantly. Just into the Indiana skies it started to rain and along with it came occasional flashes of lightning.

Trying to sleep was useless. There was no one else on board so leaving Godzilla strapped in I walked to the cockpit and climbed into the co-pilot's seat.

"Mind if I sit a spell?"

Flashing a grin the pilot said cheerfully, "Not at all. In fact, I'd like the company."

He was a young man in his late twenties. Handsome as men go with a nice smile. Like everyone else I had encountered since injecting the serum, he was surrounded by the strange colors. I hadn't figured it out yet, but I was beginning to think maybe each color might mean something special; like anger, lying, happiness, stress and other such moods. But it was only a thought and I didn't entertain it long.

We talked about flying for a while then about what it was like being a Private Investigator. I told him good and bad, then asked if he could help me pull a good joke on some friends. At First he was hesitant, so to keep from losing him I mentioned a thousand dollars cash bonus and that did it, his ears grew like twin satellite dishes.

The idea was to drop me off at the Indianapolis Airport, wait there forty minutes, then fly in alone as scheduled to the airstrip near the farmhouse.

"After you land," I told him, "wait in the plane for ten minutes exactly, then take off again. If, when you land, there are people waiting and they start approaching the plane, take off immediately, okay?"

He looked doubtful for a second then said, "that's it for a thousand bucks? Just fly in, wait, and fly out?"

Smiling I told him. "That's all, easy money huh?"

Shrugging he stared at me a second, thinking it over one last time, then said.

"Okay, you got it. But I'll tell you I feel like I'm stealing your money. I mean what if I decide not to show up?" He said it wearing the grin of a Possum eating pie. Grinning back I told him I wasn't worried; I knew he could be trusted. Then I looked away into the dark sky outside the aircraft. Rain was splattering hard against the windows.

When we landed at Indianapolis my watch read 1:10 p.m. The forty-minute wait would end at 1: 50 p.m., off again it would be another ten to the farm. That gave me exactly one hour, give or take a minute or two to grab a taxi and get to the farmhouse before he landed.

On my way to a taxi I searched for pay phones. The place was busy and Godzilla got quite a bit of attention as we made our way through the crowds. His hand in mine I pulled him along knowing time was running out fast.

We found the phones near the restaurant entrance. They were all being used, so I had to wait. Fighting impatience I leaned against the wall and folded my arms across my chest. Like a little boy imitating his father, Godzilla did exactly the same thing. It was comical and all the passersby pointed fingers and smiled. The big hairy ape was eating it up too.

After a few minutes a little girl in a wheelchair was rolled up by her parents for a closer look at him, and like a big ham he sat there making funny faces so she'd laugh.

She did too, until I thought her sides would split. In fact, she laughed so hard it started to worry me. Finally though she had to leave, and as they wheeled her away the big ape bounded over and gave her a goodbye kiss on the cheek-then looked back at me to make sure it was okay. I winked at him with a warm smile and turned just in time. A phone came open, so I grabbed it.

I made two calls. The first was to good old Jake. When he answered I spoke quickly.

"Jake, it's Al."

"Hey good buddy. How'd your case come out?"

"It hasn't yet. I've got a major problem and might need your help."

"Sounds serious, what can I do?"

"Remember those rap sheets you gave us on Mandegon and Barkin?"

"Yeah."

"Well Mandegon is dead and Barkin is holding Joe and five other people hostage in an old farmhouse just south of Indy. Here's the address so write it down."I could hear his pen scratch across a piece of paper as I gave it to him. When he was finished he sighed through the receiver.

"Sounds like you got yourself in deep shit."

"Maybe. Here's what I need. If I haven't contacted you in two hours from now, get some boys together and storm the house at that address. I'm going in by myself first. If you haven't heard from me at the end of the two hours, it means only one thing. Do this for me Jake and I'll make Joe take you dancing."

"We'll be there, Al."

"And Jake, two more things. One, just before you make the raid, call the Police Department in Rome, New York and ask for agent Lewis. Tell him everything you know, okay?"

"You got it." I heard him scribble down the name.

"Secondly Jake, and most important of all, whatever you do don't jump the gun. These people don't mess around. If they get wind you're coming, they'll kill everybody with no questions asked, all right?"

"All right Al, no problem." He said soberly.

Hanging up I placed the second call to Lewis, explaining as much as I dared while refusing to tell him where I was. When I suggested he stand by his phone and wait, he started screaming, so I hung up. He didn't like it, but I knew he'd be there when Jake's call came.

The time was now 1:28 p.m. Godzilla and I hurried outside to catch a taxi.

Rain was falling like iron balls. They were cold and stung the skin. Puddles lay everywhere and the hard droplets peppered them like bombs, making endless cascades of exploding ringlets. It was a noisy rain too, drowning out everything, even my yell for a taxi.

It took nearly ten minutes to get one and when we climbed in I looked at my watch again, 1:36 p.m. I gave the driver the address of the old farmhouse and offered a hundred bucks tip if he got us there in twenty minutes or less. He took the Hamilton and grinned at me with devil in his eyes.

I hadn't counted on the bad weather or delay at the telephones, but none of it would really matter so long as I got to the house at least ten minutes before pilot touched down.

My idea was to survey everything and get into the house while they waited for the plane; it was my diversion. Not having seen the airstrip I didn't know where it'd be exactly, but if I had to guess I'd say somewhere in the field beyond the barn. So hopefully that's where Barkin would be…at the airstrip waiting to greet me.

A quarter mile from the house I halted the taxi and climbed out into the rain. He asked no questions when I told him to turn around in the middle of the road and go back the way he'd come.  I didn't want a taxi driving past the house and arousing suspicions if spotted.

With Godzilla close behind I climbed just inside the cornrows and moved parallel to the roadway toward the long drive. When we got within four rows of it we turned left and started up toward the house. This time we were to the right of it and once in line we stopped.

Rain hammered the earth around us, falling in torrid sheets that made seeing almost impossible. Water ran over my face in steady streams and my clothes were drenched. I was cold and shivered against the air. Looking at Godzilla I told him he was lucky to be wearing a fur coat.

Placing a cold hand over the face of my watch to ward off the falling water I checked the time, 2:05. The plane would be along any minute. Now I had to worry that the weather would prevent his landing. If it did I hoped he at least buzzed the area to let them know he was there.

Turning to Godzilla, I put a hand on his hairy shoulder and looked into his face. Speaking loud enough to be heard above the pouring rain I told him slowly.

"You stay here." I pointed a finger toward the ground to reiterate my order. "STAY. Understand?"

His head bobbed for me and I ruffled his hair. Turning again toward the house I wiped water from my eyes and listened. I could now hear the muffled hum of an aircraft engine somewhere in the sky. There was no seeing it but it was there.

Reaching into my pocket I pulled out the thirty-eight. Godzilla's hand suddenly wrapped around my wrist and his head started shaking wildly. There was fear in his eyes and I knew it was for me. Ruffling his hair again I told him warmly.

"Hey champ, its all right. I'm going to go get my friend out. I'll be okay. You just wait right here and I'll be back in a few minutes, I promise". He stared at me a long time before letting go. Winking at him I turned away and climbed out of the corn.

Under the cover of the rain I ran to the side of the house and pressed my back tight against it. Water ran in a steady stream from the eves above and splattered the tops of my shoes perfectly dead center. I told myself not to worry; a hundred thousand would buy another pair with no problem. Quickly I moved toward the back of the house, the thirty-eight ready. At the far corner I peered around and saw the stone steps leading up to the back door, and just this side of it the window Joe had looked in during our first visit. Suddenly I thought about him.

Leaning against the house I closed my eyes and called his name out under my breath, hoping for a reply.

"Joe, Joe, are you there?" I heard nothing but the pounding rain.

Crouching again, I rounded the corner making my way toward the back door. Stopping, I peeped in through the window. The kitchen was empty. Moving to the steps I reached up and tried the door handle. It turned easily so I opened it gently and quickly slipped in. When I closed it behind me it muffled the noisy rain to an almost total silence.

Swiftly I darted to the far wall and peered down the long hallway to the living room with the green furniture.

I could hear muffled voices, but couldn't make them out. It sounded like three, maybe four people. I was sure in this weather the young pilot would not attempt a landing, so I had to act quickly. Those at the airstrip would be returning soon.

To my right the refrigerator motor kicked on suddenly and it made me jump. Swearing under my breath I closed my eyes for a second waiting for my heart to stop pounding.

Above my head someone walked across a squeaky floor and I followed their noisy path with my eyes. They walked halfway across a room, stopped and paused a second, then went on until their steps disappeared all together.

So, I thought. Three or four people in the living room and at least one upstairs. How many more elsewhere in the house? How many were at the airstrip? And where is Joe, the Bordenwells and the nurses? Was that them upstairs or were they in the living room, maybe with Billy.

It didn't matter. I had to do something before it was too late. So gun ready, I pulled back the hammer and started down the hallway toward the voices in the living room.

Water dripped from my wet clothes leaving behind a wake wide enough to ski in. The conversations grew louder as I approached nearer the living room. Almost to the exit I recognized three of the voices... Elizabeth, the old woman and Billy.

In my mind I knew this was it. There would be no second chance. If I failed here we would all die; dead long before Jake ever reached us.

With the thirty-eight raised to my shoulder I stood ready at the entrance. Billy was telling them about Leningrad, how beautiful and Gothic a city it was. She talked of its orthodox churches, its marble stoned architecture and of its czars and old cobbled streets. She painted a pretty picture, but failed to tell all, like it being almost a prison for its people. Its poverty and its lack of conveniences, things like refrigerators and washers and dryers, cars and televisions. She never mentioned the poor quality of goods in its stores and frequent shortages of food.

In my head I began counting to ten. At the end I would enter the living room and do what I needed to do.

One...Two...Three...Four...Five...She would die this time. Six... Seven... Eight...Nine... Here I come Billy!

With great speed I whirled around the corner, gun pulled down and ready. Every head turned and looked, startled and surprised, especially Billy. It was an expression I loved. In the room sat Mrs. Bordenwell, the two kids and one of the three missing nurses sitting beside the old Lady. Gun aimed on Billy I asked sharply.

"Where are the others?"

Her grin was wide and arrogant.

"Tucked safely away, Mr. Stone."

Shaking my head, I told her.

"No you don't Billy, not this time. I'll count to three. And if you haven't told me, I'm putting a bullet right through your heart, followed by five more at close range. No screwing around, no games. Tell me or die. ONE...TWO. Her face grew sober as she raised her chin like a noble princess. But I didn't give a shit...THREE.

Barkin came out of nowhere, hurtling himself through the air like a bag filled with heavy stone, screaming as he catapulted. In a second I caught him with the corner of my eye. It all happened in microscopic slides of time.

Pulling my eyes back to Billy I pulled the trigger just as she dove for the floor, knocking over the round table on her way down. Flowers dumped from a vase and the phone I'd once used, rang out one final cry as it smashed against the floor. The bullet missed and tore into the plaster only inches from her head. "Shit." I said the word in a fit of anger. There was no chance for a second shot.

I turned just in time to catch the cumbersome weight of Barkin's body as it took me down like a rag doll.

When we hit the floor the gun flew from my hand and went sliding somewhere within the room. He had a cast on his arm and as I rolled free of him and scrambled to my knees he slammed it into the side of my head. I saw stars and pain rocked my brain. Shaking consciousness back into my head I cleared my vision and connected with a roundhouse to his skull. He moaned and swung with the cast arm again but missed. Using his good arm for lift he scrambled to his feet and I followed suit charging him like a bull.

Head down and screaming I rammed him in the belly. Combined weight and momentum sent us crashing through a closed door into a bedroom. Wood splintered and we came to an abrupt stop by smashing hard into the far wall.

Swinging with his good fist he tried for a hit but I ducked, coming up under his chin with an open palm. His head snapped and the back of his skull smashed into the wall. I followed with a right, a left and another right, then turned and finished with an elbow to the nose. That was it for Barkin. Slowly his body sank to the floor until it ended unconscious in a sitting position.

Reaching into my back pocket I pulled out the cuffs I had taken and snapped them in place with his hands behind his back.

I remained on the floor a few seconds as my breathing slowly regulated. Then I put a hand on his head to help boost myself to my feet. His body toppled over and he lay motionless in a quiet heap.

Turning, I froze in place. Billy stood at the door, Joe in front of her. She held the thirty-eight to his head. He looked like death warmed over, weak and barely able to stand. His head bobbed as he worked his eyes, trying to stay awake. It was no chore realizing they had kept him sedated. Now I knew why he never contacted me since the motel. I asked him how he was doing and he spoke briefly.

"Sleepy, Alfie. Been out like a burned bulb." Forcing a grin he laughed lightly. "I only hope Billy didn't take advantage of me."

Not finding his remark humorous, she stared egotistically at me.

"It seems Mr. Stone, it is I who once again has the upper hand. Only this time...how was it you phrased it, 'there will be no screwing around and no games.' I shall count to three and on three I will put a bullet in Mr. Hardon's brain, although it will be such a waste. ONE...TWO... Bradley leaped like a panther to Billy's back just as she yelled THREE. I screamed the word 'no' as the gun kicked in her hands. Joe's head flopped against the impact of the bullet and he buckled to his knees, falling face first to the floor. There was no time for reasoning. No time for tears or feeling sorry.

In what seemed like slow motion, Billy bent over and threw Bradley free of her back, then stood up again pulling the gun slowly on me. I took three steps and leaped into the air. Feet first I caught her square in the face. The gun went off aimlessly in her hand, the bullet missing me only by inches. She went down hard and stayed there, sprawled on her back.

Climbing immediately to my feet I ran to her motionless body and pulled the thirty-eight free of her hand while checking her pulse at the same time. She had one and it pissed me off. But her nose was broken and blood covered her face, so I felt a little better.

Fearing the worst, I moved to Joe. As I knelt by his side he opened his eyes and gave me a puny grin. "Alfie, I got one hell of a headache." My heart leaped as I pulled him into my arms and squeezed tight. "Well, you dumb ass." I said, blinking away the wetness in my eyes, "What do you expect, you've just been shot in the head. Just be thankful it wasn't somewhere else, that could have been serious."

A close look showed that the bullet had only grazed him. Little Bradley's leap had saved his life.

Taking a deep breath, I sighed. In a few words-it was finally over.

I gathered everyone up including the other two nurses who had been locked in rooms upstairs, then went out and brought Godzilla in from the rain. Together we waited for the arrival of Jake and the others. If anyone had been at the airstrip, we never knew.

By 8:30 p.m., we had everyone turned over to the authorities and the Bordenwells back home. There were still reports to write and questions to answer, but nothing that could not be done over a period of time.

We delighted in watching James W. write our hundred thousand-dollar checks and grinned happily as we deposited them into our accounts. As soon as they were safely laid to rest, agent Lewis arrested him.

An investigation by the FBI had revealed that he too was a soviet agent, along with Emily herself. It seemed she had been making noises about defecting, so he secretly made arrangements with Billy to have her and the kids abducted. Only they were suppose to be shipped back to the USSR, not turned into human guinea pigs.

He used us as part of the plot, convinced we'd be the ideal small time Village Idiot entrepreneurs perfect for screwing things up while believing he was the concerned and distraught father and husband. But because you know what they say about sticks and stones we didn't take it personally. In fact this is one of the few times I put store in one of Murphy's sayings, 'It is morally wrong to let suckers keep their money.'

And if you like happy endings here goes. Billy lived but was deported back to the Soviet Union. James W. Barkin is now serving a life sentence in prison with a hell of a funny looking nose. The formula seems to have not only worn off but vanished as well.

Both Phieffer and Barnibin were never found...could be they discovered happiness in each other's arms. Emily was granted asylum after turning state's evidence against James W. and now she and the children live in San Diego where she teaches school.

As for Joe, he's back to his normal obnoxious self and still playing Detective. And what of Godzilla, you ask? He moved to Hawaii with me...what a babe magnet.

# ABOUT THE AUTHOR

A. Alex Come' has been entertaining family and friends with his writing for nearly two decades. A talented and diversified writer, he has delighted readers in nearly every genre, young and old alike. When creating he pulls from both heart and soul. His maxim: 'in every character created lies a little of ourselves.'

Alex lives just outside a small Indiana town with his wife of thirty-two years and enjoys long walks through the woods. As with many freelancers much of his inspiration is drawn from life experiences and real people just like his readers.

From the small boy growing up poor in the foothills of the Adirondacks to having served in the Marines, the Navy, Army and National Guard to having toured Europe, Japan, Mexico and Canada, he has developed a keen sense of storytelling. At fourteen, he left home to travel west in search of adventure. He has worked as a salesman, security officer, construction laborer, factory worker, ship titter, animal caretaker, firefighter, paramedic, and earned a degree in Marketing Management. His most admired mentors are Ernest Hemingway, Abraham Lincoln, Martin Luther King, Ben Franklin and Geena Davis.